Tampa Bay Runaway

Harriet,
what a pleasure
to meet you!
Take care,
Vik. Najjar

Tampa Bay Runaway

A Novel

Victoria Day Najjar

Tampa Bay Runaway by Victoria Day Najjar
Published 2017 Create Space, Amazon.com
Tampa Bay Runaway. Copyright © 2017 Victoria Day Najjar

ISBN-13: 9781541109162
ISBN-10: 1541109163
Library of Congress Control Number: 2017910157
CreateSpace Independent Publishing Platform
North Charleston, South Carolina

First Edition, 2017
For information, contact the author at: Literaryvicki@gmail.com

This novel is dedicated to my partner, Jeff deGrasse, who patiently served as my "I.T." man during the creation of this novel.

And to my son, Eric Teichner, who carefully edited the novel.
I recall the days, Eric, when as a young boy, you very capably edited my children's poetry. Your children, Mackenzie, Christian and Owen, are the brightest stars in my sky.

Last, but not least,
this book is dedicated to all lost and lonely teen runaways
and foster children.

There is hope.

Gratitude

FIRST, A DEBT OF GRATITUDE is owed to my wonderful brother, Donald Najjar, his wife, Sheri, and daughter, Amber, who read scenes aloud and rocked the book! Your support is awesome.

Thank you, Elaine Kirkoff, for your careful critique and excellent suggestions.

Thank you, my Wisconsin snowbird friends: Linda Fiihrr-Rudersdorf and Dianne and Rich Dvorak, who were the first to hear the story. Your encouragement meant a lot.

Thank you, Midge Shigemura, for your literary scope.

Thank you Larri and Danny Gerson (my first I.T. man) and Danny's parents, Eli and Peggy Gerson. You never fail to amaze me.

To my hairdresser, extraordinaire, Wilma Rentzel, thank you for your faith.

This process took a long time and many people, like Betty Ann Johnson, Sandi Jackson, and other members of the Clearwater Welcome Newcomer Club graciously listened while I discussed the plot.

To the wonderful author and teacher, Kimberly Llewellyn, thank you for your belief in my story. You showed me the way. Good luck with your Bella Carroll wedding wine.

To my former students and colleagues from Bloomfield Hills Schools, Michigan, I give thanks. You were all so proud and happy I was writing a novel. After all these years, here it is! Special thanks to Ed Brouhard, Jim Collins, Delphine Kolakowski, Tim Loula, Lou Ruggirello and Linda Schwartz.

Thank you, my many friends and "cheerleaders" in the Palm Harbor Newcomers Club. Your unflagging devotion has helped me enormously to keep the creative fires burning. Thank you Linda Amsden, Valerie Chittim, Ginny DiDomenico,Liz Fischer, Jacque Foltz, Marcia Giza, Linda Kaminsky, Elaine Kissel, Mary Macdaid, Cheryl McDonald, Jean North, Aphrodite Smith-Gillespie, Dorothy Shuttleworth, Dee Streitman, Lori Thebeau, JoAnn Sarpolis, and Carol Townsend for your special interest. Jim Tight, enjoy the cowboy poetry. Josie Chadwick, Chi Cook, Nancy DiMaria, Anne-Todd Eisner, Rosemary Fleishman, Carolyn Mahy, Beth McGreen, Jenny McPherson, Patti Ross, Staci Sachs, and Judy Zimlin, thanks for listening during all those Mah Jongg games.

To my former colleagues at the Oakland County Prosecutor's Office in Michigan (where I worked before

I taught school), I give thanks to then assistant prosecutors Jim McCarthy, Elizabeth Kulesz, Michael Sobel, and investigator John Meyers; thank you for your support of my writing.

Thank you, Jill Locke, former head librarian of the Farmington, Michigan Public library, for your creative influence in the showcasing of my children's poetry.

Thank you, Lee Bennett Hopkins, my first poetry editor and mentor.

Thank you, Dr. Lawrence Berkove, my eminent professor of American Literature at the University of Michigan, Dearborn campus. Your passion for great writing validated mine.

And to my "international friends," greetings to all of my cousins in Australia, particularly to my cousin Sandra Malouf Owen; Margaret and John Gilmartin, in England; Le Tianyin in China and world traveler, Anes Bajric.

A Note To The Reader

I WAS INSPIRED TO WRITE this novel by a televised news series I saw many years ago. It featured a teen runaway who lived in a city alley in a large cardboard appliance box. The years had rolled by for her and she truly wished to better herself but she remained enslaved to a heroin habit paid for by prostitution. She was a poet. Her poetry touched my heart.

I will never forget her.

I rewrote her life and named her Connie Mitchell. Connie is drug-free and working as a hairdresser at the Spa in Safety Harbor, Florida. She, like the televised teen runaway, lost her young son when her parental rights were severed. Connie now searches for her son, and in doing so, risks her life going up against a powerful man and his psychotic partner in crime, Sharon Fuller.

But Connie is not alone. She has joined a poetry group which meets at the local library, and it is there where she makes her best friends, and her worst enemy.

If you believe in the triumph of personal fortitude, if you believe in the power of forgiveness and redemption, then Connie's journey will be of high interest to you.

Thank you for traveling the road of life with Connie.

Victoria Day Najjar
Oldsmar, Florida, 2017

Prologue
Clearwater, Florida

CONNIE LEANS AGAINST THE FLIMSY bedroom door listening, alarmed by the screaming of young Celeste, "You told me you loved me! Why won't you take me away with you?"

The john sneers, zips his pants, "Are you crazy?"

"But you told me you loved me, Richard!" the twelve-year old wails.

"Hey! Not my problem if you believe all the shit you hear."

Each word a bullet to Celeste's heart. Her feet pound the floor, tiny fists work the air as she rushes him.

In a haze of meth, the john roars, grabs her wrists and heaves her across the room. Her screams of protest are cut short as her head crashes against a mammoth dresser. Celeste sinks to the floor like a broken doll. Her necklace breaks and beads haphazardly roll across the carpet which blooms magenta with her blood.

Terrified, eighteen-year old Connie Mitchell bursts into the room crying, "What have you done?" She kneels over Celeste, gently lifting soft blond curls from Celeste's blank eyes. Panicked, she scrambles to her feet, "We've got to get help!"

The john steps in her path, towers over her.

She fights him, "Get out of my way!"

His eyes blaze like a madman's, saliva drips from his matted beard. "Shut up, whore!" he bellows, pinning Connie to the bloody floor, and in a fit of hysteria, rapes her. And all the while, he chants his mantra, "Shut up, whore! Shut up, whore!"

Afterwards, dazed and bloodied, Connie watches as the gurney carrying Celeste's lifeless body is rolled into the EMS vehicle. A sweaty hand clamps her like a vice, shaking her. She hears the vicious voice of her grungy pimp. His words sound like an echo from far away, but here he is, shoving a small box into her hands. "Take this shit. Don't want nothin' of hers here when the cops show up." His eyes pelt her with hatred. "And keep your damn mouth shut, you didn't see nothin'."

The john stumbles out of the apartment house, thrusts a wad of cash into the hand of the pimp, says, "Thanks, man."

With trembling hands, Connie lifts the lid of the box, sees a tattered copy of *The Hunger Games*, a few sparkly key chains and Celeste's purple diary, her favorite color. She weeps.

Little did she know then that the john had planted a seed of life within her.

In Tallahassee, the phone rings in the governor's office.

"Your nephew," the secretary says, mincing the words as one minces garlic after chopping off the rotted sections.

The governor's face sours. He picks up the phone, listens, nods. "Yes," he says in a voice barely audible, "but this is the last time. After this, we're done, understand? If you weren't my brother's son, I'd let you rot in hell!" He slams the receiver down, barks to his secretary, "Get me the Clearwater Chief of Police."

Section One: Life In Safety Harbor

Safety Harbor, Florida, 18 years later

CONNIE SAT FIDGETING AT THE library conference table. Was there time to grab a quick smoke outside? She had, at the insistence of her neighbor Salli, enrolled in a poetry group. She wished Salli was here now but Salli was not a poet, just a fun, sweet friend. Connie now doubted the wisdom of attending this poetry group but it was too late to back out. Instead, she tapped her foot, rummaged through her purse, fingered the pack of cigarettes but settled on a mint.

Two younger women entered the room: One, prissy, the other, sultry. They were followed by an elderly woman who smiled at Connie as she took her seat. Men appeared, a different mix, the younger one, thin, wiry, sported a muscle message shirt, "Do It In Safety Harbor". He took a seat next to Connie. His breath stank of stale beer. She leaned away, knew the type, hated the type. Too many years, too many johns. His black eyes, slits, filled with cunning, leveled on hers. She squirmed. He, taking measure of her breasts, asked, "How ya doing?" Connie rolled her eyes and turned away. An older man sat quietly at the end of the table, eyes downcast, lost in reverie. Connie studied his gray, ponytailed hair and well-lined face. The quiet dignity with which he sat captivated Connie whose thoughts turned to her father. She squinted trying to picture him. It had been a very long time.

The room electrified at the roar of a Harley approaching the library, heralding the arrival of the chair of the group, Glenn Tennyson. A moment later, he entered the conference room, striding with the confidence of a lion, all the while smiling, nodding, touching shoulders. Anticipation lit the room like the 4th of July. The main man had arrived. The man with the million dollar smile, the man with the answers, the man whose law office sat prominently in the center of town. Glenn was known for his civic spirit and generosity in pro bono legal defense. His eyes sparkled with intensity as they lingered on Connie's face. She lowered her eyes, not wishing to attract undue attention. She listened intensely as group members, at Glenn's request, introduced themselves.

Let's see what we've got here, she thought, her curiosity overtaking her fear. This Sharon Fuller is a psychiatric nurse who works the night shift so she can write in "peace." If she wants peace, why is she dressed so provocatively? And at the other end of the female spectrum, Drina Alvarez, social worker. Wholesome. Connie noted Drina appeared to be about her own age, 36; Drina's eyes met hers, kind eyes, accepting eyes. Connie felt a connection, a connection she wished to deny, getting close to anyone was risky. The death of Celeste, the way it happened, gave Connie a deep-seated belief that going solo was for the best. It hurt to love. She tuned out Muscle Shirt Don Rank as he rambled his lame introduction: had a job, lost the job. Yada yada, yada.

But when Margaret Garing spoke, Connie listened. The dignified woman spoke in a soft, clear voice. Petite, and bespeckled, wearing a tailored black dress, Margaret was the image of class.

Connie learned that Margaret had been the librarian here and founded the poetry group years ago. The next to speak was the man with the well-lined face and graying hair. Connie learned his name, Sam Bantar, a Vietnam vet. "I work up at the bike shop. Big fan of Whitman," he chuckled softly, "yeah." Almost imperceptibly, Sam nodded in recognition of Connie who sensed within him something enduringly true and good.

"And our new member, welcome," said Glenn softly, "tell us about yourself."

"I'm Connie Mitchell," she said nervously, "I work right up the street at the spa as a hair stylist. I don't have a fancy writing background but I love writing poetry, so I'm here."

Glenn took note. He liked her looks, he liked her voice, his curiosity was aroused by the aura of mystery about her. She seemed shy, yet he sensed she possessed strong inward strength. She was beautiful. He said, "We have a great mix in this group and I'm expecting great things of you all. Now, please take the hand of your neighbor, close your eyes, feel the strength flowing? That's unification, what we're here for, creators and lovers of poetry. Think. Be real. Take off the mask. First assignment: Choose an object, describe the object, become the object."

Connie looked around the table, everyone immediately began to write. She felt threatened, she felt slow, she fumbled in her purse for a pen, dropped her notebook, said, "Sorry," as she reached down to get it. She gripped the pen as if her life depended on it, began to think, what shall I write about? Oh, my God! These people know the drill, started out from the gate on fire. And Glenn, obviously a man comfortable in the world of intellectual pursuit, a world of which Connie knew nothing.

She desperately wished the blinds were not pulled, perhaps something outside the window would inspire her. Maybe the moon peeking through the branches of the mighty Baranoff Oak, the tree from which she found solace and inspiration. Her friend. Sometimes dragonflies circled the tree, their gossamer wings sparkling in the sunshine. Sometimes the birds, the song birds of the northern climes, gathered in its branches. Tonight, only an enclosed conference room, a room filled with strangers.

After what seemed to Connie to be a short time, Glenn asked the members, "What are some of the objects you chose?"

"I chose to write about my trail bike," said Drina, and reached for her pink thermos.

Muscle Shirt spoke, "I wrote about my crumpled jeans lying there like a rose on the floor beside my bed where I left them before I masturbate." The women collectively averted their eyes, everyone, that is, except Sharon

Sam passed, seems he did not write, but attended the group for the love of poetry.

Margaret chose to write about a Seminole quillwork panel, part of her collection of ancestral art.

Sharon edged forward in her seat, aimed her ample breasts toward Glenn, smiled broadly, "I wrote about my baby doll heels, very 1950! Very Marilyn Monroe. As you know, she said, 'Give a girl the right shoes and she can conquer the world'."

"Yes," Glenn said, respectfully.

Sharon stewed. Yes? All he says is Yes? One syllable? Yes. She recrossed her legs, skirt crawling higher and higher, firm thighs exposed, her confidence returned. Still, she was disappointed in Glenn's lack of enthusiasm. She worked her mouth, forced a smile, forced her face into a canvas of sweetness, then she moistened her full lips. Waiting. Perhaps he would say more. He did not.

Connie's pulse quickened, nerves getting to her. Soon it would be her turn to share. Masks, Glenn had said. Masks. Connie's mind swept back to her mother's college classes, a few of which Connie had sat through as a little girl. Psych 101, something about defenses people put up. Her mother said to think of defenses as fences. She remembered thinking, people putting up fences, how strange. How do you fence in a life?

Connie's turn. "My object is an archaic volume of poetry. Henry Wadsworth Longfellow's. The inscription is Christmas, 1904, for Elise Thayer."

Sharon watched jealously as Glenn responded to Connie's words. Green with envy, she turned to Muscle Shirt Don, "Who the hell is she anyway coming in here taking over like she's somebody?"

He answered snidely, "She's something all right."

Glenn analyzed the chemistry of the group -- the change palpable since Connie's arrival: Sharon, jealous; Don, lascivious; Margaret, Drina and Sam, supportive. Though he could not hear what Sharon had whispered, he knew her well enough to know she would be antagonistic toward Connie. Glenn would not allow this. He would not allow bullying in his group.

Though Drina tried to be friendly and walked out of the library with Connie, somehow, Connie could not accept her overture of friendship. Connie was brief and polite but avoided eye contact with her.

Too many demons working full time in Connie's mind. Baggage, isn't that what they call it? Connie asked herself as she turned the ignition and backed out of her parking space, the moonlight glancing off the windshield, just for a quick second, the Baranoff Oak leaves trembling in the welcome breeze. Underway and "safe" from the others, Connie lit up, felt immediate relief that the meeting was over with. She sighed and decided that, well, she probably made a mistake attending the meeting. Some of the members were kind but would they accept her if they knew the truth about her? Would anyone? Fitting in was a crazy tough thing to do. How could she ever explain her past? The loss of her own flesh and blood, her son, Will, the pregnancy a result of the rape all those years ago when Celeste had died. Tears formed in her eyes. You don't even know where he is, she thought. You don't know if he's dead or alive. Connie choked up, gasped for air, stubbed out her cigarette. She rolled the car window down but the humid air helped little to refresh her.

Feeling down, Connie's spirits lifted when she arrived home to her rental bungalow in downtown Safety Harbor to the loving greeting of Doodle, her little dog she had loved from the minute she set eyes on her. Doodle now showered her with affection. "Mommy missed you, too," said Connie, holding Doodle close, cuddling her. Doodle had become Connie's substitute for human relationships. Doodle was safe, always there, always loving.

A knock at the door, it was Salli, her next-door neighbor, only five feet tall but a real blonde spitfire of a woman. She batted her big blues.

"So, you glad I talked you into the poetry group?" she asked, obviously fishing for a compliment.

Connie teased, "We'll see." She poured wine.

"So tell me about it! And . . . how did you like Glenn? He's a babe." Salli grinned, raised her eyebrows.

Connie sipped her wine. She shared with Salli that group had been stressful but in retrospect, kind of interesting. "What a bunch," she said. "Sharon is a hard case, thinks she's so hot." Connie continued with her impressions: "Margaret is sweet. Muscle Shirt is a pig. Drina is a sob-sister, but kind of nice. Sam, seems old and sad but nice. Glenn, hmmm, Glenn, yeah, he is a babe." She took another sip of wine and decided she might attend the next meeting for no other reason than to scope out the crazies.

La Cucaracha played on Salli's phone, "It's hubby, gotta go. I'm taking this with me!" she called out, carrying her goblet.

"That's fine. See ya!" called Connie as the screen door slammed shut.

Magnificence of the Spa

CONNIE'S LIFE DRASTICALLY CHANGED AFTER she climbed the mountain of sobriety and left the world of prostitution behind. She now worked at the gorgeous Paradise Spa and Resort which was a prominent fixture in the town of Safety Harbor. Each day as Connie arrived at the Spa, she felt as if she were entering a stately museum. The Spa seemed like an art gallery, its walls filled with massive oil paintings depicting voluptuous women posing in voluminous yards of pastel silks and satins. As Connie studied the paintings, she liked to pretend that the doe-eyed beauties were looking directly at her. Inwardly, she played a game of saying *Good morning!* to them and a smile would cross her face. For other employees, the beauty of the Spa was unimportant, but the poet in Connie responded continually to the stunning Spa setting. As she walked further into the vestibule, Connie slowed her pace, mesmerized by the forty-foot high vaulted ceiling bearing a fresco inspired by the famous Rococo artist Francois Boucher, who in turn had been inspired by Versailles. Connie hoped to see Versailles one day, but in the meantime Wikipedia informed her and the Spa inspired her. A poem formed in her mind as she pondered the magnificence of the dome. Cupids aloft on the robin's egg blue sky sporting bows and arrows playfully targeting the reclining maidens, all set aswirl amongst ribbons and flowers in lapis, scarlet and maize. Diffuse light of the encircling host of clerestory windows softly illuminated the scene. Connie felt her breathing slow as the art permeated her being.

Inherently, she understood that the Spa embodied the essence of beauty, and that its clientele sought, above all else in life: health and beauty. Connie rather innocently believed her success at the Spa was due solely to her talent as a hair stylist, not realizing her personal beauty was a draw for business. Who amongst the wealthy clientele would have faith in an unattractive hairdresser? After all, if one possessed any skill at all, why would one not be beautiful?

Time for work Connie thought as she descended the broad circular staircase to the lower level which housed the salon, exercise studios and a glass encased spillover for the mineral springs. Indeed, the spillover was part of the mystique of the Spa. For it was these mineral springs which brought fame and fortune to Safety Harbor since the 1800's. Tourists, as well as world renowned impresarios visited the Springs for their legendary curative powers. A large bronze plaque told the story of how in 1539, Spanish explorer Hernando de Soto discovered the five springs, believing he had found the fountain of youth. Now, four active springs produced a mind boggling two million gallons of water a month. When Connie would mention this to clients or co-workers, they generally shrugged and acted as if the facts were simply that, facts. But the history of the Spa thrilled Connie who felt great pride in working at the Spa. She could not avail herself of its spring-fed pools and baths, but the delicious drinking water was spring fed. Connie's well traveled clients shared stories of their world travel as she styled their hair. Rather than jealousy, Connie felt awe hoping that one day perhaps she, too, could travel. For now, she was content to be a part of something so beautiful which she held in direct contrast to the misery of the years she spent on the streets of Clearwater living in degradation.

Connie arrived at her station and tucked her purse into the side drawer, checked herself briefly in the mirror and studied her schedule for the day. Co-worker, Alice, 25, a tall, shapely brunette, rushed in without so much as a hello grimaced and whined, "Another day, another dollar, huh? Who's your first?"

"Mrs. Murray. She's due any minute," Connie answered, then forcing a smile asked, "How are you doing, Alice?"

"Ugh, how would I be?" she groaned taking a sip of her Starbucks. "My first is that cow Mrs. Paisley. God, I can't stand that woman," she wrinkled her nose. "All she does is sit here week in week out and brag about her perfect freaking life. I'm sick of it, aren't you??"

"No," Connie considered, "I figure thanks to them, I have a good job."

"Excuse me," said Alice, drawing out the words unpleasantly.

"You're excused," said Connie who could not help but smile at Alice's candor. How could Alice appreciate a good job like this when it was all she ever knew? Taking things for granted is what people did all the time. But Connie knew better and deeply appreciated her job and the goodness of her new life away from prostitution. All that was lacking was a reunion with her lost son. Her search for him was futile; he had been adopted and the records were sealed. His surname became that of his adoptive family. Were the new parents kind? Loving? Was Will happy? These questions plagued Connie. Even in joyful times, sorrow and regret lay beneath the surface of her emotions.

Sharon Fuller

MERRIAM PINES HOSPITAL, A HIGHLY lucrative member of a large Florida consortium, stood prominently on the corner of Webster and Pine. A beacon of renowned excellence in health care, it was named by *Hospitals on Review* as one of the top 100 hospitals in America. Sharon Fuller was proud to be a trusted member of the Merriam Pines psychiatric team, having won her stripes through 12 years of dependable, competent service. Sharon was entrusted with the position of night nurse on the 8th floor psychiatric ward. The ward consisted of sixteen private rooms. Dominion over the ward was hers as she was the sole practitioner on duty. Eschewing the day shift supervisors, bossy old women who'd worked there since the dark ages, Sharon was in her element, completely in charge. If a patient became agitated, a simple overdose did solved the problem. However, easy-peasy could be boring-snoring and maybe, deadly.

Sharon's solution to the doldrums, handsome 26 year old James Appleby, the apple of her eye. Depression was the diagnosis and a failed attempt at suicide had led to his commitment. "You sleep enough all day in this place, don't you?" asked Sharon, standing in the doorway, her head tilted, lips parted. "Why don't you play cards with me, do something with me, I get so bored in here," she intoned in a babyish voice, pouting.

James, friendly by nature, had sustained the loss of his fiancée in an unexpected manner. She left him the engagement ring and a Dear John letter in which she confessed that, despite her attempt to resist temptation, her tennis pro had stolen her heart. Poof! Over, just like that. The shock sent James into a downward spiral of depression. He lost faith in life. No parental lectures, no cajoling from friends, nothing could halt the dark progression in his mind. Suicide, he decided, was the way out. No painful memories to deal with, no shattered dreams, no unrequited love, no nothing. The plan for salvation failed when the gun misfired. Here he was and here before him stood a pretty woman (a bit older, yes, but so what?) offering friendship. James, lonely, isolated, readily opted for Sharon's companionship. He would be doing her a favor, after all, she was bored, too.

The games ensued and quickly moved from cards to sex. The 8th floor quiet but for the snoring of patients and the grinding of two bodies in James' room. Sharon beguiled James as she modeled a filmy Marilyn Monroe gown. "I love you," he whispered as he gently touched her face, inhaling her perfume. Hungry for affirmation, day by day, week by week, James asked, "Do you love me?" The answer always the same, "Of course I do. You're my leading man, aren't you?" Two months later when the morning shift found his lifeless body hanging, the bed sheets his accomplice, they would wonder why. The young man had seemed happier lately, to have a new positive outlook on life, even the attending psychiatrist thought so. Sharon, shocked, but somehow relieved. His proposal of marriage? Ridiculous. He took things too far. Who did he think he was?

But there were whispers, whispers from the lips of an older, wiser nurse, who suspected there was more to it than met the eye. To prove so would be difficult. No cameras, no witnesses, no love notes found stuffed in a side drawer. Nothing outwardly seeming to lack propriety. Who would believe there was foul play? But hadn't another young male patient died two years ago on Mrs. Fuller's shift? Some staff members professed sympathy for Mrs. Fuller, losing another patient like that. After all, Mrs. Fuller was a stable, happily married woman, a woman worthy of trust, this would be depressing to such a woman. Sharon accepted their condolences with grace, acknowledging that, yes, it was a loss and so sad, but "life goes on" she said. Just not for James.

Will and the Thief

ANOTHER HOT DUSTY DAY IN Florida with sky-high humidity. High school seniors, Will Stover and Chad Harn up to no good, as usual. Two guys on the frayed edges of adolescence with no hopes for a future of any kind, Chad especially bummed that his car was in the repair shop and would remain there until he could pay the bill. "Got any money?" asked Chad.

"What do you think?" Will rolled his eyes.

"Let's stop here," motioned Chad, guiding his bike to the side of the parking lot where there was a patch of shade.

"Lock 'em?" Will asked.

"Nah, this won't take long."

A bell clinked on the door of the Spoke and Wheel Bike Shop as they sauntered in. An elderly man looked up haphazardly, greeted them, "What can I do you for?"

"Nothing." Chad barked as he greedily eyed the goods, surveying which would sell well at the high school, discounted of course. Night lights, leather gloves, handy tools. The freshmen snapped them up like goldfish crackers.

A customer walked in, called out a greeting to the old man. "Hey, Sam, how're doing?" He stayed a moment or so, long enough to distract Sam.

Chad grabbed a few items, stuffed his cargo pockets. Will watched, unflinching.

Chad hissed, "Ain't you takin' nothing? Grab something, asshole."

The old man looked their way knowingly. Been there. Will tensed. The old man . . . there was something about him.

Chad turned on his heel, strolled out of the store. The old man's eyes were glued to Chad, "Just a minute there, son."

Chad continued walking, flipped the man the bird then stonily looked at Will, "Why are you such a pussy?"

Will shrugged, then defensively, "Seemed pissant stuff to me, like the electronic stuff better."

"Hey, you get what you can where you can. Got it?"

"Yeah, I got it," answered Will.

The old man stood outside watching them leave as he wiped his greasy hands with a well-worn, stained rag. Will noted there was something about the old guy. Seemed like when he looked at you, he saw right through you. Kind of amazing.

*****

"That you, Will?" called out Mrs. Maloney, Will's foster mother

"Yes, ma'am," Will answered.

"Remember to buy the milk?"

Dutifully, Will walked into the kitchen, opened the fridge, set the gallon of 2% milk on the top shelf where Mrs. Maloney liked it.

"Thank you, dear," she said. She continued peeling carrots and potatoes for the family dinner of stew. The Maloney's, well experienced in foster care, really did care for each and every child placed within their home but had learned to keep emotional distance so that when the placement ended, there was a clean break. What with raising a child of their own, a polite veneer was the best they could offer. Will accepted even this with gratitude. There was no abuse in this home. He shuddered to think of some of his past placements and gratefully acknowledged the Maloney's as the best he could have hoped for. The thought of leaving them when he turned 18 troubled him. Where would he go? What would he do? Chad said something always turns up but Will wasn't so sure. Chad's fosters were angry, brutal people; Chad would not miss them.

After stashing the milk, Will headed to the bedroom he shared with nine-year old Tommy Maloney. Tommy, the image of the all-American boy, freckles, big grin, thin frame, and casually friendly to everyone he met. A good kid.

"What's up, Tommy?" Will asked noting Tommy's sullen expression.

"Nothing much. Got homework to do or I'm in trouble."

"So do it."

"I'm stuck. I hate math, especially fractions!"

"Oh, come on, fractions aren't that bad!" Will proceeded to tutor Tommy and soon it was dinner time.

Later, after the dishes were done, Tommy asked Will if he could play a game on his laptop. Will said sure that was fine. When Will's foster parents asked him how he could afford a Sony laptop, he answered that he bought it cheap from a spoiled kid at school who'd gotten a newer model. All lies. They bought the lies. A hero to Tommy, a decent foster kid to the Maloney's, things seemed to be all right from their point of view, plus soon Will's stay would be over. Will's anxiety about his future lay under wraps, his problem, not theirs.

Secret Life

PINELLAS COUNTY IN WHICH SAFETY Harbor was located started out as a sleepy west central coastal county but within time, it had mushroomed into a viable competitor with many of Florida's most prestigious counties. The cities located within the county vied for the tourist dollars, for their attendance at the museums, restaurants, theatres, beaches and small businesses. Sharpening its focus on development, the leaders of Pinellas Country envisioned and worked to institute unparalleled growth. However, the population explosion brought with it an explosion in crime. More people, more crime, more criminal justice system expansion. The court house, prosecutor's office and jails swelled. Keeping the streets safe for the good citizens of Pinellas County no easy task. Carjackers, thugs, thieves, drug addicts, and murderers found lots of prey and lots of places to hide out from the law. Some hid out in tiny abandoned migrant worker homes, others found their way to sleazy motels where they dealt their drugs and prostitutes. No homeless tents for them, no sleeping on the park benches like "amateurs." However, not all of the criminal element emanated from the obvious sources, sometimes the criminals came from highly respectable families. Families shown on the society pages, people appearing to be exactly what they wished the public to believe they were. What went on behind closed doors was quite another matter.

Lloyd McHughes was considered a successful man, a man held in high esteem. At least that was the public image. His position as Chief Assistant Prosecutor was about to be elevated, that is if he won the pending election for prosecutor. This man, this esteemed man, now quietly strode into his home office as ice cubes chattered in his tall rum and coke. This room, above all others, his retreat. Hunter green walls, Audubon prints, barrister bookcases overflowing with law books and the classics, and a burnished leather chair snugged up to his massive mahogany desk. Every inch reflecting stateliness. A perfect background for the upcoming taping of his campaign commercial.

For a man hoping to be prosecutor, it was fitting; for a man about to go into teen chat rooms, it was not. Why a man of McHughes' position would even consider risking his career, reputation, and stature to do what he was about to do could only be explained by one word: lust. His Achilles heel and his abiding joy. He sipped his drink then carefully set his glass on the clay coaster imbued with the scales of justice. No water droplets should ever mar the surface of his magnificent desk, one of the stunning and highly valuable antiques he inherited from his dead aunt, as he called her. It was as if his mother's sister had no name, indeed, her name insignificant, her fortune not so. Not many 28-year olds inherit a cool mill from a dead aunt. But that was years ago and McHughes had invested the money wisely (thanks to his father's guidance) and though McHughes reveled in the significant growth of his investments, he lagged far behind his brother's accumulated wealth. He sneered with jealousy pondering his brother, a big-shot corporate attorney, billings huge, hours long, ego gigantic.

McHughes booted up his computer, clicked on the familiar icon and began his devilish deed. Knowing it was illegal made it all the more exciting. Arrogantly, he believed he knew enough about the various on-line stings to avoid one. He would not be trapped. He felt impervious to the law. After all, he had been enjoying chat rooms with underage girls for years. Nothing ever happened. His blood pressure began to spike, his eyes glistened and he began to breath in shallow, quick breaths. He took a long pull of his rum and coke. There was Mandy saying hello. Yes, there she was: Mandy, 14, Mandy who loved to talk dirty. Loved to post pictures of her big juicy breasts and small wicked smile. She, like McHughes' other underage victims, required very little pressure to post the porn. Both he and they enjoyed the cheap thrill.

I thought of U 2day

What did U think?

That U should C my new pantEEs pink and tinE, Cthrough so SEXEEE

Lloyd's member hardened. He touched himself. Drooled into his drink.

Wow. Some panties!
What do U look like?
I've told U B4
Tell me again, me so horny
6'2", hazel I's
A gr8 big dick 2 right?
Right and getting bigger every second, darlin'
When we gonna meet?

McHughes groaned as he shut down the site. This was where he drew the line. He thus far had enjoyed the young girls on line only. Never daring to meet them since Celeste. He leaned back into the cushy leather, touched himself, enjoying the moment of release which was just as quickly dissipated by the thought of what lay ahead tomorrow: court with the nut case Judge Bardmoor. "Oh, God," he muttered, his blood running cold. He polished off his drink and called out, "Here, kitty," calling Miss Snickers, the cat he never wanted, the cat an ex-girlfriend abandoned at his home. He kept Miss Snickers reasoning it might make for a better self-image if he had a pet. But he hated the cat as much as the ex-girlfriend. And a little animal abuse might be just the ticket to forget about tomorrow.

Seduction

Sharon rolled one more layer of Marilyn's Hot Red onto her lips, fluffed her hair, blew herself a pouty kiss then strutted out of the house. Carefully she set her white patent tote onto the passenger seat of her car. She double-checked, yes, enough copies of the poem, all spell-checked, rehearsed aloud at least six times, perfect. "A Man Who Makes Me Laugh." Glenn was sure to take note of the subtext. Sex, of course. What else mattered? She keyed the ignition, put the car in reverse while glancing down at her peek-a-boo white spike heels adorning her toes and gleaming red toe nails. Black thoughts arose as to her rival, Connie the Bitch. What piece of whiney crap will she read tonight? More moaning about a lost child? Pity-seeking bullshit. Not thinking, she took her foot off the brake. Still in reverse, the car rolled backward.

"Watch out! Are you blind?" screamed the elderly man she nearly ran over.

Sharon braked and stonily waited. Giving her energy to a crabby old buzzard wasn't part of the plan. She grimaced barely suppressing the urge to take her foot off the brake, hit the gas, kill off the old bird. Spider like, he crossed behind her muttering, "Must be blind. Must be blind."

Composed as a peace lily, she entered the conference room of the library. She surveyed the scene wishing she had arrived a bit earlier, thought, "Damn that old crank, held me up." Drina was next to Glenn on one side, and Sam, that old bastard on the other. Of course, next to Sam, Connie the Bitch. "Hi everyone!" called out Sharon, smiling, sliding into the seat next to Don, wearing his usual muscle tee. She anxiously pulled her latest poem from her portfolio. Her perfume sprang over the room, "I'd like to read tonight, Glenn," she offered.

"Sure, good, let's get started," he answered.

She read with special gusto the last line, "Make me laugh, let me feel the river of joy flow through my body, opening me in anticipation of more." She eyed Glenn. No reaction. No kudos from anyone. Just polite silence. What the hell?

"I bet I can make you laugh," offered Don.

"No need," Sharon answered crisply.

"Connie, do you wish to read?" Glenn asked.

The Bitch nodded yes. Of course she wants to read, thought Sharon. When did she not? Damn her!

Sharon slunk out of the library, deflated. It was no use, Glenn had eyes only for Connie the Bitch. She headed for home but fervently wished she had somewhere else to go instead of that inescapable prison of pathetic monotony. But she wouldn't be home long as her night shift would start in exactly two hours. She sighed, wishing James were alive. Why did he have to off himself, leave her stranded? She drove mindlessly, unaware of the smudge of red lip-stick edging her right lower lip. It lent her appearance a ghoulish effect, much like a blood-sucking vampire.

"It's all bullshit!" she croaked rolling through a yellow caution light oblivious to the pedestrians in the cross walk. She panted and plotted. How could she get to Glenn? Was it by destroying Connie? But how? Thoughts swirled in nasty little circles polluting the air in her car. She coughed. If evil were the color of mud, then she was awash in muck. She blinked, checked her makeup in the rear-view mirror. "My God! How long has my lipstick been smudged like that?" Horrified, she grabbed hold of her purse, plucked a tissue, wiped the smudge away. Did he see it? Did they all see it? Bam! Bam! Bam! A row of orange construction bar-rels went down. "Freakin' crap!" she screamed.

Glenn

GLENN TENNYSON WAS A FAVORITE with everyone in Safety Harbor and a damned good attorney. Divorced, he built his life around his law practice, his German Shepherd, Sophie, and his home in Safety Harbor in which he housed his considerable collection of turned wood objects and cowboy poetry. Glenn's luck in love had been slim. Working his way through college and law school as a wedding photographer, he met the woman of his dreams. The dream was short-lived, however, as Dream Woman left him just as he was finishing law school. He blamed himself for the breakup of the marriage reasoning that between working and law school he had neglected her. Why she could not hold on for a little while longer, he never understood, but she had hooked up with someone else and moved on with her life.

In this way, Glenn realized he was like Sam. Glenn's friendship with the homeless Vietnam vet initially came about due to their mutual love of poetry. As time went on, they learned they had much more in common than Walt

Whitman and cowboy rhymes. They shared a deep abiding sense of lost love, one not easily tempered by time. Although the reasons for the breakdown of their marriages were different, the outcome was the same. Now in his late 30s, Glenn felt life was good, but he missed the presence of a woman in his life. He filled in the lonely chasms of time with long bike rides on his Harley, mostly in Florida but sometimes he found himself riding north across the state line taking solace in the anonymity and solitude of the long rides. His thoughts would turn to memories of the great rides through the Rockies, the mighty mountains towering in their magnificent rock formations. Bittersweet memories of the artful mountain photography in which Glenn had spent many joyful hours, so unlike the regimented, cookie-cutter wedding photography for which he was paid. This, too, presented a conflict in the marriage, simply put, too much time spent away from home. His wife declined the invitations to join him on the mountain tours. Now, in his present situation, returning home from travel was a lonely business. Thankful for the companionship of Sophie and the heavy workload at his office, Glenn pushed forward, each day folding into the next.

Thunderstruck since the first night Connie walked into the writers' group, Glenn wanted to get to know her. The situation was not promising. It appeared to him she had walled herself in and carried the weight of the world on her shoulders. Glenn sighed as he patted the sofa, "Come here, girl," he called to Sophie who dutifully trotted over, hopped up next to him. Glenn scratched her ears, "Sophie, girl, I met someone. Now don't be jealous but I think she might be pretty special." Sophie barked softly and licked Glenn's hand, "Not that you aren't special, girl, because you are."

Nightmare

SOMETIMES THE INSIDIOUS MEMORIES OF Connie's life on the streets enveloped her in the middle of the night. She would toss, turn, cry out, punch the air in a struggle with an imaginary foe. Growing from the bitter roots of an incident many years prior, the black tentacles of a nightmare would strangle her. The labyrinth of her mind wove an ominous scenario: It is midnight, the air sticky, a dark car pulls to the curb, she pulls a last drag off her cigarette, grinds it into the hot pavement, slides quickly into the car. She, the hawk, the streets her hunting ground.

The john is new to her, does not speak, she motions to the side street. He parks. From there, the ghastly recollection, a gun pulled, the gun jamming, the butt of the gun pounding on her skull. Her blood, her screams, as she thrusts herself out of the car, and runs for her life.

She wakes with a start. There is nothing. She is alone. She is safe. Quietly, she weeps and shares this nightmare with no one.

Unification

DRINA ALVAREZ, A VOLUPTUOUS 35-YEAR old Cuban American loved three things: her daughter Solana, poetry, and her job as a county social worker. Divorced, independent and savvy, yet kind and trusting, Drina's big heart and sensitivity to others was obvious to everyone meeting her. Sharing her love of poetry helped Drina to feel connected to something beautiful, to suspend the harsh reality of life. Through the cadences of lyrical poetry, she was refreshed and more emotionally able to assist her counselees with their myriad of problems. Thus, when Drina entered the library, sat down at the conference table, it was with a sense of personal need and joy.

"My poem is entitled *Love is a Soaring Butterfly*," said Drina. "I wrote it in the tradition of the great Chilean poet, Pablo Neruda, whose poetry is a continuing inspiration in my life." She turned to Sam, "Sam, Pablo Neruda is considered the great Latin-American Whitmanesque father." Sam nodded with pleasure. Drina began,

"My poem is entitled Love is a Soaring Butterfly," said Drina.

The splendor of the sky beckons the anxious butterfly
Who has long awaited long sedated its desire to fly.
Its time is due to be enveloped in the silken blue.
Wings open, touch sky, bend, wend their way
From dawn till dusk delicately reaching for the cusp,
Floating Intrepidly on wings of promise upon the wind.
Casting aside platitudes transcending the latitudes of earth below,
Savoring serenity, sensing salvation, soaring, surrendering to airy motion,
The covenant, the cradle in the sky."

Connie's eyes glistened with tears as Glenn paused respectfully before asking for commentary. She spoke first, "The poem is beautiful, Drina, it painted a picture in my mind. I could see that butterfly ascending with grace."

"Humph," mumbled Sharon.

Don shifted in his seat, kept his mouth shut.

"Exquisite," offered Sam.

"I've always loved butterflies; that was lovely," offered Margaret, then she added, "Did you know that in Gainesville, we have one of the largest collections of butterflies in the world?"

"No!" said Drina, excitedly.

"Yes!" said Margaret. "It's got 5 million specimens! And," she continued, "they have a butterfly rainforest. It's really something. You should go."

Breathless, eyes wide at the thought, Drina thanked Margaret.

"Wow. Thanks for that amazing information, Margaret," said Glenn. Then, turning to Drina, he said, "That's definitely one of your best poems."

"Oh! It's beautiful!" said Connie.

"Thank you," whispered Drina glancing gratefully toward Connie. A beginning?

"Sam, are your reciting Whitman tonight?" Glenn asked.

Sam nodded. "This is a verse from Song of Myself. Hope I'm not repeating myself reciting it to you. Memory's not what it used to be.

> *"On every step bunches of ages, and larger bunches between the step, All below duly traveled - and still I mount and mount. Rise after rise the phantoms behind me. Afar down I see the huge first Nothing, the vapor from the nostrils of death . . ."*

Sam chuckled softly, "Don't want to be preachy but that section hits me hard, makes me think about how small a part I am in the stream of humanity. It's," he paused, "sort of a perspective on life. Yeah."

"So true, Sam," said Glenn. "We don't think about the millions of people whose lives preceded ours and that we're, as they say, 'a drop in the ocean of time'."

Sharon edged forward, conflicted, wanting to please Glenn but also most assuredly not considering herself a drop in the ocean of time. "Well, I . . ." she began, tilted her head, "can see Sam's point, but doesn't that discount the importance of our existence? I can't speak for anyone in this room, but my existence is supremely important to me. I don't feel that because so many have lived before me, centuries ago, I mean, that I'm any less important."

"I really don't think the poem is saying that we, the living, are not important," said Drina, "I think it means only that death awaits us all."

"Well, there's a cheery thought!" said Sharon, rolling her eyes.

Connie sighed, "Here's the thing, we all know we're destined to die, but maybe feeling a part of something greater, being a part of humanity, is comforting. I think it is."

"Oh, God," moaned Don. "This is too deep for me."

Timidly, at the end of the meeting, Connie read one of her "Poetry of Pain" poems based, she told the group, upon a woman she'd seen on a televised news magazine. The woman's life had been misspent and she deeply regretted the loss of her child.

The evening's sharing had been so serious, so emotionally charged that Glenn opted out on sharing one of his cowboy poems. Out of respect for Connie, with whom he desperately wished a connection, he released the group early that night. There simply was no follow-up to the poetry Connie had written. Everyone seemed relieved to be released early, no one suggested getting a beer as they sometimes did.

"Hey, Sam, mind if I walk with you?" asked Glenn

"You're always welcome to walk with me, friend."

"Well--"

"It's about Connie isn't it?"

"Who else?" Glenn swallowed hard, trying to swallow his pride.

"I think--" Sam began.

"Seems like I'm invisible to her. I'd like to talk to her, get to know her."

Sam studied the sidewalk, dark with black mold, "Give her some time, seems like she's been through a lot somehow. May need time. Yeah."

"You honestly think I have a chance?"

"Only time will tell," Sam said. "One thing's certain, if you give up, you'll never know."

Beginnings

"Knock, knock," Salli called through Connie's screen door.

"Come on in, Sal, I was just pouring myself a glass of wine."

"I'm bored stiff," Salli said and accented it with a dramatic sigh.

"What else is new?" said Connie handing Salli a goblet of merlot.

"So, tell me, how did poetry group go? Anything new with that cra-cra Sharon? Oh, better yet, what's new with Glenneeeeee?"

"Oh, stop," Connie said, "But, since you asked, I kind of would like to talk about the group but not about the two people you mentioned."

"Then, who?" Salli curled up on the sofa, anxious to hear gossip.

"Well, you know that woman I always make fun of?"

"Goody two-shoes?"

"Yes, well, her name is Drina," Connie winced, "tonight she read this poem she'd written about a butterfly--"

"A butterfly?"

"Yes, it was actually quite beautiful. It was," Connie paused to gather her thoughts, "it was like floating to heaven."

"Really? So you mean now you don't think she's so dorky?"

"Exactly."

"You like her?"

"I don't know if I like her. But that poem, I liked that poem."

"So maybe liking the poem can mean that maybe you like the person who wrote the poem?"

Connie considered Salli's comment, "Yeah, I guess it can mean that."

"Well, then," Salli raised her glass, "to butterflies!"

"To butterflies!"

Insanity

Sharon Fuller was pissed, though no one would sus-
pect it by the demure manner in which she left the poetry
group. She smiled and waved to Glenn, her crush. Alone
in her car, as she pulled out of the library parking lot,
anger fomented toward the new group member, Connie,
who commanded all of Glenn's attention with her commentary on Drina's pathetic little jingle about butterflies.
Give me a break, she muttered. If she makes one move on
Glenn, I swear . . . Her face contorted with anger as she
slammed the gear shift lever, then fearing wrinkles on her
porcelain skin, she immediately released her frown, raised
her eyebrows and made the letter "o" with her lips. All
this as she eased her car along the narrow streets of Safety
Harbor. Tiny houses, cracker boxes she called them, sat
in neat rows of pastels, homes painted mango, tangerine,
lime or lemon, accented by shutters in hues of eggplant,
avocado, or peach. Flower gardens, yard sculptures, and
hand-painted mailboxes graced the homes. But none of
these adornments graced Sharon's faded brown rental,

trimmed haphazardly in peeling white paint. Sharon hated it, hated living in it, and hated the man she lived with, Ray Fuller, her husband.

She edged up the broken patch of driveway, cut the engine, grabbed her purse, and hoped her husband had already fallen asleep on the couch. No such luck, he sat there wide awake, like a dog waiting to be patted on the head and given a treat. She tossed out a quick hello and went straight to her bedroom where she closed the door. She gazed at her reflection in the etched silver mirror. Dazzled by her own brilliance, she carefully reapplied a coat of radiant red to her lips, taking special care to make the heart shape prominent. She stepped back to admire the effect. Perfect. What could Glenn see in Connie the Bitch when he could have her? She ran her hands over her breasts and down onto her thighs, as she did so, studying her collection of Andy Warhol posters, his iconic images of Marilyn Monroe. Garish in some respects, their size enormous, the room not so. A macabre bodiless chorus line sat on the dresser: Five life-size glass heads, each topped with a Marilyn Monroe wig. Their lips, bright red; cheeks bearing black moles; their eyes, black pits; their lashes, spiked, stabbing the air. Each gruesome master-piece painstakingly created by Sharon who then stepped over to the small closet which groaned, crammed with reproductions of Marilyn Monroe dresses. She felt calmed fingering the folds of her favorite, the white dress with the plunging neckline, worn by Marilyn in *The Seven Year Itch*. The poster of Marilyn, her skirt billowing in clouds over the subway grate, hung there, next to the closet. Sharon giggled, struck a pose imitating Marilyn. Yes, All Things Marilyn website supplied Sharon with chunky, shiny, fake diamonds, long black gloves, strappy high peek-a-boo heels. The bedroom, a museum of another woman's life, a life, an identity Sharon emulated to her core. She sauntered into the living room, bent over the coffee table, pawed through the stack of magazines, admiring the glint of red on her nails as it touched the shiny white paper.

"I got the VISA bill today," Ray grunted. "How do you propose we pay it? Got any money?"

Sharon turned, snatched it from him, "Give it to me," she spit out, her red lips curling, "I'll take care of it, don't I always?"

She looked at him with disdain, regretting having married him twelve years ago. Initially, he was a brawny construction worker with high hopes and a big desire to make her his. But Ray had grown tired of the long hours and low pay. He complained that the crew bosses were idiots. Fed up with his nightly temper tantrums magnified by his drinking, Sharon had requested the night nursing shift in an effort to avoid as much contact as possible with her husband.

"Answer me! Hello! Earth to Sharon!" Ray said. "If you're paying these bills, how come I get all those nasty calls all the time then, huh?" His voice a metallic clone, " Your bill has not been paid for three months."

"Shut up! If you earned a decent living, they would be paid. I certainly pull my weight around here, working in a loony bin every night, not what I bargained for when I married you!"

"Hey, it's not my fault I got laid off! Plus . . . it was your decision to be a psycho nurse."

The blaring sound of an EMS truck ate up the air in the room. Sharon paused before screaming, "Psychiatric nurse, asshole!"

She stormed to the bedroom, slammed the door. Five glass heads trembled in disapproval. Ray shook his head, exasperated, regretting stirring her up. He'd pay for opening his mouth. He sighed; she kicked him out of their bedroom weeks ago and now, he realized he would have to work harder yet to get back in her good graces. He pulled the tab on his can of generic beer, leaned back into the scratchy, stained recliner, his heel nestling into the familiar gap where the upholstery was torn. He guessed he could sleep in the chair. It beat the lumpy mattress in the spare room. The "Star" would be holed up in her quarters for hours now watching "The Seven Year Itch" for the hundredth time. He snapped on a baseball game, the score was tied. The Rays were giving them hell. Something caught his eye, something protruding from the cushion in his chair. He smiled. Forgotten beef jerky. Ha! he thought, I've got myself all set up and she can go to hell. Boom! He brushed the air as if sweeping away the problems of the world.

Then, moments later, Ray timidly knocking on the star's door, "You know I love you, babe."

Friends

DRINA ALVAREZ TOOK HER SEAT at the library conference table, keenly observant by nature and by professional training, she closely studied Connie. From what she could determine, Connie was an extremely self-reliant person who feared intimacy. Judging by Connie's nature poetry and her "poetry of pain," this made perfect sense. Connie represented a dichotomy as she faithfully attended the poetry group but held herself back emotionally from the group communicating instead through her deeply personal lyrical poetry. This intrigued Drina who admired Connie's stalwart, yet sensitive stance toward life. She wished she and Connie could be friends.

Though her overtures of friendship had been rebuffed, Drina thought she would try yet once more. As the poetry group concluded for the evening, before Connie could rush out the door, as was her pattern, Drina turned to her and asked, "Connie, can we talk?"

"Talk?" Connie answered, skeptical. Though she had loved the sentiment in the butterfly poem Drina had read at the last meeting, Connie felt intimidated by Drina, because of her stature in life, that of an educated woman.

"Well," Drina began, "I thought maybe we could get to know each other better if we--"

"Why would you want to know me better?" Connie gathered her notebook and purse.

"I kind of know you already a bit through your poetry and thought maybe--"

"We're worlds apart, Drina, I don't think we even speak the same language." Connie, very nervous, began walking. Drina followed.

"Oh, but we do," Drina asserted, hurrying to Connie's side. "It's the language of the soul, of desire and frustration, of how to stop the . . . " she paused, looked squarely at Connie.

"Hammers?" Connie said. Drina's impassioned answer had opened Connie's heart. She felt she could trust Drina.

"Yes, exactly, thoughts hammering our brains repetitively," said Drina, encouraged.

Connie paused, swallowed her pride: now it was she who studied Drina, saw nothing but kindness and hope in her eyes. "Okay, I was heading home for a glass of wine. Want to join me?"

Drina followed Connie the short distance to her home.

"Come on in," said Connie nervously, as she unlocked the door.

Drina smiled as she entered, "Connie, I love your place!"

"Thrift shop chic."

They both laughed. Connie poured the merlot and the women were no sooner seated when Salli knocked.

Drina raised her eyebrows, "Expecting someone?"

"Come on in, Sal," Connie called out. "She's my neighbor."

"Oh!" said Salli seeing Drina. "Am I intruding?"

"Course not," said Connie. She introduced the two women.

Salli seemed upended for a few moments but regained her composure and began to enjoy the camaraderie of not one but two women friends.

Connie felt relieved. Salli's appearance lent a casual air to the sharing of the wine. She'd worried for nothing about how the evening would go. The visit was fun. She hadn't laughed this much for a very long time. The three women, all very different in background, education, and careers, hit it off magnificently. Doodle, Connie's Shih-Tzu, strutted into the living room after hiding under the bed the first hour.

"Oh, my God! What an adorable dog! Where'd you get her?" exclaimed Drina.

"Come here, Doodle," Connie said. Doodle obliged and hopped up onto her lap. "From a customer who was moving to a no pets apartment. I got lucky. I got Doodle."

"Doodle! I love that name!" said Drina, reaching over to pet her.

"She likes you!" said Connie.

"She likes me, too," said Salli, at which all three laughed.

Afterwards, when the women left, Connie sat stroking Doodle's chin and throat. "I tell you what, puppy dog, mommy's feeling very good right now. Yes, I am. I think we'll make a regular thing of wine night. What do you think?"

Doodle replied by licking Connie's hand.

Mentor

WILL HAD A DREAM, A dream of someone reading to him . . .
Green Eggs and Ham --turning pages, looking at pictures,
laughter, ice cream cones. The wheel of dreams turns to
the other side -- where's mommy? Mommy is gone.

Saturday morning, the dreams forgotten, Will got up,
and since no one was home, he freely drank milk straight
from the container. The note Mrs. Maloney left indicated
that she had taken Tommy to baseball practice. This was
good. A chance to relax, have the house to himself. But
soon after flipping channels on the television, soon after
eating peanut butter on toast, a familiar nagging feeling
of discontent filled his heart. The house became a tomb.
What to do? He wheeled his bike out of the garage, hopped
on, began to ride no place in particular, just pump the ped-
als, keep moving.

Sam was tired. Another night of nasty nightmares in which his legs march as he shoulders his rifle, peering left and right, aware that the quiet of the jungle masks danger. He stumbles in the marsh, leeches attach to his legs. He peels them off: Then, rocket fire." Get down!" he cries, startling himself awake, next the proverbial head ache. Old news to Sam. He dresses perfunctorily and heads over to the Spoke & Wheel. Working would make the day pass quicker and working somehow always cheered him up. The familiar sound of a bike on the pea gravel out back stirred Sam from his work bench. He recognized the patron, it was the boy who was with the shoplifter a couple of weeks back.

The boy stammered, "I wonder if you could help me with something? I got a problem with this chain not working right. I thought maybe . . ."

Sam stuffed a greasy rag into his back pocket, warily crouched beside the back wheel.

"Doesn't look too bad. She's got a lot of wear, all right."

"This is all I got for transportation till I can get a car anyway," Will said glumly.

Sam groaned as he got to his feet, "Well, you're in luck, it's a quick fix."

A distant train whistle filled the air, then the bell, the lowering of the gates.

"Live around here? I thought I'd seen you around." Sam waited.

Will, edgy, shifted his weight, the pea gravel sinking, "Kind of, not too far out of town. Go to the local high school," he said, tossed his head in the direction of the school.

"Yeah, I thought I'd seen you. Where's your buddy?" Sam's eyes narrowed.

Will winced, "Oh, hanging out somewhere, I guess."

Sam turned the wrench, "You're set."

"What do I owe you?" Will reached into his jeans.

Sam waved off the cash Will offered. "Nothing."

"I sure thank you," Will said as he studied Sam's face, a face reflecting wisdom, kind of like some of the characters Will had seen in movies, weathered, trustworthy, strong. "By the way, I'm Will."

Sam nodded, "Will. You got some spare time? I could use some help, I could pay you from my wages. It ain't much but it might help you to buy that car, bike, or whatever it is you want."

"You're offering me a job?" said Will. "Amazing. I've been looking but they're hard to find." Then he added, "I guess you'd show me what to do. Train me I mean?"

"Sure, sure, you'll need training, I can see that," he chuckled and extended his hand to Will.

Will reached out and shook Sam's hand, "I sure thank you . . . you didn't tell me your name."

"Sam. Call me Sam."

Sam watched as Will rode away. So young. The kid was so young. Seemed lost somehow, Sam thought to himself. He shook his head and began making the next repair.

Sam, an African-American man, a man once very handsome, had returned from Vietnam broken, the ravages of war having taken their toll. His wife, a good woman, tried vainly to lift him from his devastating depression. Eventually, she gave up and moved on. Though it pained him that she did so, it relieved him of the pretense that he could overcome the deep sadness which pinioned him every day without cessation. With her leaving, he was free to think his thoughts and reflect upon the horror of watching his friends die before his eyes, one in his arms, eyes blank staring up at the cruel blue sky. Though primarily at peace now, Sam lived his life through the filter of his memories. The past unalterable. The Vietnam War so ugly, so fierce in its magnitude, it had wreaked everlasting destruction upon Sam's body and soul. He contented himself now living on the outskirts of town with others like himself in a makeshift camp, their fires burning at night like distant starts.

Sam's skill as a mechanic provided him with work at the small bike shop in town. He frequently hummed tunes from the 60s as he handled the spoke wrench or chain rivet extractors. Working helped pass time and his friendship with Glenn provided a new avenue of human companionship. Despite this, sadness emanated from his heart, not from regret but rather from the repetitive thoughts which always came down to the same question: Where did my life go? The answer elusive, no matter how many hours he spent reviewing the decades. They were simply gone, like the plaintive cry of the mourning dove, fleeting, lovely, but temporary. Though Sam did know joy through the poetry of Walt Whitman, somewhere deep inside, he knew he was waiting to die. And when he felt especially sad, he would dig into his tattered backpack and remove the ancient treasure, a bottle of Chanel No. 5, which was the one thing his departing wife left behind that fateful day. Its scent, though weak now, had once been hers. It sustained Sam reminding him that, yes, once he was young, he did love, and someone loved him. The mean streets, the endless wandering dissipated.

Advice

IT HAD BEEN SEVERAL MONTHS since Connie and Sam had met. At first their relationship progressed, both learned quite a bit about the other and liked what they learned. For Sam's part, Connie was a decent woman who had gone down the wrong path in her teen years. No need to suffer for the rest of her life for those mistakes. It was evident she was self-correcting, moving on, working hard to make her way. For Connie's part, Sam represented an era in American history of which she knew little. Never a student of history and having dropped out of high school at age 14, she was anything but an expert on the Vietnam War. But she'd seen movies which impacted her greatly, "Born on the 4th of July" and "Coming Home" and she'd gleaned a sampling of the misery of that war from the films and the news retrospectives. Though Sam did not write poetry, he often recited Walt Whitman's poetry especially from *Leaves of Grass* written from the point of view of a transient who loved and respected all people he encountered. Sam's soft voice reciting at the poetry group enthralled Connie, who knew nothing of Whitman until Sam introduced her to his work. This enlightenment filled Connie with sincere respect for both Sam and Whitman, her keen intellect and lyrical sense of language previously unhappily shaped by the dark side of life. Like rings of growth on a mighty oak, Connie was ingrained with the history of her mistakes, regret, growth, hope for a different outcome than what might otherwise be. In short, Sam and Connie deeply respected one another for the suffering they'd endured, the emotional pain having scarred them deeper than one might imagine. Poetry their balm. And so it was with perfect trust and faith in Sam's friendship that Connie would sit beneath the ancient and majestic Baranoff Oak just outside of the library and talk with Sam. Since they both worked in town, they would sometimes take a break from their work schedules, sit on the bench by the Baranoff and have coffee.

Connie turned to Sam as she lit a cigarette, "Sam, do you mind if I ask you a personal question?"

Sam nodded, stared off into the distance, anticipating the question, "I lost full use of my leg in Nam."

"That had to be horrible. You were so young."

"It takes a toll, yeah."

"Are you bitter about the war, the way things went, Sam?"

"Used to be, did a lot of hitch hiking, thinking about life," he sighed, "but at some point, I had to acknowledge I was lucky to be alive. Most of my friends died over there, little lady."

A young mother and her children crossed their path. "Hold tight to your books, don't drop them now," she cautioned.

Connie waited. "Were you married then Sam, have kids? I don't mean to pry." She lowered her head, exhaled a puff of smoke, brushed imaginary lint from her slacks. In the distance white clouds billowed forming a scene worthy of any artist's paint brush.

Sam stroked his chin, "A wife, no kids."

"Where is she? Is she . . .?"

"Dead? Don't know. She gave up on me a long time ago. I wasn't easy to live with, too many demons I suppose."

Connie absorbed this, appreciated his opening up to her. A slight breeze stirred the jasmine scented air.

"How 'bout you? Is there anyone?" Sam asked hesitantly.

"No," Connie shook her head, "I don't know if there ever will be."

"That's one way to go," offered Sam, "but take it from me, it's a lonely, hard way to go. Sometimes, little lady, it's okay to give someone a try, see how it goes. Yeah."

Connie nodded, extinguished her cigarette. She sighed realizing exactly who Sam was talking about. Maybe she should trust Sam's veiled suggestion, give Glenn a chance. Maybe she would do that. Maybe life could take a suitable turn but still, deep down, Connie held fast to her resolve that her chief purpose was to locate her lost son. She stood. "Thanks, Sam, I know you're trying to help me. I know that." She bent down and quickly hugged him.

Though Sam did not know this, Connie looked upon him as a father figure. Guiltily, she would ask herself why she had failed to reconnect with her own father. Was he still living? She often wondered about herself, doubted herself, her validity as a human being. Why did she feel connected to Sam, but not attempt to see her own father?

Thieves

CHAD HARN WAS A GUY used to hard knocks, foster homes, and living on the edge. Seemingly, he made a perfect companion for Will. They had met the previous year in the high school cafeteria when a bag of chips happened to slip off Will's lunch tray. As Will bent to pick it up, the jock Michelson, kicked it across the floor. "I guess you think that's funny!" Will said, facing the jock. But suddenly Will found himself surrounded by the jock's buddies. He readied himself for a fight knowing all eyes were on him, especially those of Liz Webber, a beautiful brown-eyed girl he spent a lot of time thinking about. Yes, Liz would see him defend himself. Things changed quickly, however, when Chad stepped in.

Will remembered it well: "You fuckers want a fight?" Chad yelled, "You've got one!" With that, he dropped the lead jock with a sucker punch. The other jocks soon lost courage and backed away from the crazy man, fearing him, all too familiar with his reputation. A badass who loved to kick the shit out of someone with his wicked black

boots, brutally thrash the victim with a heavy chain, fil-
let the victim's flesh. Reputed to own a gun, not afraid to
use it. Chad hated the jocks, thought of them as spoiled
punk-ass cowards and made no secret of it. Derisively, they
called him Bad Ass but he liked the name, added it to the
tats on his arms and chest along with the guns and skulls,
Gangsta Tats. The lines between the Haves and Have Not's
clearly defined: The jocks drove expensive cars Mommy
and Daddy leased for them. Chad drove an old junker he
bought with his own money from working part-time jobs,
that is until he learned theft was far more lucrative than
work. Stealing from the rich gave him a sense of power, a
feeling he was leveling the playing field. Retribution. He
took pride in his cunning, his innate ability to survive;
when the privileged asses were touring castles in Europe
or skiing Aspen, Chad hit their homes. Disarming alarm
systems, over and over again. The strategy: hold steady,
don't panic when warning tones blare, hold firm, disable.
Hit after hit -- Chad stole -- Chad marketed -- Chad pock-
eted cash. Lots of it. But he wanted more. Breaking and
entering, the most lucrative job he ever had, but he might
be able to steal more, earn bigger bucks if he had a partner.
Was there someone he could trust? Was that guy Will?
After all, they were two of a kind: Outsiders. Will's reverie
broke at the sound of Chad's voice.

"Hey! Wanna make some money?"

"Doing what?" asked Will, chomping down on his
burger. He knew Chad but only from the fringes; they hung
out a bit now and then but not that much. Chad, upstairs

in the special education room for his academics, Will in mainstream courses. Will wondered, looking at Chad now, why would he be wearing a leather jacket in this heat? Will guessed it was Chad's way of looking like a tough guy. Jet black t-shirt, jeans, boots, leather. Everything black, his signature color. When someone dared to call him Johnny Cash, Chad had broken his jaw. Chad sported one more thing besides black, a sneer upon his face which gave him an ominous look much like that of an attack dog. Yes, that was it. Chad was an attack dog. Will naively believed he knew what Chad was about. Believed he only put on a tough facade to make a statement. Will appreciated that Chad stepped in, backed him up that day in the cafeteria.

Chad leaned in, "Michelson's parents are outta town. Golden boy has a game tonight so I'm going over to his crib to see what I see. Interested?" Chad's dark eyes flashed with devilment. His lips formed a crooked grin which slid across his stubbly, pock marked face. Will continued to study him. The guy looked 25, not 19. There were student teachers in the building who looked younger than Chad.

"Yeah? So what's the deal?" Will asked.

"I'll let you know the details, that is, if you're in," said Chad with suspicion. Maybe he should not be so quick to trust Will Stover; after all, he might be a foster but he had not served time in juvy the way he had, three months last year. Bunch of real jerks and crazies in there. Chad had no desire to repeat the experience, got beat up pretty bad but did plenty of damage himself. Chad's blood ran cold remembering the long, dangerous nights there.

"How much cash we talking about?" asked Will. While it was true he'd just landed a job at the bike shop, he knew the pay would not add up to much. You couldn't take a girl out on a bicycle, he reasoned. No way. He longed for a car, envied those with cars. He would settle for a motorcycle. He spotted one on line and learned that for $175.00 a month, he could get a used Triumph or an Indian. This appealed to him -- girls liked guys on motorcycles. But the insurance and the license would cost him. He needed cash.

"Depends, don't know till we get there. You saying you're in?"

Will looked across the lunch room at Liz's sweet face, "I'm in."

"See ya at nine. Be out front. I don't wait for nobody."

"Piece a cake," said Chad. "Piece a cake."

"I'll say," said Will relieved that the Michelson's failed to set their alarm system. Will had gotten away with shoplifting, got off with a warning once, but never a heist anything like this. Awed by the sheer size of the home and the elegant furnishings, "This place is something," he said to Chad.

"Look at this shit!" Chad shouted.

Will joined Chad in the living room where they observed a HigherFi--Ultimate sound system, each speaker had to cost $100,000. Chad lifted his foot, kicked a speaker over, then kicked another, and another.

"What're you doing?" yelled Will.

"Having some fun before we leave. You got a problem with that?"

Will said nothing.

Chad sidled up to Will, "I call it RETRIBUTION."

"Okay," said Will.

Soon the two boys stripped the house of laptops, tablets, a Google watch, video games and equipment. Chad baptized each room with his urine, kicked over tables, chairs. Will remained focused on discovery of portable, expensive items. Will was both amazed by Chad's wild abandon and apprehensive about it. Chad, fueled by hate, believed in the validity of his anger and that others should pay for the hard-scrabble life he'd lived and yet would live. They would pay as he had.

"Check this out -- Fuck-up Michelson's old lady's got lacey drawers with about a grand stuffed in them. Mine now," said Chad pocketing the cash. "What's this shit?" Chad asked, fingering a lilac sachet. "MaMa Michelson got some coke stashed, too?" He ripped the sachet open and was dusted with its sickly sweet scent of lavender. Pissed, he threw it across the room, wiped himself off with the bedspread. Will knew better than to laugh, stifled the urge, left the room.

The boys went out the way they came in, through a back patio door they simply lifted off the track. Wisely, they did not remove their latex gloves until they were ensconced in Chad's old Buick. Chad began to laugh, feeling powerful, successful, avenged. "Bastards," he mumbled half to himself as he tossed the X-Box into the trunk of his car. "One for you, one for me," he said, adding the Play Station 4 to the stash.

"Oh, my God," said Will, "this was like taking candy from a baby." Jubilantly, he realized that once they fenced the stuff, he would be ahead at least $500, maybe more. What a haul. Maybe he would keep some of it. Play some video games with Tommy. Ask Liz out.

"I know! Dumb fuckers! The richer they are, the dumber they are!"

"Thanks, buddy; this was very cool," said Will as they drove away.

"Oh! The best part is when you hear 'em at lunch whining about the robbery. I want so bad to walk up and say, 'Yeah, fucker! I took your shit! Whaddaya gonna do about it?'"

Cowboy Night

THE NIGHT AIR WAS UNUSUALLY cool this Friday at Sam's camp site. The men had gathered around the camp fire to savor the strains of *The Last Cowboy Song*. They waited expectantly for Sam to begin his recitation of his favorite cowboy poems, a Friday night tradition. This night, a friend of Sam's sat with them and he seemed to be an okay guy; Sam was fond of him so that made things all right. This camp of homeless men, a community unto itself, welcomed few outsiders to its fireside.

Sam began and his usual low, somewhat shy voice became bold and confident as he recited *Hell in Texas*.

The devil in Hades we're told was chained,
And there for a thousand years remained.
He did not grumble nor did he groan,
But determined to make a hell of his own
Where he could torture the souls of men
Without being chained in that poisoned pen.
So he asked the Lord if he had on hand

**Anything left when he made the land.
The Lord said, "Yes, I have lots on hand,
But I left it down on the Rio Grande."**

Sam continued with the verses of the poem, flawlessly reciting for the men. One of them poked the other and whispered, "Here comes my favorite part."

**He put thorns on the cactus and horns on the toads
And scattered tarantulas along the road.
He gave spiral springs to the bronco steed
And a thousand legs to the centipede . . .
Oh, the wild boar roams the black chaparral,
It's a hell of a place he's got for Hell.**

"What'd you think of that, Glenn?" asked one of the men.
"I think it's great poetry. Sam, who wrote that?"
"It's anonymous."
"Oh, okay; by the way, you nailed it."
"Why, thank you," said Sam and he doffed his hat.
"Heard this one?" asked Sam. *The Gol-Darned Wheel by Anonymous.* With a look of mischief, Sam said, "I'd like to meet Anonymous sometime. I like his poetry."

I can ride the wildest bronco in the wild and
woolly West,
I can take him, I can break him, let him do his
level best.
I can handle any cattle ever wore a coat of hair,
And I've had a lively tussle with a tarnal griz-
zly bear.
I can rope and throw a longhorn of the wildest
Texas brand.
And at Indian disagreements I can take a lead-
ing hand.
But I finally met my master, and he really made
me squeal,
When the boys got me astraddle of that gol-
darned wheel.

Sam stopped, laughed, asked Glenn, "Do you know
what a wheel is?"
"Ah, yes . . . "
"No, you don't. Bicycles used to be called wheels!
Ha! Yeah!"
"That's a new one on me. You got me!"
"Let's drink to that," said Sam.

A Chance

GLENN SHOWED UP ON CONNIE's front porch with a sense of trepidation -- this was to be his first "date" with Connie. On previous occasions when he had suggested that they dog walk together, she had declined. This time she said yes. Glenn was thrilled. He figured Sam had something to do with her change of attitude. Whatever the reason, he was grateful.

"Whoa, girl, settle down," he cautioned Sophie.

Connie pushed the screen door open, "Come on in." She looked at Glenn, then looked at Sophie, two of a kind, she decided, both lean and muscular. Glenn's dark hair was almost a perfect match to Sophie's mottled fur. Interesting. Did people see connections between her and Doodle? She wondered.

"Hi," Glenn said, smiled and added, "this is Sophie."

"Nice to meet you," said Connie. Connie held tight to Doodle for her protection. Would the big dog go after her?

"How is she with --"

"She's great! She won't hurt your dog," Glenn assured Connie.

So off they went, to beautiful Philippe Park which was located nearby to see what they would see. The day was clear, yet warm, so their early start made great sense.

"Let's take this path," suggested Connie, "it's shady here."

As they walked, they talked and discovered common ground on issues of overbuilding in Florida and the threat it presented to the natural beauty of the state. The ensuing endless stream of high rise condos, and more condos.

"You know, John MacDonald forecast this problem in *Condominium*," Glenn said.

"*Condominium*," repeated Connie, "I haven't read it."

"You should. It's a classic, came out in the '70s. It's about Florida being overbuilt and condo's being built on sand and a Category 5 hurricane taking them out. I mean, take a look at Clearwater Beach, all those hotels, condo's, pretty soon it'll look like Ft. Lauderdale, no view of the water. It's sad." Glenn shook his head.

"It is sad, paradise expired."

"What?"

"I said, paradise expired." She nodded gravely.

"I've heard of *Paradise Lost* but never *Paradise Expired*."

"Is there a difference?" asked Connie.

"Wow. I'd have to think about that but my gut reaction is no."

"Anyway . . . " Connie said to relieve the tension.

"So what do you do in your spare time?"

Connie thought for a moment. What did she do in her spare time?

"Well, I keep pretty busy at the Spa and writing poetry, walking Miss Doodle here. I guess that's about it," she said. Connie said nothing to Glenn about her past, her efforts to locate her son. She said nothing about how things stood with her parents, that they were estranged. Best to keep personal issues to herself, she thought.

"And you?" she asked, stepping up onto the tiered walkway by the water. "Come on, girl, you can make it," she said to Doodle who hesitated before hopping up onto the embankment.

"Same as you, work and writing, although you write much more than I do. Actually, when I lived in Colorado, I was into photography," he said.

"Really?" said Connie. "What did you shoot?"

A squirrel crossed the path; Sophie charged aggressively. "Sophie!" Glenn commanded, "Stop." Sophie obediently resumed walking with Glenn, knowing full well that when he used that tone, he meant business.

"Good girl," said Glenn. He reached down and patted her. He explained to Connie that he had been a wedding photographer and how it had paid his college and law school bills. "But my real interest was in photographing the mountains in Colorado. That was amazing."

"Wow!" said Connie, impressed. She thought for a moment, "And now? Do you photograph Florida? I mean we have no mountains but --"

Glenn hedged, "Not exactly . . ."

"Not exactly," Connie repeated.

"I haven't had the camera out of the case since I moved here."

"What a pity," said Connie. "We'll have to do something about that, don't you think?"

"Yes, we will!" said Glenn, his face filled with joy. Was this a beginning? He hoped so. He had not met anyone like Connie before. Her very presence gave him unspeakable happiness, a happiness he had not experienced in many years.

Tarot Predictions

"WHAT'S THAT, SAL?" ASKED CONNIE.

"Tarot cards!"

"Oh, I've heard of them but never seen them before," said Connie.

"They're very cool," said Salli. "I'll tell you all about them."

"Why don't we wait for Drina?" asked Connie, uncorking a bottle of merlot. "Here, try this," she poured Salli a goblet of wine.

Salli had no sooner agreed the merlot was delicious when Drina arrived. The women settled in for Friday night wine. Connie sank into the sofa, curled her legs and popped a chocolate into her mouth, "Mmmm . . . these chocolates are so dark and rich, Drina. Thanks for bringing these tonight."

"Ditto," said Salli. "Yum."

"Okay, Sal, shoot, tell us all about your Tarot cards." Drina and Connie waited, curious.

"Well, some people play card games with them but mostly people use them to tell the future; they read them," said Salli.

"And?" asked Drina.

"And, they're cool, that's all. See?" Salli spread the colorful deck out onto the coffee table. "This one says: Be relaxed. Restful healing."

Drina picked one up: "Great inner strength. Release judgment."

"That's kind of nice, I like that," said Connie.

"Take one," said Salli.

"Okay," said Connie, "Review and evaluate. Be thoughtful when you weigh the consequences."

"This stuff gives good advice," said Drina. "I had no idea."

"Yes! The pictures are gorgeous, too. Look at this one!" Salli held up a watercolor impression of a unicorn and a maiden.

"This is art!" said Drina. "Really." Drina looked over at Connie who sat spellbound, "What?"

"Listen to this," Connie read: "Challenging information. Delays may occur. Persevere. You will win in time."

"Hmmm," Salli teased, furrowing her brow, "I'm looking for a card that says: You should not withhold information from friends."

Drina and Connie looked up, puzzled.

Salli continued, "If a handsome man appears on your porch with a dog . . . "

"Oh, come on!" said Connie.

"What's this about?" asked Drina.

"Tell her!" said Salli.

"Oh, my God, I don't believe this." Connie looked at their expectant faces, "Sometimes Glenn comes by with Sophie and we walk our dogs. No big deal."

"If it's no big deal, why haven't you said anything?" asked Salli, smiling, pleased with herself.

"Con, that's awesome that you guys hang out," said Drina.

"I guess so," said Connie. "Sorry. It isn't supposed to be a big deal or anything."

"I bet it is to him," said Salli.

"Oh, yeah," agreed Drina.

Pseudo Wife

From the minute he walked into her office to discuss the child mentoring program, MentorBond4Kidz, Drina was attracted to Chief Assistant Prosecutor Lloyd McHughes. An unhappy marriage had rendered Drina Alvarez a single parent, one struggling to support her teen daughter. Life was not easy. She found it difficult to meet a good man and she was lonely. McHughes' bright penetrating eyes, shy smile, broad shoulders, firm hand shake all bespoke a man of credibility. His well-tailored suit hung in casual elegance on his well-built frame. He appeared relaxed, gentle, yet when he spoke, his words revealed a current of energy and focus, a man of vision. She found him fascinating.

For his part, he found her to be sensuous, sweet. They exchanged amenities.

Then, he said, "May I ask you a personal question?"

She said, "Yes," quite happy to accommodate.

"Your name, Drina. It's unusual. I assume it's Spanish?"

She smiled, pleased that he was interested, "Drina means helper, defender in Spanish, yes."

"And your last name, Alvarez, is it Mexican, Cuban, or ?" He leaned in, waiting.

"Cuban," she answered.

It was his turn to smile: Perfect. The Cubans were known to hold a 70% voting rate amongst the Hispanics in Florida. By the time he had left her office, he had secured a position in the MentorBond4Kidz program as well as one in Drina's life.

The Chalk Festival

I<small>T WAS</small> S<small>UNDAY, THE DAY</small> of the annual Safety Harbor chalk festival. Main Street was closed to traffic and filled with food vendors, artists, and musicians.

"This is so cool! I love this!" said Salli, as she stood watching an artist sketch an outline of Beyonce onto the asphalt street. "Wow, they sketch so quickly!"

"That's for sure," agreed Connie.

"I can only stay a little longer; I have to get to work," said Salli, wrinkling her nose. Just then Drina joined them, "Salli, your ice cream is melting!"

Salli attended her ice cream, still sulking, "Aren't you guys going to some tea party or something like that today?"

Connie nodded yes and checked her watch; she did not want to be late to Margaret Garing's tea party at two.

"Oh," Drina said sourly, "look who's here strutting her stuff," she tossed her head in the direction of Sharon.

"Wow! That's her, isn't it? The one who's after Glenn. The slutty one!" said Salli, thrilling to the moment.

"Um-hmm," said Connie.

Sharon looked magnificent, gleaming blonde curls peeking out from the rim of the broad-brimmed, white sun hat. She wore the Marilyn Classic Playsuit -- $200 -- white cotton pique sweetheart neckline top, tucked into crisp white, boy-leg short-shorts. Her legs tan, long, curvy, her feet strapped into cherry red espadrille's, matching her red patent tote. She leaned over a chalk depiction of Clark Gable, whispered to the chalk artist, "Do Marilyn Monroe right next to him, okay?" she batted her long eyelashes.

The young male artist readily agreed. "Anything for you," he said.

She smiled and dropped a twenty into the tip canister.

"Thank you!" said the young artist, keeping his eyes locked on Sharon.

Maybe he was lonely, too, she thought. Since James had inconsiderately taken his life, Sharon existed in a sexual desert. Though men constantly hit on her, none of them stirred her libido or heart strings like Glenn. Where was he anyway? She scanned the street: There he was, walking toward Connie the Bitch, big happy grin on his face.

"Humph," she muttered.

"What was that?" asked the young artist, hurrying through his chalky Clark Gable, anxious to do Marilyn for the gorgeous blonde standing nearby.

"Oh, nothing," she said. She trained her eyes on the little group. She saw they were heading to Margaret's apartment. It was time. "I'll be back soon," she promised and headed right for the apartment. She wouldn't miss this for the world.

Margaret hummed "Tea for Two" busying herself for her little party. How she loved a party. Why, when Herbert had been alive, they were known as the premier party mavens of Philadelphia. She looked lovingly at his photo now. Ah, she thought, he was so dapper. She blew him a kiss, "Oh, my love, how I miss you."

The ring of the door-bell was joined by the whistle of the tea kettle, braced by the sound track playing the "Best of 1940's" music.

Margaret welcomed her guests and announced, "I have Earl Gray, green tea, orange-cinnamon spice."

"Sounds wonderful," said Drina.

Margaret studied the flushed faces of her guests and realized they needed cold drinks not hot tea. "I can ice the tea and," her eyes sparkled, "I can spike it with -- brandy, rum, anything you like." Thus, the tea party began.

"Your place is darling," said Connie. "I love all the tea pots, the tea cups. You must have collected all of your life!" She stood in amazement and gazed at the array of designs and shapes of the tea pots.

"Yes, I did, or, rather we did," she nodded toward Herbert's picture, "we traveled the world and we collected our tea pots joyfully." She picked up a Russian beauty, gold, royal blue, a fluted spout, "This one's from --"

The doorbell.

Connie and Drina stiffened realizing it was probably Sharon.

"Oh, Sharon, dear, welcome," said Margaret, herself stiffening a bit at the sight of Sharon.

The tension in the room palpable, Margaret offered her guests a view of the bay from her large casement of arched third-floor windows.

"Wow!" said Glenn, "This is wonderful. The sunsets must be spectacular from here."

Margaret smiled and began to recite Longfellow from *The Song of Hiawatha*, everyone became still to listen:

> **The Son of the Evening Star**
> **Can it be the sun descending**
> **O'er the level plain of water**
> **Or the Red Swan floating, flying,**
> **Wounded by the magic arrow.**
> **Staining all the waves with crimson,**
> **With the crimson of its life-blood,**
> **Filling all the air with splendor,**
> **With the splendor of its plumage?**

"That is so beautiful," said Drina.

"It is beautiful," Margaret said. " I read Longfellow each morning and never tire of the beauty of his work. I sit here," she pointed to the bistro table and two chairs positioned strategically for the view. "I watch the sun rise. This is also where I write. Also," Margaret pointed to a bank of windows across the room, "I see the sun set over there. It's perfect." There was a pause as the guests appreciated the splendor of the views.

"Margaret," asked Glenn, "didn't you just publish again in *Seminole World*?"

Margaret smiled, "Yes, I did, but enough about me now. Everyone, please help yourselves," she gestured to the table laid with goodies. She turned to Glenn, "By the way, is Sam coming? I haven't heard from him," she shrugged, "of course, I didn't expect to, I know he has his own life." Margaret cared for Sam but the time had passed in her life that she wished to have a significant other and it was obvious to her that he felt the same. "And Don?" she asked, "Where's he?"

"Neither of those guys are the tea party type, Margaret," Glenn said. He put his arm around her, "But I am." The friendship between Margaret and Glenn went way back; it was she, in fact, who had been the founder of the poetry group when she was head librarian, a post she held for 30 years. They shared this history with Connie, Sharon, and Drina.

Glenn said, "She roped me in. Yes, you did, Margaret! You roped me into chairing by asking if I would 'just do it for a little while'."

Margaret broke into laughter, "It worked, didn't it?"

Glenn looked into her eyes, eyes that held metaphysical secrets, "It worked!" said Glenn who towered over this diminutive Seminole woman who had steered the success of the library from its infancy to the large, incredible facility it now was. Under Margaret's tutelage, the library system purchased twenty acres of land, part of which now housed the library, part leased to the Spa for guest parking, which was a great source of income for the library. A shrewd businesswoman, a highly literate woman, a lovable woman, Margaret Garing was the backbone of the Pinellas County Library system.

"Glad it worked!" added Connie.

Sharon sat quietly observing the merriment, her face pale, her mouth grim. She felt alone, closed out. She watched Glenn's eyes dance with affection for Margaret, saw him train his eyes on Connie and the look of love he gave to her made Sharon feel envy to her core. Why could it not be her he loved? Is it because I'm married? she wondered. Her next thought was of Ray and she felt sad, cheated. Tears formed and she blinked them away, inhaled deeply and tossed a smile across the room to the others. She sat there alone, on Margaret's brocade sofa, sipped tea in a room filled with others, none of them her friends. Friends. Do I have any? She pondered this, tilted her head, put her finger to her cheek, thinking, forgetting for a moment where she was. I had a friend once; what happened to her? Once more, she thought of her husband who had been her friend once. But now . . . nothing, no one. No one except The Glass Heads, they cared about her, yes, they were her friends now. She cheered at the thought. They understood her, listened to her.

After her guests left, Margaret rinsed the tea cups and glasses, emptied the ice bucket, poured herself a brandy and sat down at the bistro table. "Oh, my," she said, "I almost forgot Herbert." She went to the sideboard and lovingly picked up his picture. She could hardly wait to tell him all about the party so she began telling him as she walked back to the table.

"Herbert, dear, my little party was a success." She set his picture facing her across the table from where she sat, as was her custom at the end of each day and she sipped her brandy. Herbert had been her love from the time they had met. He, staunch, straight-backed, very British, she, warm and loving. The contrast worked for forty-two years. Now he was gone. Though Margaret's father was British, her mother was Seminole and had named Margaret Hachi Akcawhko meaning river water bird; privately, Herbert would call her Hachi all of their lives. Hachi chose the name Margaret for professional reasons, but now regretted that she had done so. Herbert never did understand her decision but he supported her in all things. Her love of tea pots stemmed from Herbert's mother's love of tea pots, and when she had passed, Margaret had inherited many beautiful pots. She and Herbert added to the collection as the years passed. She rose and changed the music, inserting a CD of *Hiawatha's Wedding Feast*.

"This party was my farewell, Herbert, I'm coming to you very soon now."

Herbert's warm smile and kindly face encouraged her to share her secret, a secret she'd been keeping from everyone, especially her cardiologist. "I've stopped taking the meds, my love." She paused, "I know it won't be long now, and I'm relieved. You see my dear, since you passed seven years ago, I've tried, you know I have," she emphasized to Herbert that, indeed, she had tried to enjoy life but without him, it was lonely. She sighed, "Yes, the poetry group has been a comfort, but . . . " Margaret shook her head, "It's time to go. Hachi is coming to you."

Margaret took pen to paper and wrote out her wishes: The immense collection of tea pots and small Seminole collection of artifacts would be given to Glenn Tennyson. As chair of the poetry group, it would be his responsibility to bestow tea pots upon her designees and to find a home for the rest. "I trust his discretion, Herbert. You know full well no one in the family cares about my silly tea pots."

Showcase

Glenn listened intently as Margaret's executor explained that it was he she had chosen to oversee the dispensation of her tea pot collection and her collection of Seminole artifacts. At first, Glenn wondered why Margaret chose him instead of the one of her nieces or nephews in Philadelphia, but the executor assured him that Margaret had been quite specific in this regard.

"I see, thank you," Glenn said and hung up the phone, feeling frustrated. Collections, collections, what do I know about collections? Guiltily, he realized he owned several collections: The turned wood bowls. The cowboy poetry books. The photography equipment and extensive library of photography books -- the list went on and on. "I guess what we collect defines us." He sighed, "Okay, where do I go from here?" He puzzled only momentarily when he had what he considered to be a spectacular idea. Some of the tea pots were highly valuable. They would be an excellent addition to the library's annual silent auction, the proceeds of which went directly to the children's book room fund.

Margaret would love this. Still, some of the tea pots should be preserved. But how? How could he do this and honor Margaret?

Glenn decided he might be inspired if he did a simple thing, make a visit to the library which was a short walk up the street. Most of the time, he simply walked to the back of the library and into the conference room for the poetry group meetings but today, he would take a good look around. As he approached the library, he noted the mosaic patterns on the exterior walls. How had he failed to notice them before? Sprinklers turned on and danced sprinkling drops of sparkling water into the air. Inside, he saw a large glass showcase. It was wonderful. It was empty. Why? He learned that a scheduled quilt display had been rescheduled, possibly cancelled, by the quilt group. There it was, the answer: He would fill the showcase with a grouping of Margaret's tea pots. That was it, he would give a brief history of each of the tea pots, and donate a large bronze plaque in tribute to her. This plaque would delineate Margaret's heritage as that of a descendant of the great Seminole War leader, Chief Osceola. He would see that the small collection of Seminole artifacts would be housed also but in a separate showcase. She deserves that and more, he thought. Without her, he would never have met Connie, or Sam. His pace quickened as he walked back to his office. Yes, he would make arrangements right away. A nagging thought wove its way in and out of his mind as he plotted the course of Margaret's tea pot collection. Did she specify any specific directives? He would call the executor back, ask him.

Tea Pots

GLENN CAREFULLY PACKED THE TEA pots Margaret speci-
fied be given to each of the poetry group members and
arrived early at the library for their meeting. He was right
in calling the executor back: Margaret had not forgotten
her friends; she had chosen certain tea pots for each individual. It was these that Glenn would now disperse. He
would always cherish the cowboy tea pot Margaret left to
him. In fact, it now sat on his office bookshelf in a prominent position.

He quietly greeted Connie, Drina, Sam, Don, and
Sharon. The group seemed diminished without Margaret's
smiling face; her patient, supportive manner would be
greatly missed.

"I know all of you feel what I feel," he began, it was
more difficult than he expected to get the words out.
He cleared his throat. "Our dear friend is departed." He
tapped the box next to him on the table, "But she left each
of us a remembrance."

To Connie, the exquisite grapevine tea pot. To Drina, the pink lady tea pot. To Don, the Corvette tea pot which had been one of Herbert's favorites. To Sam, a copper tea kettle. To Sharon, the Marilyn Monroe tea set.

Each of the members of the group admired their tea pot. Each pot unique to the individual, but no one expected Sharon's emotional reaction.

"For me? This is for me?" she gasped and wiped away tears. Embarrassed, she shrunk back into her seat. Quiet, unable to speak further, her need to be the center of attention unspooled. Unusual for her.

When Sharon got home, she heated the kettle and hurriedly searched for the tin of tea she kept in the back of the cupboard. There it is, she thought. She carefully set the Marilyn Monroe tea pot, cups and saucers on the table, stood back and admired them. She sighed and poured herself a cup of tea.

Ray walked in, "So what're you doing?" he asked.

"What does it look like?" she answered coldly.

"What's that thing?" He pointed at the tea pot.

"A tea pot, you dolt," she said sourly.

"Really? the leg is the spout? What the hell?" He laughed.

"You're spoiling this for me. This tea set was a gift. You wouldn't understand." She sniffed.

No, he would not understand. For once, Sharon felt someone remembered her, someone gave a damn, someone understood her. Now that person was dead. She wished it was Ray who was dead, not Margaret.

Later, she would discuss her feelings with The Glass Heads, they were her fall-back support system, uncritical, smart, always there for her.

High School

Lunchtime at Clear Springs High was a zoo. Most days, seniors piled in cars, took off for fast-food restaurants which they circled like hungry sharks. Today, repaving of the student lot meant off-campus parking. There simply wasn't time to get to the car, drive to a restaurant, eat, drive back, park, and get back to class on a 45 minute lunch break. The cafeteria festered with grumbling over the crappy burgers, fake cheese, limp lettuce, frozen fries and watered down soda. "This sucks. Why didn't the idiots wait till school's out to pave the lot?" "Anything to piss us off." Blah. Blah. Blah.

Chad and Will slumped over cokes and greasy fries staring with disdain at their classmates. Snobs. Entitled bastards/bitches. Going away to fancy colleges, not interested in anyone but those within the confines of their own cliques.

Suddenly, Will's eyebrows shot up, his posture straightened.

"Oh, she's here, eh?" said Chad.

"What if she is?"

Liz Webber, the dark-haired beauty with an irrepressible smile, approached Will, balancing her lunch tray and shouldering her purse. "Hi, Will," she said, smiling.

Will felt himself blush, said "Hello".

"Are you going to the spring play?" She lowered her eyes onto her wilted salad, "I'm playing the lead. You may have heard?" she asked, tilted her head coquettishly. Though Will was not part of the clique, she was interested in him all right. Tall, good looking, a quiet, confident manner of speaking in English class. His discourse proved he was intelligent. He was different from the other guys.

"Oh, yeah, I did. That's really cool," Will nodded. "I'll, I'll try to make it."

"There you are!" the voice boomed, cold eyes darting Will's way.

"Robert, you know Will," Liz said. Stonily, they greeted one another.

"Liz, come on, we gotta go." Robert cocked his head toward the table across the room.

Will's gaze lingered on Liz as she and Robert turned to go.

"Yes," spouted Chad, "hurry on to the Harvard and Yale bound assholes' table."

Will frowned, "Was that necessary?"

"Oh, did I insult your Lady Love?"

Will picked up his lunch tray.

"Where you going?" challenged Chad.

"Anywhere you aren't," said Will.

Will dumped his uneaten lunch into the giant trash barrel, threw the tray onto the shelf above it, then briskly headed up the stairs to the outdoor student lounge. Thoughts circled his mind. He liked Liz. Liked her a lot. He clenched his teeth and his fists just thinking about Chad's crude remark. No, Liz wasn't Harvard bound but she was college bound. Where? He seemed to remember her saying something about the University of South Florida. Remorsefully, he reviewed what his foster case manager advised: If the Maloney's were willing to continue being fosters, then Will's college expenses would be paid for by the state. But the hitch was (wasn't there always a hitch?) the Maloney's had declined. Will sighed. The Maloney's raised the question was he college material? Their polite non-committal manner had indicated that no, he was not. They aptly pointed out that he had not shown intellectual curiosity nor had he earned the high grades necessary for college entrance. Desiring privacy, Will sought out a bench hidden away beneath a giant magnolia tree. The familiar feeling of hopelessness crept in. Sometimes putting up a good front, hiding feelings worked best, other times, like now, he felt exhausted by the effort.

"Hey, here you are," Chad sat down next to him, "sorry, man, if I rained on your parade."

"Okay," Will said, his tone icy.

At the sound of the bell, the young men rose as one. The foster bond they shared transcended their differences. Their perceived status as outsiders reinforced their disconnection from the student body. Though not as hard shelled as Chad, Will's faith in a positive future faded. Nothing ever worked out. Why should it now? Liz would meet some hot shot at USF, fall in love, marry him. One more thing Will could not have. Someone to love.

Suspension

TROPICAL SHADES OF MANGO, HIBISCUS and lime shimmered in the freshly remodeled main office of Clear Springs High. Decorative palm leaves festooned the walls and repeated in the upholstery of the chairs and carpeting. Things were looking up at Clear Springs High which had gone through a dry period of funding, poor parent perceptions combined with an influx of lower performing students. Things were on the mend now with the new administration in place. The office bristled with energy as teachers stopped in quickly to retrieve their mail from the bank of staff mailboxes, counselors met with parents, and rule breakers sat awaiting their hearing with the associate principal, Miss Havercane. The students, of course, called her Hurricane. This was due to the speed with which she talked, walked, turned red and screamed when provoked. A perpetually on-the-muscle toughie. Her skirts, so short, that the staff whispered they knew what brand of underwear she sported, some snickered she probably went without.

The principal, her polar opposite, a man of quiet refinement, a man of letters, a man of lust. Every good looking woman was fair game. His glistening steel gray hair, bronze skin, lantern jaw, the stuff of heroes. A GQ model all right with his impeccably tailored suits and silk paisley ties. (Though he was careful to hide the truth that his wife worked in a pricey men's store and got all his duds at a deep discount.) Father of four, all nearing college age, made Wayne Phelan an ambitious man. His eyes never wavered far from the prize: district superintendent. He felt most excellently endowed for the position. Word was out that the current super was moving on to another larger district. Therefore, Phelan culminated each meeting with whiny, critical parents with a firm hand shake, a smile, and a promise to take care of the problem. Most people liked him, some did not, "I don't trust that guy. He's weak is what he is. Agrees with whoever is in his office."

But one person both trusted and lusted Phelan, hitched her wagon to his star: young Miss Havercane. His were the deep set dark eyes she loved to look into, like star gazing; his voice was the voice she loved to hear, the voice of approval. Work was work for most of the staff, but work was life for Miss Havercane. She centered every iota of her being on enforcing the rules of the school. Making enemies was not a problem for her, neither with staff nor students. Parents? she treaded more lightly with them but a few of them also knew the wrath of Havercane. All she cared about was pleasing Phelan.

"Wayne," said Havercane leaning over him, breasts exposed, "take a look at this study, the results of the latest parent community's perception of our staff and administration. We rock and you know why . . . our take-no-prisoners method is working. We're looking good."

"Looking good is right," he said, grinning ear to ear, enjoying the view.

From Phelan's office, Havercane strode down to her office, quite displeased to see Chad Harn in the seating area. She beckoned him into her office. "You're here . . . again," she said tersely. Quickly scanning the teacher's note, she added, "Same offense. You just don't learn, do you?"

"I learn what I like, not what other people tell me to learn."

Havercane glared. Her eyes flashed. His met hers in defiance. "This is the third time I've had your ass in here on the same issue. What's your problem?" She lowered her eyes to the baseball he rolled in his hand.

He opened his mouth, about to speak; when she blasted, "YOU ARE NOT TO BRING A BASEBALL INTO CLASS!!"

Undaunted, he spit out, "Why not? I don't do nothing with it. Why's that a problem?" He smirked and continued to roll the ball in his hand.

Will's friend. Partner in crime.

"That's a lie! Mrs. Jensen reported you're bringing it to class, and I quote, 'repeatedly rolling it in your hands, sometimes feigning throwing it at her.' She also said that you told her to fuck off."

"Yeah . . . so?" he smirked, eyes dead.

"So, this time you will know I mean business," she scrawled on a form, "you are hereby suspended for five days. Out. Of. School." She accentuated the words.

He stood, shaken, the slick act dissolved, "Wait! Out-of-school? That means I can't make up finals. I won't graduate!" Fists clenched.

Havercane stood, leaned over her desk, leered, "That's right! Should have thought of that before. You'll find we have an excellent summer school program."

He headed straight for her, circled her desk, she faced him squarely, her reptile eyes gleaming, neck veins swelling, taunting, "Want to hit me? Go ahead, hit me! DO IT!"

Disarmed, he backed off, promised, "I'll appeal this. Bitch!"

"Go ahead," she sniffed, "you'll lose." She lifted the phone, advised security to escort Mr. Harn out of the building.

Forgery

THOUGH SAID TO BE ONLY one of the metrics used to judge Florida's schools, the reality was the Florida Comprehensive Assessment Test (FCAT), was a huge determinant of a school's status. Status impacted every aspect of a school. Parents wishing to enroll their students in the best, most competitive colleges, read the scores before choosing a home in a school district. Grants and awards were impacted by the scores, not to mention the reflection on the school administrators. Their performance as educators was directly linked to the almighty state exams because the axis upon which the state rotated with regard to the ongoing national competition between states wishing to boast that theirs was the best educational system. The daily papers posted the scores routinely on the front pages. The noble governor would post first-hand, detailed analyses and every taxpayer in the state would crow about how "They're not doing their damn job!" Thus, Havercane believed in the virtue of what she did as she sat at the computer screen adjusting student answers:

delete, add, move. Supposedly safely encrypted, it didn't take her long to hack in and adjust things to reflect oh, such a great student body, brilliantly prepared for college, the FCAT being the proof.

She muttered, "Social studies, why is it always the worst of the scores? Can't these idiots remember anything, any prominent dates, wars, generals?" Her face tightened with disdain as she flipped through the student tests, applying correct answers gleaned from the answer booklet. (Sometimes she herself unsure of an answer.) Principal Phelan will see when I show him these scores, she mused, spreading her lips into a wicked smile that my take-no-prisoners, zero-tolerance policies WORK. She inhaled, felt aroused just thinking about him. No one will ever know. No one. It would take all night, but there she sat, making Clear Springs High the gem of the gulf coast.

Video Prank

A THOUSAND TEENS BURST OUT the door of Clear Springs High, free at last, another school day ended. The circular drive clogged with every make and model of car -- parents picking up their precious cargo. The student lot, filled with expensive cars, cars more pricey than those of the teaching staff, roared with noise as engines fired up.

Will sprinted down the concrete steps, his backpack slung over his shoulder, looking for Chad. There he was, parking further down along the curb. Will jumped in the car, "Didn't know if you'd show."

"Why not? I just can't go in the building. I'm allowed out here. It's a free country!"

"Wow, when I heard what Havercane did, man, I was in shock," said Will as Chad aggressively eased into traffic. He got the horn, returned it, along with the finger.

"Pick you up later?" Chad asked.

"Definitely," answered Will.

"I love Friday night," Will exhaled slowly, feeling the burn. "This is good stuff, man, where'd you get it?"

"Can't say, you don't wanna know." Chad paused, "Changing the subject, Havercane, can you believe that bitch? Havenobrain, Haverslain, I wish I could kill that bitch," Chad's eyes narrowed.

Quiet, then . . . "What the fuck? Did you see that?" Chad asked.

"What? See what?"

"I swear I just saw Haverslain and Fuck-up Phelan drive by."

"You're seeing things, man." Will took a drag.

"No! I know what I saw." Chad suddenly awakened from his slump, started the car, creeping along, tailing them.

There, parked beneath the sago palm they could see Havercane's car. "What are they doing here?" Will asked.

"I don't know but I'm finding out." Chad crept out of his car, Will followed. "They're going at it, those fuckers!" Chad whispered.

"Let's give them a moment . . ." Will grinned, "This will be your ticket out of suspension."

"I knew there was a reason I kept you around," said Chad.

With that Will pulled out his stolen cell phone and hit record. Quietly he laughed, loving the sting. Chad thrilled, the bitch would get her due. Retribution.

Still laughing over the events of the evening, Will uploaded the sex video on his laptop as soon as he got home. He reflected, Havercane favored the jocks, shunned the rest of the students, she deserved to be humiliated. How this was to occur was not yet clear in Will's mind, but he knew she would be brought down and that he would be a vital part of the process.

$$✣ ✣ ✣ ✣ ✣$$

Monday morning, over the objections of Havercane's secretary, Will pushed into Havercane's office, shut the door, sat down.

She rose, tense, "If you're here to plead your good buddy's case, forget it, his punishment stands. No deals. Now, get out!"

Without a word, Will hit play. Before Havercane saw the screen, she heard herself moaning on the sound track. Mortified, her jaw dropped.

"I assume my friend's suspension is hereby revoked?" Will cocked an eyebrow, his blue eyes burning.

Speechless, she nodded.

Will called Chad, "You're in," got up and walked out. She, frozen.

Chad strutted into the building savoring revenge. Will wasn't seated in class very long when there was a message from the main office, he was to report immediately.

"Sit down, Mr. Stover," ordered Phelan, "I believe you have something that belongs to me."

"No, sir, I have nothing of yours."

"Let's not play cat and mouse. You got what you wanted, your friend is back in school, he will graduate. Now give me the cell phone."

"Why would I do that?"

"Look you little bastard, I want that phone and NOW," he pounced from behind his desk, sweat beads on his forehead, eyes bulging.

"You got it old man," Will said setting the phone on the desk.

Phelan grabbed it, "You better not play fuck-around with me again or I'll make sure neither you nor your friend graduate. Got it?"

"Bullshit," Will spat out.

"No bullshit. At the flick of my wrist, your school records can be altered to reflect you lack the necessary credits to graduate. You see," he grinned, "you're not the only one who's capable of using technology to his advantage."

Will and Chad were immediately placed on out-of-school suspension.

Will got home, uploaded the sex video onto YouTube. Next, he called his study hall seat partner, a friend, Janine, asked her to go to the media center and call up Havercane on YouTube. She did so, and went the extra mile putting it up on the large screen for all to see.

News spread across the study body as fast as high-speed internet. Phones rang in thousands of households.

Parents gasped, many unbelieving of what they saw. "This must be some sort of joke. Whoever concocted this should be punished severely." Others said they thought the media center computers had filters to screen out this sort of nonsense. Havercane's moans were heard in homes, cars, work places, any and everywhere technology and gossip could go. Within two short minutes, 1500 people had seen Havercane and Phelan in action in the car, beneath the Sago palm. The lovers.

Exposure

Havercane burst into Phelan's office. "The video's on YouTube!"

Phelan calm, "What are you talking about? I've got his phone right here in my desk."

"It's on YouTube," she gasped, "they, they've all seen it!" Blood pressure screaming.

"Wha . . . what?" Phelan bug-eyed. Then, "My wife, she'll," he gasped, ready to faint.

Noise, strange voices, cluttering the air -- "You can't go in there!" "There they are!" "Move it! I was here first!" This amid the churning hallways, students engaged in disparaging their noble leaders. Laughter, cheers, and an eerie atmosphere as if time stood still. Phelan's door burst open. Reporters piled in. Microphones shoved in their faces by a sea of media hounds, drooling. All was lost.

Havercane backed away, decided to run. But how? She could never traverse the crowd of reporters. The window. Phelan's office window -- it was open. She hitched up her skirt and pushed herself through the opening, spilling onto the lawn. More reporters. Her black lace panties on video now. She ran for her life, which, as a professional, was over. Panicked, Phelan failed as he tried to escape, his bad knee giving way. Collapsing in his stately chair, he covered his face and dissolved into a very small heap. Shoulders quaking, low-pitched moaning. Beaten.

Chad and Will were triumphant: They had beaten the enemy. Will slid into Havercane's office and deleted their suspensions. They were back, home free.

Confession

ONE OF THE NICEST FEATURES about the town of Safety Harbor was the long wooden pier which stretched itself into Tampa Bay and with immediate ease thrilled its many visitors with a wide, expansive view. Manatees frequently nestled beneath the pier and dolphins played in the near distance. The Marina Fishing Pier was frequented by locals as well as tourists and was flanked by Veteran's Memorial Park. Fishermen and women who cast lines and waited patiently, were often rewarded with any one of a variety of fish: pompano, mullet, bass, bonefish, amberjack and others. This Marina pier had become a favorite spot with Will and Sam.

"Sam, I've been waiting for you. Look at the size of the mullet I caught!" called Will over the cry of the sea gulls.

Sam smiled when he saw Will, "Hey! You're starting to be real competition, boy!" Sam squinted and pulled the brim of his baseball hat down further, shielding his eyes

"I was hoping I'd see you today. I kind of have something on my mind and . . . " Will hesitated, his eyes trailing a few passersby.

Now curious, Sam asked: "What's that?" He set his bait, cast his line, tossed Will a curious look.

"There's this guy, actually, he's my buddy, and he got in some trouble and I fixed it for him. I guess I wonder if I went too far."

"That's not much for me to go on, Will."

"I videotaped some people having sex. Then I published it on the internet."

Sam's eyes darted back and forth, "You did what?!" A fisherman standing nearby moved closer. Sam edged away, Will followed suit, lowered his voice.

"They deserved it. They treated me and my friend really badly. They're scum."

"Who the hell are these people?"

Will proceeded with the back story, Sam listened, and even though Sam was a bit hard of hearing, he was the best listener Will had ever known. Will opened up to Sam telling him how Havercane had instituted a zero tolerance attendance policy at the high school, kids like Jennifer Breen who was under the treatment of a psychiatrist for three years and had tried suicide once already being told she would not graduate, did not have the credits. She had to be institutionalized she was so distraught. Stories about one unkind action after another like Will's favorite teacher being disallowed to attend her own daughter's Pre-Olympic swim competitions.

"How'd you know about that?" Sam croaked.

"The door of the teachers' lounge was open; I heard her crying and talking about it."

"I see," said Sam, satisfied it was the truth.

"There's lots more, too." Sam put up his hand, a motion for Will to quiet down. "That's enough, I get it," Sam sighed. "What's done is done, boy. I can't condone what you did, but I understand why you did it. Mean people bring out mean behavior."

"I've done some other things I'm not too proud of, Sam." Will hung his head.

Sam hesitated, "Was the guy you were protecting the guy that came in the shop that day -- I know he stole stuff."

Will edgy, sighed, "Yeah. It was him."

"Careful," Sam cautioned, "when you lay down with dogs, you wake up with fleas."

The Cat

McHUGHES SWIRLED THE ICE IN his rum and coke. He had just finished a phone call from his older brother, Bryce, aka, Mr. Perfect, who was not only two inches taller than McHughes, but much richer than McHughes, being in private practice and billing 90 hours a week at a cushy law firm in Tampa. Another brag session, Bryce's two sons, both stars, of course, on the field in their never-ending sports teams, and in academics, the pride of their parents and grandparents. McHughes' mother also never seemed to get enough of raving about the boys, now 8 and 10. She claimed they favored her side of the family in their looks, and obviously in their intelligence. No matter her own husband had graduated summa cum laude from Duke. Other than her eldest son and his sons, she disparaged everything, her lips frozen in a permanent scowl.

McHughes took a long pull on the rum and coke, chewed his mustache, spit out "fuck her." The one memory of his childhood that repeatedly made an entrance into his little world was the morning his brother had spilled a quart of milk on the kitchen floor. Mother had been very upset, asking Bryce to help clean up the mess. But Bryce said he'd be late for school and walked out leaving her with the mess. McHughes felt quite the hero for staying and helping her but she never acknowledged he did so. Never did, never would. As usual, he got no credit for anything, not from her. Apparently being the youngest was a detriment, a negative which he could not overcome despite his Herculean effort to do so. Oftentimes he felt as if he were invisible. Birth order was a bitch.

What did Mr. Perfect want to talk about this time? Oh, yes, the BBQ, the infernal, miserable, let's pretend to be a family BBQ. Again, the phone rang. McHughes, cursing under his breath, banged back another gulp and took the call. Mother. Same topic, same nagging pressure, yes, he would be there, yes, he would bring Ryan, his assigned child in MentorBond4Kidz, yes, he would be bringing his lady friend. Yes. Yes. Yes. McHughes had learned that this was the only acceptable answer to her: yes. But there was a no included also, in fact, several, no he wouldn't be late, no, he would not forget the salad from Fresh Market, no, he wouldn't make Ryan the center of things and ignore his very special nephews. Miss Snickers walked into the room, tentatively. She was hungry.

"Come here, kitty," McHughes beckoned. When she failed to do so, he clicked his tongue but Miss Snickers knew better than to get too close. McHughes scooped her up onto his lap, smoothed her fur for a few seconds, then, something snapped. Anger bubbled to the top of his gullet,

"I hate those people!" He began to squeeze Miss Snickers hard; she struggled and in the process drew blood from the back of his hand. "You piece of shit!" he screamed as he threw Miss Snickers at the wall. She fooled him, however, landed on her feet and managed to escape. Hungry, yes, but safe.

Drunk Again

IT WAS 2:30 AM WHEN McHughes carefully pulled his white Lexus into his clapboard garage located in the back of his deep yard. How careless he'd been not to stock enough of his favored spirit, rum. He'd made a run for more despite his present state of inebriation. The liquor store was nearby; he chanced it. Quietly now, he picked his way up to the house along the narrow, tree-lined driveway. A seam in the concrete caught the tip of his shoe. "Shit!" he hissed as he caught himself from falling. However, his fine Lopez Leather loafer flipped off and landed in a puddle, face down. McHughes ground his teeth as he bent his powerful body to retrieve it. His hand trembled as he grabbed hold of the shoe, once again, too much to drink, and for a man of his stature, so foolish. People would love to read how the governor's nephew, now the chief assistant prosecutor, had been arrested for driving under the influence.

He stood at the threshold by the side door, his body swaying. Vainly, he tried to insert the key into the lock; finally, using his left hand to steady his right, he succeeded.

Turning gently, he eased the door open, staggered to the sofa and promptly passed out.

The blast of the ringing phone jolted him awake. "Hello?" he slurred as he squinted at the clock. It was already nine in the morning. Drina was calling for the details regarding the BBQ his parents were hosting that evening. He quickly filled her in, ended the call, shuddered, then fell back to sleep.

This bachelor of sorts, one who loved his routine, privacy, power and wealth disdained completely the idea of sharing his life with any woman. But the election was coming and Drina could be useful. Eventually, he got up, swallowed his daily dose of aspirin, grabbed a quick shower. Observing his reflection in the mirror, he admired himself as he dabbed water droplets from his curly hair, his trademark. He carefully trimmed his mustache, pulling his jaw this way and that, the ladies' man. His small paunch was no problem, the ladies liked his broad shoulders and height. He liked to think he had style. McHughes was known as an icon of sorts in the courtrooms of Pinellas County. His stealth legendary. Young attorneys sought to emulate his minimum gestures and movement, preferring to rotate his eyes rather than turn his head. He rarely lost a case, keeping extremely calm. Yes, he was known for his calm demeanor by everyone, everywhere. The exception, of course, was when he had dealings in Judge Bardmoor's courtroom. McHughes loathed the verse-spouting maniac. The hate was mutual.

McHughes was somewhat pleased. He was about to do the right thing for his image. He was picking up Ryan, his mentee, and taking him along to his parents' home for the BBQ. Ryan was a good kid, he lived with his mother and Melissa, his gorgeous 16-year old sister, on the other side of town in a modest stucco ranch. McHughes had actually grown fond of the 12-year old boy. The boy made him look good. The secretaries at the Prosecutor's office swooned when he told them he had taken Ryan to a Gator's game and had bought him a University of Florida football jersey. McHughes could be a knight in shining armor in these stories. Indeed, he frequently planned events with Ryan so that he could report his latest benevolence. After all, most of his colleagues were married, had children. Ryan provided a shield, an appearance of normalcy for McHughes. Now all that was missing was a faux wife. The election was coming; Drina was oh, so convenient, so beneficial to his image.

BBQ Misery

It was hot, humid, above and beyond what was typical for Florida in August. Lloyd McHughes mopped his face with his monogrammed handkerchief, leaned over and brushed Drina's cheek with a kiss as she slid into the front seat of his car. "Careful you don't spill that now," he warned.

"Don't worry, I've got it. You did say I should bring bean salad, right?"

"Yep," he frowned, "just not all over the front seat of my car."

"What's bugging you?"

"What do you think? I hate these afternoons with my parents."

"Well, having Ryan with us will soften things up, won't it, don't you think?"

They turned onto Gulf to Bay and McHughes eased over into the right lane, then down a side street to Ryan's. "I hope he's ready. Mother can't abide tardiness."

The front door opened and Ryan's sister popped out. She sprinted down the drive, long legs, short shorts, leaned into the car, ample bosoms rising above her hot pink camisole. "He'll be out in a second." Drina started to greet her but the expression on Lloyd's face as he observed Melissa stopped her cold. She wanted to accuse him of something, but what? She held her tongue. Was it his fault the girl dressed in such a provocative manner? Perhaps she had misread him. Maybe he was just happy to hear Ryan would be out shortly.

Ryan hopped into the car, called out warm greetings while he did so. Then added, "Hey you guys, guess what? I just got a special delivery."

"You did?" asked Drina. "What is it?"

"Don't know, mom said I have to wait until my birthday to open it. She put it away, but I know where."

Both Drina and Lloyd laughed. Ryan had already eased the tension.

Bryce, Lloyd's older brother, pulled up in his new Lexus SUV a minute after Lloyd. He got out of the car and removed a three-layer cake and a bottle of wine, carefully balancing them while calling out greetings to his brother, Drina, and Ryan.

"Hi," called Drina, then asked, "where are the boys?"

Mary, Bryce's wife, answered, "We have a free pass today, they're at soccer camp." Then, turning to Ryan, she added, "You'll be the center of attention today!"

Bryce and Lloyd followed the two women and Ryan into the house where Bryce and Mary were welcomed by Mrs. McHughes, who wore a starched apron and a pinched expression. Lloyd, Drina, and Ryan received a cool reception which was the way of things, the pattern in the family. Lloyd wore a blank expression, Drina feigned joy, Ryan, guarded. Ryan's father had long disappeared and Ryan was grateful to Lloyd for the time and money spent on him. Ryan's mother often reminded him that, "Mr. McHughes does this out of the kindness of his heart, not because he has to." What neither Ryan nor his mother surmised was that Lloyd McHughes had more motive than kindness in his actions. The election was coming.

The room warmed immediately with the entrance of McHughes' father.

Mrs. McHughes excused herself to the kitchen accepting Mary's offer to assist with dinner but declined Drina's offer. "No, too many cooks spoil the broth," she said, trying to add a cheery polite note, to her dismissal of Drina. Mary and Mrs. McHughes turned and left the room. Lloyd's father, clasped his hands together, smiled, and invited the others to the Florida room for drinks. "I have soft drinks, Ryan, and I believe, lemonade."

"Thank you, sir, I'll take a coke," Ryan answered politely. Ryan was a smart kid, he understood he wasn't really accepted by the family. He was an outsider let in for an occasional party. Other than that, he never saw the elder McHughes. They never came to see one hockey game, even though it was Lloyd who bought him his own hockey stick for Christmas, and paid for his membership on the team. Hockey was joyful for Ryan, meaningful, he appreciated Lloyd and he would do his best to represent himself in a respectful manner. Thus was his loyalty.

"Drina, come sit by me, I haven't seen you for a while, what've you been up to?" questioned Mr. McHughes. Drina smiled and sat in an adjoining chair. Lloyd's father saw a great deal of character in Drina and was pleasantly surprised when his son brought her to their home. He remembered feeling a bit ashamed of himself for thinking that his son, while an accomplished attorney, had not formed a mature, personal life. He felt he was extremely fortunate to attract a beauty like Drina. A beauty with brains. He realized his wife could not abide the fact that Drina was, to her thinking, unsavory on two counts: Hispanic and divorced with a child. However, Mr. McHughes never dared disagree with his wife knowing he would regret it. She would give him the silent treatment for weeks at a time. She would consider any opposing opinion as an assault on her dominion, that of the home. He had a career, she had the home. She stayed out of his business, he had better stay out of hers.

"Where's your daughter, Solana?" asked Mr. McHughes.

"She's at a friend's birthday party."

"Sorry to miss her."

Polite conversation ensued. The brothers had cocktails, talked about a wild and crazy judge who made rhymes and made fools out of any and every attorney he could possible attack.

"Yeah, the tiniest thing, a word out of context, anything and he's all over the poor sap unlucky enough to draw him on his case," said Bryce, shaking his head.

"A nightmare. That jerk should be removed."

"Well, he's always reelected you know. How many terms has that guy had?"

Just then, Lloyd's mother stepped into the room, Drina noted she was wearing high heels. A curious thing at a BBQ. "It's time for you to start the grill, dear," she said to her husband.

"Yes, dear," said Mr. McHughes, rising.

Ryan, bored and hungry, went to the kitchen to see what was going on. "Oh, Ryan," asked Mrs. McHughes, "would you please take these dishes? Just set the stack on the table there." Ryan dutifully obeyed carefully picking up the fine china dinner plates.

Drina stood with the brothers assessing their common features, yes, they looked a lot alike except Bryce, thinner, taller, hair straight, while Lloyd had curly hair. He hated the curls until he realized the women loved them. Then, a crash. An awful sound.

"How could you be so stupid?" roared Mrs. McHughes. Drina, Lloyd and Bryce rushed into the kitchen just in time to see Ryan getting up off the floor trying not to step on any of the dishes laying there, many chipped, several broken.

"Those precious dishes were from my aunt! They can never be replaced," Mrs. McHughes huffed, "but how would you know anything about family heirlooms, precious dishes?" She scowled at Ryan who clung to Drina for shelter.

"I'm sorry, I think the edge of my sneaker got caught on the edge of the tile or something," he whimpered.

Lloyd's father knelt to the floor claiming indeed, the tiles were uneven there, that it wasn't Ryan's fault. All were silent, but the harsh words hung in the air.

"Mom, why would you give a 12-year old kid a stack of 'priceless dishes' to carry anyway? Why would you do that?" Lloyd asked, challenging his mother. Then he took it further, "Everyone else uses paper plates for BBQ's anyway, you know?" He glared.

She scowled, said nothing.

"I don't know what you're implying," Bryce retorted acidly. "Mother is entitled to serve any way she wishes. She certainly didn't expect Ryan to trip and fall." Lloyd's mother moved to Bryce's side whereupon he put his arm around her.

The lines drawn, as usual, score one for Bryce, zero for Lloyd, and certainly zero for Ryan.

Posturing

Mrs. McHughes' new black Lexus crept up the long, winding ribbon of asphalt to Faith Hammock Cathedral. She drummed the steering wheel as she braked at the crest waiting for the parking usher to direct her to the appropriate parking lot. Irritated at the thought of having to make excuses as to where Mr. McHughes was, she silently seethed at his decision to stay home and read the *Tampa Bay Times*. She studied her manicure, then gazed upward taking in the magnificence of the Gothic Revival cathedral, modeled on Scotland's Melrose Abbey. The parking usher signaled her forward, motioned to the appropriate lot where her Lexus fit right in with the plethora of Mercedes and BMW's. Every car spotless, windshields gleaming in the morning sun. The McHughes, longtime members of Faith Hammock Cathedral had indeed chosen to settle in the city of Dunkirk as it housed the singularly most status driven church in west central Florida. The cathedral, a bulwark in the community, boasted a carillon tower reputed to be one of the tallest in the world. Its hymns broadcast the air with the call to worship, its heavenly notes programmed to perfection by a quartz timer. Inside, Mrs. McHughes took her customary seat up front in the family pew bearing the McHughes' brass plaque. Surreptitiously, she peered about the sanctuary, eyes darting left and right. Being seen and seeing others, every Sunday a fashion preview, eyes attuned to the glitter of twenty jet black Gothic chandeliers, each bedecked with 3,000 Vienna full spectrum crystals.

The cathedral, sanctified by mediocre divinity but transcending in wealth of spires, land holdings and exclusive parishioners reflected elite society in microcosm. The parishioners appeared benevolent but most lacked empathy. Mrs. McHughes fit right in. Her English ancestry dating back to the Earl of Essex and the Earl of Carlisle lent her immediate entry to this social arena and her Irish husband's money, though considered to be "new money" -- lent her attendance at the cathedral all the more desired. She was a huge donor and, therefore, a respected pillar of the church.

※※※※※

McHughes and his father huddled together on the lanai, steaming mugs of coffee and a half-eaten coffee cake between them. McHughes relished being alone with his father, a rare occurrence.

"From what I've been reading, son, you'll need to get yourself a social media person if you want to win this election."

McHughes nodded thoughtfully. "I've got a couple of people in mind but if you've got any suggestions, I'd like to hear them."

McHughes genuinely liked his father as a person and respected him for his intuitive approach in the field of computer architecture. Mr. McHughes' secret to success: Give your employees plenty of intellectual freedom to run with fresh ideas, which in turn brought about innovative software marketed worldwide.

Mr. McHughes paused, considering people he might recommend, when he heard the sound of the garage door opening. "Your mother's home," he said between compressed lips.

McHughes winced. "Already? I think they should lengthen that church service." Father and son looked into each other's eyes and smiled, conspirators.

The sound of Mrs. McHughes heels clicked on the travertine as she approached. "Well, isn't this a cozy little get together?" Mrs. McHughes said sarcastically. "Having a party without me?" her comments aimed at her son, but it was her husband who answered.

"Of course not, dear, there's no chance of a party without you," he chuckled. He accepted a peck on his cheek while he briefed her.

"Well," she said turning away, unfastening her diamond bracelet, "Anything you put on social media? It better be that you're a happily married man, or at least engaged to be married." She paused. "Having said that," she turned and faced her son. "What's the deal with this Gina?" Mr. McHughes' turn to wince.

"Drina," McHughes said correcting her as he sucked in the hot air, avoiding her challenging visage, "for the thousandth time," he said slowly in measured cadence as if she were mentally challenged, "Drina, her name is Drina, not Gina."

"Excuse me," she huffed. "How dare you use that tone on your mother! Don't blame me because her parents named her something, so . . . so," she shook her head, found the word, "offbeat! I mean, look at your brother and his beautiful family, what a picture that would make for the media, consider that!"

Smack down. One more time. McHughes excused himself, trudged out to his car when he realized he had to go back to the house for his car keys. Quietly, he pulled open the side door, hoping to escape notice, just get the keys and get out, but hearing, "You know, you could give your son some encouragement. Why is it you always compare him to his brother, bring him up short like that? I don't understand."

The reply, "Whatever. Get showered, we're meeting the Hoffman's for lunch at the club."

Section Two: Danger Awaits

Wine Night Confession

DRINA AND SALLI STROLLED INTO Connie's house for their traditional Friday night get together of chocolates and wine, their cherished escape.

"Oh, no!" they exclaimed, feigning fear, "the jigsaw puzzle!" referring to the huge unfinished project which lay prominently before them on Connie's coffee table.

"Oh, stop, you know you love it!" teased Connie.

Drina and Salli dutifully marched to the kitchen, each uncorking the bottle of wine they had brought. There was pleasant chatter and the pleasant sound of the wine pouring into the goblets. They returned to the living room where Connie was already kneeling, working on the puzzle. Salli knelt to work on the puzzle but her face was in a pout. "I'm stumped," she whined..

"Me, too. I'm guessing this piece goes here," Drina said as she locked the piece into place, cocking her head as she looked to see if it looked right.

"How can you tell? All the pieces look the same, they're white!" complained Salli, grimacing.

Drina pointed, "See the little bit of yellow there and the green there?"

"Oh, my God," moaned Salli while plopping a gooey hazelnut chocolate into her mouth.

"You guys don't have to do it if you don't want to. I can do it alone," said Connie, taking a sip of merlot, her merry mood changing by the minute.

"No, no, we're in this together," asserted Salli.

"Yep, we're in it together, all right," said Drina.

Salli asked, "But, Connie, why did you have to pick a puzzle that's so hard?"

Drina chimed in, "I'm wondering the same thing. This is tough."

Connie flinched, "It's kind of something from my childhood."

"You mean when you were a kid you had a white puzzle? How horrible. Kids like color!" said Salli, incredulous.

Drina studied Connie sensing there was a lot more to the story.

Connie rose, "Just never mind."

"Tell us!" demanded Salli.

"You know what, Salli, you've got no tact, none at all," said Drina.

"Why would you say that to me? I am tactful," Salli said turning to Connie for verification. "Right?"

But Connie did not answer.

Drina clenched her jaw, got up, "Look what you've done! You've upset her! Sometimes, Salli, you really need to just keep quiet!"

"You've got your nerve," said Salli rising to face her.

"Stop!" Connie held up both hands. "It's time you knew anyway, even if it means the end," she cleared her throat, "of us."

The silence was static.

"Sit down," Connie gestured to the sofa. "My mother had this," Connie paused, "this garden that was all white. No color except for the green leaves. She called it her Moon Garden. When I was a kid, I liked sitting out there at night with her." Connie's eyes focused on a tiny piece of lint on her yoga pants. "Oh, except for the bougainvillea tree, she made an exception for that."

Afraid to speak, of being intrusive, Salli sat like stone.

"Your mother? You've never mentioned her before," said Drina who recognized that tonight would be a different kind of wine party, one more of a confessional nature, a true sharing without constraint.

Salli ventured a question, "Where is she now?"

"Can you let her talk without interrupting?" Drina's eyes bulging, staring at Salli who shrugged.

Then stillness as Connie took a deep breath. "I was a fool and ran away from home. I was 14," she paused gathering the courage to continue, "I made a mess of my life . . . I had a baby, a son," she wailed, "but I lost him."

Salli whispered, "You had a little boy? What do you mean, you lost him?"

Connie studied their faces. Their obvious compassion moved her to tears.

"I was an idiot, hanging out with an idiot, a drug addict. I thought I was in love," she drew out the word as if it were a curse, "I ran away with him," Connie's face a pattern of misery, "to do heroin." The words rushed out, "When he took off, I did what I felt I had to do to get it," she nodded her head as she stared into space replaying the scenes of her life. "To get the heroin. I prostituted myself, I had a kid, a little boy." Connie broke down. Drina and Salli reached out to her.

"I was a bad mother," Connie reached for a tissue, blew her nose, tears streaming down her face. "Department of Children and Families took my kid. I begged my mother to adopt him but she refused . . . I never saw him again, or her either, I was so mad at her."

"You poor thing, carrying all that sorrow all alone," said Drina

"Oh, Connie, we're so sorry," said Salli as tears spilled onto her face.

"He'd be 17 now, if he's even alive," Connie murmured.

They cried together, the three friends.

Drina whispered. "Why haven't you told us before? We love you, we --"

"I was worried," Connie gasped, struggling to speak, "that you'd think less of me."

"Oh, my God, no!" said Drina.

"Why would we think less of you? You're our friend. We understand, I mean everybody does stuff that they wish they didn't," said Salli, her voice choked.

"We've got to find your son," resolved Drina, desperately looking about the room as if he might be there.

"We need a plan," said Salli, sitting forward on the sofa, alert. "Yes," she wagged her forefinger at Drina and Connie, "a plan."

"You guys," Connie cried and shook her head, "what would I do without you?"

"What would we do without you? You give us chocolates!" said Salli.

"You give us wine," said Drina.

"You read us your poetry," said Salli.

"You make us laugh with your hairdresser escapades!" said Drina.

Salli stood, opened her arms and called, "Group hug!"

Meaning of Friendship

AFTER CONNIE, DRINA AND SALLI hugged, they wept quietly, each taking a turn at needing a tissue. It was a supreme moment of realization between them that theirs was a special friendship, one to be cherished. For Drina, being a single parent, mother of Solana and holding down a demanding, and emotionally draining job as a social worker, there wasn't much time for personal friendship. For Salli, wife of Bill, Walmart checker, young, and even she would admit to being a bit "flaky," friendship was a much desired but not easily obtained treasure. For Connie, brutally fighting her insecurities while putting on an act of being impervious to what others thought of her, it was a gift to be able to share her secrets, her fears, and her wish to find her son. Friendship became a cathartic experience for these three women, women facing the pressures of daily life to the best of their abilities. Each day rolled up so quickly, many times before events and pressures of the previous day had been handled. Life was demanding. Friendship helped ease the pressure, gave vent to frustration, lent credence to the fact that, yes, there were challenges to be met and not all of them desirable challenges.

Connie sighed as she hugged her friends goodnight. She closed the door softly, then sat down to reflect upon the intensity of the evening. How did it happen? she asked herself. Where did all this come from? But she knew the answer even before asking herself the question: she trusted these women, felt secure with them, knew that her best interest was theirs also. She felt remorse, even shame, in not believing in their dedication sooner. They did not judge her. They did not turn on her, find her past so disgusting. They rallied to support her, even offering help. Amazing, she thought to herself. One thing led to the other: The overdose to a successful rehabilitation, from that, the cosmetology training, from that, the excellent position at the spa, and from that, the little rental home in Safety Harbor. She laughed remembering seeing Salli that first morning as she backed her car down her short driveway, Salli shaking feathers from a pillow into her garden. Salli encouraging her to join the poetry group. There, she met Drina, a dear and kind soul. And Sam. And Glenn. She thought about Glenn but pushed him out of her mind. Her energy must be focused on finding Will. This she must do.

Now, in the quiet of her home, she lowered her head and said a prayer of thanks, a prayer which came from the heart. How long had it been since she'd said a prayer? She pondered this also. She remembered that after Celeste's death, a cold dark shroud of bitterness dwelled in her heart, that darkness seeped into every fiber of her body.

She had lost hope for a better life, even increased her use of heroin, until she was arrested and jailed. She reflected on how the arrest was instrumental in saving her life, bringing her to a better place if only for a short time. She was off drugs and Will was born healthy. She understood that for most addicts, rehab was not a one-shot deal, so why did she hate herself for backsliding? It was a difficult process. Eventually she beat the heroin, didn't she? Now, the focus: find her son. Make up for the past. Fix things. Be brave. Persevere.

Celeste's Treasure Box

CONNIE AWAKENED SATURDAY MORNING FEELING that she was moving in slow motion and in a rather negative mood. Why was this she wondered after the supportive love her friends had shown her? She slept reasonably well, considering the seriousness of last night's wine session with Drina and Salli. Though the summer heat permeated the small cottage home, Connie felt a chill, the chill of remembrance, the sad death of Celeste. She made a quick cup of coffee, sipping the heated brew enlivened her and she went for it -- straight to the spare room -- knowing exactly what she sought -- Celeste's trinket box.

She stood on tiptoes to reach the top shelf of the closet. It was there all right, just as she'd remembered. Tenderly, she took hold of the faded purple silken box. The mere touch of it brought memories of sweet Celeste cascading into Connie's mind. She sat down on the sagging twin bed, held the box on her lap, "Oh, God, " she whispered as she brushed away tears. Sunlight pierced the white lace curtains, its beams bounced off the colorful glass stones inset in the lid of the box sending a myriad of colorful shapes onto the walls. But Connie did not notice. Transported to her life all those years ago, she pondered how much Celeste loved her little trinket box. She could almost see her delicate fingers opening the lid to tuck her treasures away. Connie took a deep breath and raised the lid.

Inside lay silver key chains bearing charms of hearts, dogs and cats. Gently, Connie grasped a pair of beaded earrings. She smiled sadly, remembering beading with Celeste, those few happy hours they would steal when they could, but she stifled a sob as she raised a faded package of bubble gum to her nose, inhaling, hoping for a residue of scent. Yes, Celeste liked her bubble gum and was quite proud of just how huge she could blow bubbles. Connie carefully laid each item down on the soft chenille bedspread. Through tear-filled eyes she saw it: a lock of hair tied with a narrow purple ribbon. A ringlet of red hair. Connie's mind spun with sensation remembering Richard. She wept thinking of how Celeste, in her childlike trusting way, loved him so. The diary Celeste kept, the delicate gilt-edged pages, the purple ball point pen festooned with purple feathers. All in the box.

Connie cautiously opened the diary recoiling as she did so remembering the pain it evoked years ago when she had read it after Celeste's death. The childlike printing, Celeste's script, neat and tidy embellished with circles dotting the i's. The first random entry:

I love Connie. Shes the nicest person I know and shes fun.

Connie trembled, wiped her eyes and read further:

Today I did a sneaky thing but I'm not sorry! My boyfriends name is Richard Nevelson. Ha! I found out his name. He would not tell me his name only would say call me Mr. Wonderful. I snuck in his wallet when he was asleep. It was pretty easy. He says he's my boyfriend, too. Harry says hes just a john. I don't like Harry he's really mean. Connie says all pimps are slime balls. Ha. Ha. Ha.

Connie's mind spun back, peeled away the layer of the years, remembering in great detail how she had lived as a prostitute in the seedy two-bedroom apartment in Clearwater, how she had dreaded the new "roomie" assigned to her. Connie, 17, had worked for Harry the Pimp for three years. Though she was seasoned in the business and hooked on heroin, her heart had not hardened. Connie hoped it never would; indeed, she feared a few of the hardened prostitutes who would slit her throat if she dared to walk within ten feet of their territory.

When Harry moved Celeste into the apartment, Connie could not believe how young, how tiny, how doll like she appeared. Connie raised her eyebrows and blinked several times when Harry introduced Celeste as the "latest addition to the family." Sure, thought Connie, some family. But within no time at all, she came to like Celeste very much. Celeste was cheerful, happy in her own little world and considered the price of prostitution well worth escaping her horrible home environment.

"They took away my dog -- Fluffy was mine and they gave her away when I was at school." Connie listened with rapt attention to Celeste's descriptions of her home life, a night mare. Celeste's divorced mother hooked up with a mean man, early 30s, swarthy, cocky, bossy. Celeste and he became instant enemies. He banished her to the garage, setting up a tiny cot there where at night, shadows, spiders, and trailing headlights frightened Celeste. But nothing frightened her as much as when he would open the door to the garage and call out to her mother, "I'm taking out the trash." That meant he was coming for her.

He was rough, he was crude, he held her down as he forced himself on her, a hungry, wild animal. When Celeste complained to her mother, she was told to stop lying, to shut her mouth. On the lonely, frightening nights, Celeste's only comfort was Fluffy. She held her tight as she fell asleep. One day, when Celeste returned from school she asked where was Fluffy. Her mother and the evil man harshly replied that Fluffy was gone and she should forget about her. It was then Celeste decided to run away. "I ended up here, with you, Connie," Celeste said. At twelve, she had worry lines well beyond what any child should. "Do you like Richard?" she asked one day as they sat beading earrings and bracelets, Celeste's favorite pastime.

"He's okay I guess, Connie conceded.

"I do, he's my favorite one; he brought me these beads and the new key chains, look!" Celeste held up three shiny key chains, dangling them from her slim, white fingers. Kewpie doll, Connie thought looking at tiny Celeste. Richard Nevelson had been her regular but abandoned her for the petite Celeste which was fine with Connie. She squinted as she threaded a purple crystal bead onto thin wire. "You know, I never beaded anything till you moved in here."

"Are you happy I'm here, Connie?"

"Yes, I am, sweetheart," said Connie smiling, "but this is no life for you. We have to get you out of here and into a good home."

"But I don't want to leave you," Celeste insisted.

"Well, maybe we can both work toward getting out, you know?" said Connie. "We'd have to go to rehab -- me for heroin, you for those pills Richard brings you."

"Oh, my happy pills? I guess, yeah. But would we still be together?" asked Celeste.

In fact, Connie did find the relationship endearing, sister like. Yes, that was it, Celeste was like the little sister she never had. Now, sitting cross legged on the carpet, enjoying a break between johns, beading had become a tradition for her and Celeste.

"You know I love your poetry, Connie," Celeste smiled shyly. "I don't understand a lot of it but I like the sound of it, you know?"

Connie had been penning poetry for as long as she could remember. It gave her a release, even joy. On occasion, she would share a poem with Celeste, and had written one about Celeste, which Celeste treasured.

"Well, you're a writer, too," Connie commented, encouraging Celeste to talk about her diary. "How long have you been keeping a diary?"

Celeste paused, held tight to a heart-shaped charm, "Since I came here, I guess," she looked sad, shrugged.

"Why'd you say it like that?" asked Connie. "Don't you like to do it?"

Celeste answered, "He took it."

"Your mother's boyfriend?"

"Yeah. He said if I wrote about him being a beast again, he'd kill me, that I should write he was nice and that I was glad he lived there. So," Celeste sighed, "I didn't write anything anymore, until now."

"I see," said Connie. Then, trying to cheer her up, "Hey, that charm bracelet is looking good! Is it for me?"

That brought a smile to Celeste's face, "Yes, it is!"

The smile vanished when surly Harry burst into the room, "Clear up this shit! I got guys who want action! I don't pay you to sit around all day!"

Doodle marched into the room, hopped onto Connie's lap, brought her back to the present. Richard Nevelson. Connie mused, squinting her eyes, trying to remember all those years ago, after her release from prison, searching for a man by that name, coming up with no one. No one at all except a 64-year old guy who lived in Indianapolis. Must have been a fake I.D. Of course it was.

Too many years. And yet, his son, her son . . . he was such a sweet little boy. Where is he now? she asked herself and stumbled to her feet seeking cold water to calm herself. She splashed it on her face, drank from her cupped hand, choked on it, coughed harshly, dropped to the floor of the bathroom, sat with her knees drawn up, hugged them hard, rocked to and fro, whispering, "What can I do? Heaven help me."

Signs Over Their Heads

CONNIE, DRINA AND SALLI SAT around Connie's kitchen table as rain fell softly and darkness enveloped the sky, making it quite cozy for them, a chance to relax. As the evening progressed, the women enjoyed light conversation but Drina grew serious.

"Hey, I shouldn't burden you guys with this but sometimes I feel like a fool," she kept her eyes on the base of her wine goblet and traced its shape with her forefinger, "you know?"

"And why would a smart woman like you feel like that?" asked Connie taking a sip of her chardonnay.

Drina paused, then plunged in, "I can't get enough of sex with Lloyd even though I feel deep down, he's strange."

Salli wanted details, "Wait, what do you mean strange?"

Connie nodded, offering encouragement for Drina to continue. At times like this, the three women felt as if they were one person. The connection that strong.

"I've never had better sex!"

"All right!" said Connie. She and Salli clicked their wine goblets. But Drina was serious.

"So what's the problem?" asked Connie.

"He doesn't talk about anything much except how much he hates his mother and his brother. That and the election. Sometimes I feel like I'm being used."

"In what way?" asked Connie.

"Well, it's kind of like all we are is a couple of bodies that meet, sweat and grind."

"Ooooh, you're turning me on." Salli giggled.

"I can't get enough of this guy but there's something insincere about him. I'm telling you."

Connie got up, threw a frozen pizza in the oven, set the timer.

Connie, concerned now. If goody-two-shoes Drina smelled a rat, well, there probably was a rat. Her face reflected her concern.

Drina began to discount her suspicion. "Oh, I don't know, maybe it's just me. Maybe I just want more attention."

"Well, he looked real cute in the pic's you showed us, didn't he, Connie?" Salli asked.

"Let me see the picture again, I kind of forgot what Lloyd likes like," Connie admitted.

"Here," said Drina handing Connie her phone, "that's us at a campaign party."

Connie studied the picture, he was a good-looking guy, his hair, short, light brown, curly, a large walrus-like mustache dominated his face. He appeared pleasant natured from what Connie could see. A bit overweight but nice looking. Was there something familiar about him? Maybe so. She shrugged and decided that she'd probably seen a campaign poster or something. Interestingly, she thought he and Drina looked good together. She told Drina now, "You guys look good together. But," she added, "I'm concerned that you sense something is off with this guy because your instincts are dead on, accurate. After all, you have a degree in social work, right? You would know if something was strange, I would think."

"Well, if you think he might be a wacko or something, why do you go out with him?" asked Salli.

Drina's face flushed, "Let's change the subject, shall we?"

Connie turned to Salli, "Believe it or not, sex and good looks aren't everything! In fact, you know what there should be? A sign over their heads that only we can see like, 'I'm a fool -- don't trust me!'"

Drina howled, "Or, 'I'm a pathological liar!' Boy, wouldn't that save time?"

"Here's one," said Salli, 'I'm a dud in bed!'"

Connie said, "How about this one? 'I'm cheap, lazy, and stupid. Wanna go out?'"

"Well," said Drina, somewhat seriously, "why limit the head signs to men? There are plenty of witches out there, in fact -- coteries of witches. No! On second thought, I mean covens of witches!"

"I know what a coven is, but what's a coterie?" asked Connie barely able to keep a straight face.

"Let me explain," Drina answered, "but first, a toast to us, because we're not witches!"

"And we're not bitches!" said Salli turning to Connie, teasing, "By the way, Miss Connie, do you have anything you'd care to share about Glenneeee in the sex department?"

"One word," said Connie as she poured more wine, "no."

"I've seen the way he looks at you," agreed Drina. "He's in love."

"Oh, please," said Connie

Salli let it go, "Okay, I get it. It's private. I envy you being in the flirtation part of the relationship, Connie. I just get so bored."

"So let's review, ladies: Drina senses her boyfriend is using her although she loves jumping his bones, Salli loves her husband but she's bored, and I certainly find Glenn attractive but with my trust issues, who knows? We sound pathetic!"

The oven timer buzzed. Connie rose to serve the steaming pizza.

"Let's change the subject, ladies," said Drina.

"To what? What could be more interesting than men?" asked Salli.

"Have you forgotten? Miss Connie's going to read at the poetry slam Saturday night!"

"Well . . . " Connie hedged.

Drina continued, "Saturday night is the Open Mic Poetry Slam at the Clearwater Library!"

"Really?" said Salli.

"Really? I invited you!" said Connie.

"Oh, I remember now," said Salli, embarrassed.

"Um-hum, let's eat!" said Connie.

Clearwater Open Mic

THOUGH THE EVENING WAS STULTIFYING with heat and humidity, Connie changed from shorts into a long black t-shirt dress. Maybe it was the desire to protect herself, her clothes becoming a form of armor, or maybe it was the chill she felt, the chill of fear. Tonight was the night, no getting around it, she had promised her friends that she would read her poetry at the Clearwater Library open mic night. Connie brushed her hair and stepped into flip flops. Pink. A touch of whimsy, perhaps to calm herself. Then, at the sound of Drina's horn, she grabbed her sheaf of poems and ran out the front door.

Drina read the anxiety in Connie's face, "You'll be fine," she said, patting Connie's knee.

"I don't know about this, Drina," Connie lit a cigarette.

"Oh, please, no, not in the car."

Connie extinguished it. "Sorry, just so nervous."

"Don't be that way. Remember how much fun you had when you read at the Poets Mingle and Open Mic night at the Safety Harbor Library? Everyone loved your poetry. Think about that, why don't you?"

"I know, but the intimacy of the Safety Harbor Library is so different from this venue."

"This is just the beginning: Next we should get you into Safety Harbor Art and Music Center. Think about that," Drina said.

Connie raised her eyebrows and thought, wow . . . SHAMc, the bohemian, gorgeous arts center.

Salli came charging toward the car, yanked the door open and slid onto the back seat, breathless. "Let's go!"

Drina accelerated.

"Hit the gas!" yelled Salli.

"Whoa! Calm down, girl!" said Drina and the three women laughed. Off they went to the library. The foyer throbbed with excited voices, a peek into the meeting hall revealed many people already seated, many of them motioning to friends to seats they had saved. Connie's tension increased; she took air in quick, shallow breaths. As she walked, she felt her legs turning to concrete. She willed them to work.

"There's Glenn!" said Drina, taking Connie's arm, steering her to the front row. Glenn stood smiling, sought eye contact with Connie to give assurance, encouragement. She appeared dazed and did not respond.

"I didn't expect such a big crowd," she began, clinging to her poems.

"This is a big night all right. I haven't seen it like this before," Glenn said.

Drina gave him a Be Quiet! stare and said, "This'll be fun, you'll see." Connie groaned and sat down.

The crowd hushed as the lights dimmed. The host opened the poetry slam with a blasting voice and recitation of a slick limerick. The crowd exploded with laughter but Connie did not hear a word he said.

Glenn leaned in close, touched her shoulder, whispered, "You'll be fine."

One of the regulars, a guy in his late 60's stepped up to the mic, shouted a greeting and wowed the crowd with a five-stanza ode to his motorcycle. Glenn joined others shouting, "My man!"

"Get up there," commanded Salli, "show them what you've got!"

Connie's reply, a deer in the headlights stare.

Another reader approached the mic, this time a twenty-something female with purple and black striped hair, piercings galore and a swagger full of piss and vinegar. Knocked them dead with, "I wear pink panties when I sleep at night."

Connie sat puzzling, should she read nature poetry? To this crowd? Maybe not.

Sam tiptoed in, whispered an apology for being late, hugged Connie and said, "You can do it."

So she did. At first her words tumbled out too quickly. Sensing it, she slowed her pace, allowed the cadence of the poems to carry the moment. One down, "Jacaranda," next, "Sea Glass," and last, "Flowers at Sea." She began,

Sandy beach and misty sky
Give way to pier, long and gray
Heralding the seaward day
Beckoning me to come along
While breezes bend the air to song
Much like a lullaby.

Connie finished the last verse and waited. The audience, stone silent -- she stepped back from the mic, lowered her head, wishing she could disappear.

Then it came: Thunderous applause.

Slowly, she lifted her gaze to see members of the audience climb to their feet, cheering. Cheering *her*. She felt as if she was floating away to another dimension and stood transfixed. She searched the faces of her friends. Their faces beamed with pride. Drina proudly noted the use of the word lullaby in Connie's poem, and believed it was a tribute to her butterfly poem in which she had used the word lullaby. It was that poem which had stirred Connie's heart, brought them together. Poetry, a vehicle of communication.

❧❦❧❦❧

But in the back of the hall, one person did not applaud. One person, hate-filled, vengeful, did rise to her feet, but only to sneak out before others saw her. Echoes of her spiked heels stabbing the terrazzo floor were muffled by the sound of Connie's success. Sharon drove home in silence. Ray, asleep in the recliner, did not hear her come in, quickly change into her nursing clothes. Nor did he hear as she chanted a vow she made to the Marilyns, a vow to get Connie the Bitch. The Glass Heads chanted, "Get her!" Sharon listened and looked with love at the way their hard glass faces gleamed in the lamplight. Sharon, taking pleasure in the acknowledgement of the axiom: Revenge is a dish best served cold, asked herself -- Did I hear that somewhere? Did I? Did Marilyn say that? No matter. The Bitch would be dealt with. How? When? Where? She pondered these issues, these details, these much-needed necessary plans to destroy the eminent enemy stealing Glenn's ardor.

Marilyn would never tolerate another woman's interference with her love object. Would she? Of course not. Marilyn always, always, always, got her MAN.

Sam's Advice

THE CROWD BEGAN TO DISSIPATE and Connie found herself being shuffled along with Glenn, Sam, Drina and Salli, everyone in a jolly mood, especially Connie herself feeling relieved the slam was over with and apparently a success. She hugged each of her friends but still felt a bit numb from all the excitement.

"Next performance should be the Safety Harbor Art and Music Center!" called out a voice from the crowd."

"Here! Here!" called another voice.

"They love you!" exclaimed Drina. "Hear that?"

Connie was speechless at first, then muttered, "Oh, my God! I don't know . . ."

"One thing at a time," said Sam, "one thing at a time, little lady."

She hugged Sam.

"Let's celebrate!" cried Salli.

"How about we meet you guys at the Whistle Stop?" Drina suggested.

The three women piled in Drina's car while Glenn and Sam headed out together. It appeared to be a festive moment but Glenn was faking it, secretly hurt that when Connie hugged everyone else with such intensity, his hug was rather weak, standoffish. His ego bruised, his desire for her burning, yet his belief in his ability to capture this rare and beautiful woman, flagging. Was there any hope? Probably not. he concluded.

"She'll come around, she's got a lot on her mind," Sam said sensing Glenn's somber mood, Glenn driving mechanically, brow furrowed.

"It's that obvious?"

"Yeah," Sam said and gestured to the red-light signal up ahead.

Glenn eased the car to a stop, "I don't know, seems like she's not into me. She's friendly but not real warm. I'll put it that way." The light changed, Glenn sighed, hit the gas.

"Don't give up now," Sam cautioned. "Women are different than us, they need more time," Sam shrugged, added, "just the way they're built."

Glenn took heart, smiled, "I love the way she's built!"

"That's the spirit now!" said Sam.

Ruth

RUTH MITCHELL, CONNIE'S MOTHER, MIGHT have been envied by many of those who did not know her circumstances. A very private woman, she played her cards close to her vest. Elegant by all standards of society, Ruth moved through each week bearing a heavy load, seemingly effortlessly. But the burden had grown more cumbersome, the days longer, more tedious, and increasingly -- frightening. How long could she hold on? Was there no help? None at all except for an Alzheimer's facility for William, her beloved husband.

She thought of her daughter Constance and a restless reflex pushed her up from the tapestry winged armchair. Should she try again to establish contact? Other efforts over the years had been rebuffed, unwanted, her daughter disinterested in a relationship. She wondered, was she never to be forgiven for not adopting Will? Was there no understanding of her position? Her duty toward her husband? Apparently not. She shook her head as if to clear it and mindlessly headed for the kitchen to plug in the tea kettle.

She reached for the tea tin which contained a labyrinth of tea bags. She, unable to decipher the labels through a fog of tears. Did it matter? Chai or vanilla cinnamon? Any tea would do. Just something, something calming. Minutes passed and the cry of the steaming kettle echoed Ruth's cry, "Dear God!" She pictured her daughter, an angry teen, and the screaming matches, her accusations: "You don't even know I'm alive! Why'd you even bother to have a kid? All you care about is your husband!" Ruth's answer, "My husband is your father, have a little compassion, won't you? You know he's ill!" The outcome predictable, a door slamming as Constance ran out to hang with her reckless friends. Constance reveling in breaking curfew, skipping school, using drugs, urged on by that monster Jack Rank. "Oh, God," Ruth stammered as she trembled and poured scalding water into the chipped china mug emblazoned, "World's Best Mother," a gift from Constance eons ago.

Ruth put William to bed and felt relieved that he fell to sleep immediately. She headed for the bathroom where she glanced briefly at her image in the mirror, the woman before her gaunt, the eyes weary, sunken. She lay in bed, whispered prayers as the familiar sound of the grandfather clock filled the hallway. She drifted to sleep. William, softly snoring, lay in his adjustable bed a few feet away.

From below, French doors rattled tested by a petty thief. His prey, luxurious homes. Tonight: Ruth's.

Choosing a moonless night, using a pen knife, he carves the slot needed for quick entry. With stealth, opens the door. Holds his breath, listens. Nothing. No dog. No alarm. Drive-by observations correct. Smugly, he thought, research pays. Theft, his forte from which he takes pride. Holding a small LED flashlight, he illuminates the room noting the abundance of mosaic tables filled with orchids, obstacles to his escape route. Stepping into the next room, surveying the contents of the highly polished cabinets, he rejects the fine china and silver. Too bulky. The cash and the jewels had to be upstairs. Cautiously, he mounts the staircase wary of creaking stairs. All silent. Just the ticking of the clock. Pats his pocket taking courage from the Magnum 357. Just in case.

A swift tour of the upstairs: Spare room, girl's room, home office. He enters the office and with gloved hands, rifles the desk drawers. No cash. Following the sound of the snoring, he tiptoes into the master bedroom. Asleep, both of them. Malevolent eyes lock on the massive carved mahogany jewelry chest. Bingo. He stuffs his black velvet bag with gold galore, diamond dinner rings, diamond and emerald necklaces, rubies, and pearls, shooting sideways glances at the sleeping couple. There, amongst the treasure, a vintage pocket watch. His fence would be happy. He could hear him now, "Get the vintage stuff, people go for that crap."

The canvas of William's mind roughens. He moans, "Ah . . ." The thief turns. William thrashing violently from side to side. Louder, "Aaaaaaaaaaaaaah." The thief freezes, reaches for his gun. William screaming, boxing the air, "No! No! No, I say!" his mind playing hideous scenes. Ruth awakens with a start, eyes focusing on William but picking up a shadowy image as a sliver of light from the bathroom guides her vision. What is it? The shadow moves quickly out of the bedroom.

Ruth throwing off her bed covers, screams, "Who is it? Who's there?"

Hearing his wife's scream, William roars, leaps from the bed.

The thief panics and flees, his heart racing as he plunges down the stairs seeking escape. He trips as he bounds across the Florida room and smashes into the line of small tables each covered with pots of orchids. The impact upends the tables and the pots of orchids break as they crash to the floor. Bark and plant debris scatter in the process. These orchids, a tribute to Connie, each purchased and nourished by Ruth in memoriam for all the birthdays she missed with her errant daughter. Now they lay broken.

The thief struggles to his feet, desperate. Where is the black bag? His ears ring with the terrifying sound of William's bellows. The French doors, his escape route, are but a few feet away, but where are the jewels? He can't leave without them.

Upstairs, a frenzied Ruth rakes her hands through her hair.

William, a mad man, pummeling the walls with his fists.

Ruth screaming, "Stop!"

William protesting hysterically, "No! No! No!"

Ruth lunges for the phone.

William, out of his mind, throws her to the floor. Stands over her body, panting. He is now a predator. His eyes blazing, voice pulsating, "Why? Why?"

Downstairs, the thief is vexed, wonders, "Is that guy going for a gun?" With renewed desperation, the thief drops to his knees, paws the floor, sifting bark and soil, gasps with relief. Got it.

The question enters his mind, "Should I run or go up there and shut him up?"

Connie's Conscience

"Did you happen to see Jane Fonda in that televised movie last night?"

"No, Mrs. Harper, I missed that. Was it good?" Connie asked politely. Mrs. Harper was one of her favorite clients, a carefree sixty-something in the prime of her senior years, still energetic, interested in life.

"Good? Good isn't the word! It was great, and she looked great," Mrs. Harper said with gusto, her brown eyes sparkling. "In fact, I got to thinking I'd like a makeover."

Connie smiled as she adjusted the velcro closing on the beauty cape, "A makeover?"

"Yes, dear, I want to wear my hair like Jane Fonda wears hers."

"I see," said Connie avoiding Mrs. Harper's sincere gaze.

"Is that possible, dear?"

Connie nodded yes and listened intently until Mrs. Harper finished her description of what she wanted.

"Layered here . . . "

It was then Connie felt herself freeze in place, her ears cocked as she heard a familiar voice, her mother's voice coming through the perforated screen which separated the work stations. *Could this be?* She knew that years ago her mother frequented the Spa occasionally for massages but not this, not for her hair. *My God.*

"This robber, he came right into the bedroom, it was terrible," said Ruth momentarily wiping a tear. "He took all my jewelry. I screamed, my husband, well, he, he isn't himself."

"I'm so sorry, Mrs. Mitchell," intoned the hairdresser.

Connie's mother stood, "I, I can't do this today, please accept this," Mrs. Mitchell pressed a large tip into the hairdresser's hand and quickly exited the salon.

"So you can tint my hair this color, Connie," continued Mrs. Harper pointing to a magazine photo of Jane Fonda. "It would be perfect for me."

Connie snapped back to attention. Robotically, she created Jane Fonda. Her mind zoomed in on what her mother had said. A mixture of shame and guilt permeated her being. Her head throbbed as thoughts ricocheted in her mind. Laser blasts of purple and black fired at her memory and cognition, confusing both. Burning.

Mother, why is she here? I don't understand how she --

"Yes, the color match is lovely, Mrs. Harper, I'm so happy you like it."

Robbery. This is terrible, terrible. Oh, my God. Panic creeping in, gaining ground.

"Connie," Then again "Connie!" the receptionist raised her voice. "Patti Nichols is on the line asking if you have time to do her hair Friday."

Mechanically Connie checked her calendar, replied, "Yes, fine, 2pm."

"Oh, she also said and I quote, 'Get ready for a Beyonce look. Hair extensions.'"

"Block off the rest of the afternoon for her in that case," Connie said dully.

Frustrated, Connie thought to herself, Isn't anyone content with their looks anymore? I'm not a magician. She placed her hand to her throat to suppress her desire to scream. I'm not a magician, she told herself, but I am a coward. Here I stand, like a frigging block of granite instead of going to mother, to help her. Coward.

William Wanders

Ruth pulled into the garage grateful to be home. Sharing the burglary story with the hairdresser renewed the feeling of horror she'd experienced that night. *Get a grip* she told herself as she got out of the car. She shook her head as if to wake up to present time. Her next thought was of William. She hurried inside fully expecting him to have fallen asleep as he watched his favorite movie, *Tom Sawyer*. Thankfully, his fascination with the film provided Ruth with an instant caretaker whenever one cancelled last minute, like today. He never tired of the movie, alert to every nuance, seeming to be in the picture as if he were living it. It engaged him, rather than enraged him as most stimulation was prone to do. For Ruth, it was a godsend. Simply settling her husband into his arm chair, putting *Tom Sawyer* on gave her a much needed respite.

"Hello!" Ruth called, setting her car keys on the hall table. The soundtrack loud filling the house. But something was wrong. Repeatedly, it cycled, the words, "I'm just runnin' away from home." She hurried to the living room. William's chair empty, eerie words again repeating, "I'm just runnin' away from home." Ruth snapped the television off. "William! Answer me, where are you?" She ran from room to room, her panic escalating. She bolted out the front door, questioned the gardener. "Have you seen William?" The gardener nodded, "Why, yes, about an hour ago. He took a walk."

Ruth felt the blood drain from her face, "Oh, God." She scrambled back to the house, frantically dialed 911 and screamed into the phone, "My husband is missing! Help me!" She sobbed, "He has Alzheimer's!" The Silver Alert was immediately posted. This public notification system an invaluable tool in the rescue of missing persons. Soon William's face would be posted on local news channels. He would be found.

Earlier, William, free, free to follow his gnarled logic, walked through the sub-division, turned a corner and crossed a major highway, cars honking, drivers waving. William waved back, smiled. Mesmerized, his goal close at hand, proceeding to the unmoving sea of cars. Lots of cars, cars parking sideways, cars parked backwards, cars all colors, big cars, small cars, orange, green, blue cars. Then, something very big, very wide. Shiny glass, something bright, something enticing. William cocked his head, curious, pushed then pulled on the silver handle. The door opened. Walking inside the shiny box. Balloons! Music! Party? Birthday party? The young salesman approached, "Would the gentlemen like to be a part of our store's anniversary?"

William said, "Birthday party?"

The young man nodded, "You could call it that. Would you like me to take your picture? Make a movie of your visit?"

William moved joyfully toward the camera waving his arms, calling out, "Happy Birthday!" The salesman uploaded the video on the store's closed circuit, soon William was projected onto 30 televisions. William walked the aisles ecstatically, moving from one screen to the next seeing big Williams, little Williams, Williams everywhere. The manager approached immediately understanding what was happening, signaled his salesman to call the police.

"Party," said William as the manager handed him a balloon and a bottle of water.

"Yes, a party," agreed the manager, gently guiding William to a seat.

"I'm just runnin' away from home."

Silver Alert

"AND HERE'S THE LATEST FROM Klystron 9, the most advanced radar system in the world." Bay News 9 blared its irritating sound effect as a spray of yellow blobs marched bravely across the map of Florida.

Connie glanced at the screen, grimaced, stirred her coffee, sighed and sat down to rest at her little kitchen table. Glad to be home after cutting, coloring, blowing out other women's hair all day long. She rolled her shoulders, took a sip of coffee, lit up and inhaled deeply savoring the taste. She smiled reading the side of the coffee mug *Girls Get It*, a gift from Salli. Then out of nowhere, frighteningly, her father's aged face materialized across the room. She might not have known him except for the eyes. The eyes.

She leaned in listening hard, "A Silver Alert has been issued for this man, 77 year old William Mitchell, of Tarpon Springs, last seen wandering on the shoulder of U.S. 19 at Klosterman, if you have --"

"My God!" Connie screamed, slamming the coffee mug down then yelping with pain as the hot liquid scalded her hand. She rushed to her feet.

"My God!" she repeated, circling the kitchen.

Doodle trotted in, danced from one foot to the other, sensing the panic in Connie's voice. Alert, Doodle waited and watched as Connie stood at the kitchen sink and ran cold water over her burning hand and wrist.

White Garden

RUTH IN HER WHITE GARDEN, seeking solace, collapsed into the floral cushioned chair, crossed her legs, clasped her knees, and rocked to and fro, pondering the painful process that lie ahead, that of committing William to a memory care facility. The delicate fragrance of jasmine, the pungent fragrance of the calla lilies, lent comfort. She sighed. William. The final blow would be losing him. Could she withstand it? As fear stalked her, she began to whimper, reached to pluck a single white rose. The bittersweet remembrance of William carefully covering the rose bushes with netting protecting them from the deer. She clasped the rose and her tears cascaded onto its petals. Despite Alzheimer's erasing William's mind, his physical presence had comforted her. Now she would lose that. Managing his care gave her life purpose, an outlet for her love. A chance to be useful. The multitude of home care specialists provided a rhythm to the daily life of the household. Once he was committed, she truly would be alone. Ruth shivered as her mind played a recording of the hideous vocabulary of the disease:

tangles in the brain, plaque, and with progression, the possibility of psychosis. Like slow moving lava, the disease eradicated William. He, once a tycoon in the world of business, now a man who'd lost control of his physicality and worse, his mind now projecting terrifying images causing violent outbursts. The unrelenting distortion of reality, disorientation, the unflagging war-torn territory of mind.

Was all lost?

As the disease spiraled, taking all from William, so too it took from Ruth. One activity after another abandoned. Volunteer docent at the Leepa-Rattner Museum of Art. Monthly "catch-up" lunches with old friends. Water aerobics at the YMCA. Only shreds of her life remained. Had she become invisible to everyone except him? Would she one day also be invisible to him? He recognized no one but her. When that was gone, what was left? Isolation? Memories of her youth, her career as curator at the St. Petersburg Museum of Fine Arts, William, in his 40s, dashing, divorced, available, she 28, swept her off her feet. Married quickly, a dream come true. "Ah," she ruminated, "a fairy tale beautiful." But the early onset of Alzheimer's encroached dissipating his genius, turning the fire to ashes, the sparkling personality into one of introspection, estrangement. A mind filled with vacant rooms.

Cruel Confrontation

Late one evening, Chad at his house, Will at his, both bored out of their minds. Chad calls, "Hey! I'll pick ya up, there's something I wanna do."

"What's that?" asked Will, perking up.

"You'll see soon enough. Got a baseball bat?"

"Baseball? Since when are you into baseball?"

"Since now. Be out front."

Will called out to his foster parents that he'd be out for a while. No big deal. They didn't really feel it was their responsibility to monitor a guy his age anyway.

Curious, Will yanked the car door open, "So what's up?"

"Just get in, will ya?" said Chad impatiently. "You know those bums livin' outside a town? You know, that shitty camp? We're going over there to have a look-see." The tires squealed as he pealed out.

Will tensed, "Oh, yeah?"

"What's a matter with you? You got something better to do?"

"Nothin'," Will shrugged, "nothin'."

The camp was home to about twenty or so men, who for reasons of their own, preferred to live on the fringes of society. There were few rules here: Don't steal from one another. If you get stinking drunk and are abusive, you will be turned out. Eat what's provided without belly aching. The residents, mostly Vietnam vets and even a few Korean War vets, lived in the makeshift compound primarily comprised of tents, small fire pits and just enough water for their needs from a small spring near their field. The authorities left the men alone, rarely making an appearance. The vets, self-sufficient, bothered no one and wanted no one to bother them. This camp was Sam's home, his refuge. When he cried out from night terrors, no one asked why, they knew why. When he patrolled the camp perimeter carrying on his shoulder a massive "rifle," no one asked why, they knew why. Indeed, his silhouette in the late evening was soldier like and the halted gait of the man carrying the large, thick oak branch carefully stripped of its bark, was a comfort to the men. Tonight, it wasn't Sam on patrol; however, it was Edward, a well liked decent sort of man who kept to himself, did his share of the work without fail.

Chad doused the lights, eased the car into the thicket, pulled his bat from the back seat, commanded, "Get yours."

"I don't like this, dude. This is too weird."

"Shut the hell up, you pussy, get out of the car. We're doing this." Chad slammed the car door angrily and immediately regretted the noise it made. "See what you made me do, Wilbur."

Will did not correct Chad. Chad knew full well his name was William. Wilbur was just one more form of sarcastic manipulation. Will ruefully exited the car, glared, "I'm not bringing the bat. I told you, I don't like this."

"Look, asshole, every time you want to use my wheels, I let ya, don't I? You owe me."

Will sighed. Trapped in the logic of a maniac.

Chad led the way, a predator anticipating the kill. Begrudgingly, Will followed to the camp site where several small fires burned, some men sat in makeshift chairs or on tree stumps. A couple of vets dozed on bed rolls. A sound from the far edge of the camp drifted on the night air, the mournful notes of a harmonica. Only a sliver of the moon in the dark sky.

Chad spotted Edward patrolling and viciously swung the bat into the back of Edward's head. Edward went down, hard. "You bastard!" Chad cursed, as Edward's blood dripped onto the scrubby tufts of grass.

Will froze in fear. What was happening? This was not what he bargained for. His eyes scanned the camp. Who heard? Who saw? Anyone?

There, by a small fire, a vet, one arm lifeless, squatted, patiently stirring a pot of stew. Chad advanced, cracked the man's one good arm. The man fell back, cried out, writhing in pain, his cries unheeded as many of the vets were stone deaf, shell shocked from war. They were unaware of the sound of Edward's cry, others in for the night asleep in their tents oblivious to the danger that await them. But Sam heard. Sam was not asleep, nor was he resting. He heard the cry, saw his friend on the ground next to the fire, writhing in pain, saw Edward bloodied, laying still as a statue. Then Sam spotted the intruders, recognized Will. Sam scrambled for his oak stick, screaming an alarm to the camp as he did so and charged Chad with everything he had. Will watched in horror as Chad bested Sam, who now was the third man down. Chad, on his feet, shrieking, "You're next grandpa! Retribution!" lifting the bat high, ready to split Sam's skull. Sam, raising his arms to shield himself, his face contorted with fear. Will, panting in terror, threw himself against Chad, halting the killing blow meant for Sam. Two friends, now enemies, one cursing and brutally swinging his bat, the other dodging the bat, but then grabbing hold, hanging on, lifting his fist and smashing in Chad's face.

"You'll pay for this asshole! Retribution!" Chad threatened as the blood gushed onto his black t-shirt, and dribbled down onto his jeans and boots.

"I don't think so," said Will slugging him in the gut for good measure, "get outta here. You make me sick."

Their mutual pact against the cruel world ended. Chad had gone too far.

Some of the men stirred, one reached for his cell phone. Another said, "No police, don't want 'em here." Others agreed. The police would not be summoned.

Will stood in awe of the men who gently carried the wounded to their tents for care. They were fortunate that within their ranks was a former army medic, a competent vet who would administer care to the wounded men.

One vet, stronger and younger than the rest chased Chad, tackled him, pinned him to the ground. He huffed, "You bastard!" as he slugged Chad in the nose, breaking it. Blood gushed and Chad began to choke on it. "You ever show up here again, you're dead," the vet promised.

Others gathered around, "Hell, he's dead now!"

"No, we won't kill him but we'll teach him a lesson he won't soon forget," said another stepping forward.

"Not here," cautioned one vet. His eyes narrowed, "Take his wallet, just the driver's license. That's all we need."

The vet handed him the license and threw Chad's wallet into the camp fire.

Chad, panicked, heard, "Now we know where you live. You had better keep your eyes peeled for company, 'cause we'll be comin' for ya. You bet. You invaded our territory; we'll be invading yours. Get ready!" The vet put a fist the size of an anvil into Chad's gut. "That's for good measure, you bastard."

The vets backed away, some having to hold back others who wanted to finish him off. Chad lay writhing in the dirt, bleeding and puking. He pushed himself to his knees and struggled to his feet. His big plan, his retribution, had back fired. Cursing under his breath, he stumbled to his car. He would drive straight across the state line to Georgia. There was nothing left for him in Florida. Nothing. No one. For the first time in his life, he was genuinely afraid.

The Pervert Strikes

It was late afternoon and Drina was excited. McHughes was due shortly and he, a master at the grill, was cooking for her and her daughter, Solana. Solana saw him differently and complained that she wasn't comfortable around him.

"How can that be? You met him twice for two minutes each time before he took me out."

"I don't know," Solana answered, "he's just weird, mom." She added that her friend Allison was over and asked, "Could she stay for dinner?"

"Of course," Drina replied.

Drina had shared Solana's dislike of McHughes with Connie, also offering that Solana never liked any guy she dated. Connie thought that perhaps Solana was jealous of the attention the men received. Solana, at 15, possessed the body of a woman and dressed to accentuate her ample bosoms. She enjoyed the appreciative looks of the many young and older men who noticed her. But McHughes was a sleaze, she had caught him checking her out when Drina was in another room or when her mother's back was turned. He was sneaky and he was scum. Solana believed this with every fiber in her body.

"Girls, I'm making a quick run to Publix for garlic bread, let Lloyd in and be polite, Solana," Drina cautioned.

"All right," Solana grumbled, shot a look to Allison.

"So I finally meet this guy, huh?" asked Allison.

"Yeah, lucky you." Solana stepped over to the chopping block, began chopping the scallions. Sure enough, within minutes of her mother's leaving, McHughes pulled up onto the driveway. Solana called out, "Door's open." She did not look up when he entered the kitchen. "Mom ran to Publix."

"Aren't you going to introduce me to your friend?" McHughes asked letting his eyes roam Allison's body.

"Allison, Lloyd McHughes; Lloyd, Allison." Solana pursed her lips, blew a puff of air up off of her face. She sniffed, scowled, had he been drinking?

"What're you girls up to tonight?" The girls shrugged their shoulders, mumbled, "Nothing."

McHughes poured himself a rum and coke, leaned against the counter and took in the view of the gorgeous young women, downing the drink quickly without attempting further conversation.

"There's nothing for you to do here," Solana waved the knife gesturing to the Florida room.

"Excuse me a second," said Allison, scooting down the hall toward the bathroom.

McHughes fixed another drink, "I'll relax out here," he said and walked toward the Florida room.

"Good." Solana pushed the bowl of scallions aside and began chopping the cucumber. She kept her eyes on her work, finding the sight of him disgusting.

McHughes had a plan. Allison was a hottie and he wanted some. He followed Allison and waited outside the bathroom door. Listening, salivating. Allison came out. He smiled. She frowned. He stood in front of her, blocking her exit. When Allison tried to pass, he reached out and fondled her breasts.

"Stop it!" she screamed.

He did not stop. Electrified, he pressed his groin into her. Again, Allison screamed.

Solana ran down the hall, tightly clasping the knife, "What's wrong?" she challenged, searching their faces, Allison's blotched red -- McHughes' placid.

"He touched my boob and pushed himself against me. He's a pervert!"

"Oh, please," McHughes said sarcastically, "I bumped into you, I'm sorry, excuse me," he bent his head in mock supplication. Then, as cool as the cucumbers Solana was chopping, he stepped into the bathroom and closed the door.

Doubt

Drina arrived at Heilman's Beachcomber, an established gem of a restaurant close to the legendary Clearwater Beach. She loved the place, always entered with sense of joy, but not today, today it was with a sense of foreboding. She arrived early hoping to calm herself before McHughes arrived. This would be a difficult conversation. She slid into the leather booth and reflected: Solana seemed trustworthy, not subject to the wild mood fluctuations and general craziness most teen girls displayed. But Lloyd McHughes, a man of substantial influence, education, a man held in high esteem? How would he do such a thing?

What had happened? She reviewed: She was expecting Lloyd for dinner at her place. Solana and Allison were in the kitchen preparing a salad. A quick trip to Publix was necessary and she had told the girls to let Lloyd in and let him know she'd be right back. Then what?

"May I bring you something to drink?" asked the waiter.

"Oh, not just yet," Drina answered, embarrassed realizing the waiter had been waiting patiently tableside. She, in a daze. Pensive.

He turned to leave, "Yes, ma'am."

"No, wait," she said, snapping back to present time and despite seriously wanting a glass of wine to calm herself, she ordered iced tea with lemon. She would need a clear head, for this lunch she scheduled with McHughes. She did not want alcohol to interfere with her ability to think.

The waiter served her. "Are we expecting another guest today, ma'am? Or, would you like me to take your order?"

"Yes, a friend will be here soon. We'll order then, thank you." What was that tremble she felt in her throat? She lifted the glass of tea. Somehow she could not coordinate her lips to the rim, missed and dribbled tea down her chin -- it rolled down her neck. She set the glass down, the white tablecloth stained now with tea. Embarrassed, she wiped her throat and chin with the napkin. She looked around, no one noticed. It was her private faux pax. Calm down, she commanded herself.

Then, McHughes came into view. There he was. Drina shifted her view to two women seated a few feet away. The one studied Lloyd, commented to the other who turned to see him, their faces showing interest in the good looking man. The sky blue polo shirt stretched across his shoulders and back so nicely. His long stride, sweet smile. What a catch. Drina herself watched with appreciation and asked herself how there could be any truth in what the girls said? This man could have any woman he wanted. Why bother with kids? She rose and greeted him with a kiss. He slid in next to her, cozying up. Disarmed by his apparent relaxed demeanor, his warmth of greeting, she felt silly even approaching the subject. Maybe she wouldn't.

Challenge

Connie peeled open her fourth packet of butter and spread it on toast, crispy, just the way she liked it. Drina signaled the waitress to bring more butter. They sat relaxing at the Sunshine Grille, glad to score a booth at the popular restaurant, well known for its omelets and waffles. Connie's face took on a strange, bemused expression. "Did anyone ever turn in your jogging suit?"

"What?"

"You know, the jogging suit you said was stolen when you were in the shower at Yellow Sneakers."

Drina stiffened, "No. Apparently no one turned it in. I left my information at the front desk."

Connie lifted her steaming mug to take a sip, "Of course not, someone's wearing it right now." She took a bite of her fluffy omelet, lifted her eyebrows, nodded to a nearby table. Drina followed her gaze.

"Wasn't that the color of yours? Peach with a gray hood?" She buttered a second piece of toast.

"That's ridiculous, there must be hundreds of the same jogging suit sold every day. What makes you think that one's mine?" Drina irritated now.

"Didn't you have a patch or something to cover up where you stained the sleeve?"

"Yes, a butterfly appliqué, but I can't see the side of the sleeve from here and neither can you." Drina stabbed a fork into her sausage.

"Ah, yeah, I can. I can see it. She's the thief. There's your suit!" Bingo.

Drina made a sour face, "I doubt that but if it's true, she can have it."

"What do you mean, she can have it. It's yours."

"You think I would wear it after she has? Come on!"

"Aren't you a teensy, weensy bit angry? I mean, the woman stole your jogging suit."

"Maybe she needed it."

"Oh, my God," Connie put her fork down, "When do you stop being the victim, Drina?"

Drina's answer, a frown.

"Didn't you just tell me just last week that your supervisor was overloading your case load making it tough for you to investigate the child abuse cases you already have? Didn't you? And did you confront her? No, of course not. And your daughter tells you what your boyfriend may or may not have done to her friend, but one lunch with him and it's all smoothed over.

Drina locked eyes with Connie. "That's enough Connie," she said, rising, "this *victim* is going home. I'm sorry I disappoint you."

Across the room, the thief rose, ready to leave, brushing toast crumbs off herself. Her male friend glared at Connie and Drina, whose eyes now fixed on her.

"Aren't you going to say something to her?" Connie asked.

Drina froze.

"I am." Connie got up, followed the thief and her friend outside where they were lighting up.

"Nice jogging suit."

The woman looked at Connie, squinted, "What's it to you?"

"Do much shopping at Yellow Sneakers?"

The woman huffed smoke at Connie. "Let's go," she said to her friend. They jumped into a beat-up pickup truck and sped off.

Drina turned to Connie, "I don't care, she can have it. I told you, I won't wear it now anyway."

"Okay, but I'm just saying."

"I know what you're saying, and again, I'm sorry I disappoint you."

"Are you angry with me? You should be angry with her."

Drina sighed, "I'm not angry. But Connie you can't fight the world all the time. Sometimes it's easier to just do your best, walk away from confrontation."

Connie thought for a minute, answered, "I can't do that."

Instinct

WINE NIGHT OPENED ON A serious note when Drina announced, almost immediately, "Connie, there's something I'd like to talk about." She looked guiltily at Salli, "I'd like your input, too, Sal." Drina had done a lot of thinking since she and Connie had argued at breakfast a few days ago. There was something about Lloyd McHughes, something that caused doubt to lurk continually in her mind. She now wanted to talk about it with her friends.

"What is it?" Connie and Salli asked with concern. It was quite obvious to both of them that Drina was upset. Connie surmised the discussion would be about Drina's boyfriend, Lloyd. She was right.

Drina sighed, "Lloyd, of course. There's just something about him that doesn't add up, you know? Something I can't quite figure out."

Connie considered what Drina had said. "Trust your instinct, that's what I recommend. If you think there's something off with this guy, don't waste your time with him. You've had concerns before about him, haven't you?"

Drina knew in her heart that Connie was right but she felt sad when she thought about breaking off the relationship with Lloyd. There was so much about him she admired, yet there was his strangeness. She sighed. It was tough dating one guy after another, each time hoping for the best outcome, but most men proved unworthy. Some were nice guys but there was no chemistry. And chemistry could not be overrated. Still a young woman, Drina had needs. Lloyd satisfied those needs, yet once the sex was over, he seemed distant, inscrutable. Yes, something was there, something he was hiding. That was it: He was hiding something. What could it be? Thoughts of the incident with Solana's friend haunted her. Had he been lying about that? She turned to Salli, "Salli, you haven't said anything, what do you think?"

Salli looked thoughtful, "I think you should date him, have sex, but be on the lookout for another guy. That way you avoid a dry spell."

Connie listened thinking how the little wine nights made a real contribution to the mental stability of each one of these women who trusted one another, shared their innermost fears and desires. Connie validated Drina's intuition: "Dump him. Do like Oprah says, listen to your instinct. It knows things your brain doesn't. You don't feel that you can trust him, right? This feeling isn't new; you felt this for a long time now. Dump him. He's expired." She paused, "Sorry if I sound harsh but that's what I think."

Drina resolved she would dump McHughes, the sooner the better. Time to move on. She felt remorseful, a bit guilty. Had she let his wealth and position influence her unduly in assessing his character? Why did she not believe her daughter when she said he came on to her friend in a highly inappropriate manner? Was she so flattered to be dating a powerful man that she was blind to reality? Was she that shallow? That foolish? She felt violated somehow, as if her strict moral code had eroded bit by bit by permitting Lloyd to be in her life. Yes, he would have to go. That much she knew. Expired.

Dumped

IT WAS GETTING TOUGHER ALL the time for McHughes, balancing work with play, maybe too much play. So many hotties out there, all anxious for play. But now, he needed a stable relationship, something marketable for the media -- a wife or at the very minimum, a fiancée. No contest there, it had to be Drina Alvarez. Respectable Drina. Cuban-American Drina. Educated Drina. He poured himself a drink, surfed on-line porn sites for a while plotting how he could have his cake and eat it too. The phone rang. It was Drina:

"Lloyd, I've been doing a lot of thinking--"

"I have, too," he interjected, confidently.

"I've appreciated our friendship, I really have, but I don't wish to continue seeing you."

The news hit him like a sledge hammer. He stammered, "What?"

Drina said, "I wish you well and hope you understand." With that, she hung up.

He was dumped. Just like that.

Sharon's Attack

I just can't take that bitch anymore Sharon decided as she drove to the library for the poetry meeting. She's been in the group a couple of months, acts like she owns it, gets all this attention, all this sympathy. Bitch. One more poem about her long lost son, and I'm . . .

Oops. She saw Glenn as she pulled into the parking lot, rearranged her face, "Hi, Glenn!" she called out. Glenn cut the engine on his Harley, removed his helmet, nodded to Sharon.

"I didn't know you wore a helmet, you don't have to by law, you know, but you would know that," she giggled, "you being an attorney."

"Well, you're right but I've handled enough liability law to know there's definitely virtue in the helmet," he reached over and patted it like it was a buddy. Sharon, excited as a school girl, quickly grabbed her sheath of poems off the seat of her car hurrying so that she could be seen walking in with Glenn. That would kill Connie. Ha!

Truth was, Connie was late and not exactly in the mood for group but with Salli's urging, she walked the few blocks over to the library. Pulling the door open, Connie sighed. What she had overheard her mother say at the Spa was greatly upsetting. Guilt and self-remorse crowded her mind, the bitter taste of regret palpable.

Glenn was overjoyed to see Connie, as she tiptoed into the meeting room, but when he saw that her eyes were red-rimmed and sunken, he felt despair. Sam glanced knowingly at Connie, shifted in his seat, whispered, "Hello." Sharon looked triumphantly across the table at Connie and thought good, she looks like shit. Sharon, feeling invincible wearing her new bullet bra, pulled herself up ramrod straight, aimed the torpedoes at Glenn.

Glenn greeted the group members and quietly asked, "Who would like to read?"

Sharon shot her hand up like a rocket. "As you all know by now, I take inspiration from my idol Marilyn Monroe and one of her most famous quotes was, "Sex is part of nature, and I go with nature; therefore, this poem came straight from my heart." She looked longingly at Glenn. He lowered his eyes. She cleared her throat and read the sensuous poem, a poem she had written during her night shift, with Glenn in mind, so arousing that she had pleasured herself during the writing process. Now that James was dead, she was adrift with no sexual outlet. Damn him.

Commentary was minimal, everyone anxious to move on from the constant barrage of Sharon's sex poems.

Sharon again boldly looked into Glenn's eyes, sending a signal: I Want You. Signal received: Discarded. Nervously, she pawed through her purse as if looking for something. Connie's turn to read. She shared a poem from her Poetry of Pain collection. Her voice faltered as she read:

"The poem is entitled, *Bereft*."

I carried you nine long months, suffered the pain
Writhed as my belly grew, much to my disdain
Wept when you were born, a most untimely birth
And now, I wonder, where you are
Where on earth.
For you are gone, and nothing is the same
I look for you but your face is a blur
A tiny child is what you were
When last I saw you, I knew your name
They took you from me, changed your name.
Others have children, I have none
I made it that way, and so it is done
But time brings regret, faces carved in stone
I just wish that you would come home.

Connie, with downcast eyes, waited for the critique. Sharon jumped in ensnaring Connie. "Just who is this mythical mother searching for her son?" she asked, her face a mosaic of anger, jealousy and hatred. She continued, "And judging by your previous mean streets poetry, I guess we know who you were and what you did with your life."

Connie gasped as if she was slugged in the gut.

"You can stop right there!" shouted Glenn, his face flushed.

Connie waved him off, raised her gaze to meet Sharon's, "No, let her finish. Go ahead, what else do you have to say?" Let the enemy speak.

"You sit here and read this poetry of pain," her lips curled as she emphasized the words with the sharp edge of sarcasm, "Obviously, *you* chose to be a street walker. *You* abandoned your child and *you* expect us to feel sorry for *you*. Well, I don't!"

Tears formed in Connie's eyes but stood her ground, "Who the hell are you accusing of abandoning their child? Mine was removed, taken from me," she swallowed a sob, "do you understand the difference? I never abandoned my son."

"Oh, but you did," Sharon savored each word. "The day you shot up one more time, screwed one more john, that was the day you abandoned your son!"

Connie rose, "I'm done here." She gathered her things.

"I am, too," said Drina who turned, staring with loathing at Sharon.

Sharon returned the hateful stare, glaring, unblinking.

"This is not good," said Sam rising, he touched Connie's arm as he walked out beside her.

Glenn, devastated, threw up his hands, "Sharon, you're out. Your presence in this group is no longer desired. You're out." He shook his head in disgust. "What you did was vicious." He walked out.

Margaret followed Glenn out of the room.

Don sat there for a moment but even he, this crude excuse for a man, stood, and without saying a word, walked out.

Sharon was stunned as she looked about the empty room. No one to talk to but the walls, she quoted Marilyn Monroe: "I'm selfish, impatient, and a little insecure. I make mistakes, I'm out of control, at times hard to handle. But if you can't handle me at my worst, then you sure don't deserve me at my best!" Sharon, redeemed, now raised her head imperiously, spit out, "Tough shit! Piss on them! Isn't it a pity I told that little bitch the truth. Who does she think she is?" The room, eerily silent but for the sound of the ticking of the clock. The air in the room, gray and cold from the icy blast of the air conditioning. She sat transfixed, unseeing, unhearing. She crossed her arms, heaved a sigh, took out her compact, checked herself in the mirror, thought she saw blood on a tooth but it was only Marilyn's Screaming Red lipstick.

Outside, Drina implored, "Let me drive you home, Connie."

Connie shook her head. "I need to be alone." She left the scene trying with all her might not to dissolve into tears in front of her friends.

Drina, Glenn, and Sam stood together watching Connie walk away. From above, the street light illuminated their faces, faces pale with pain and bewilderment.

Drina waited until Connie was out of earshot, then lashed out, "I can't believe what Sharon did in there! I want no part of this group if she's in it."

Glenn's eyes flashed, "I told her, she's out, we're done."

"All I got to say is the little lady didn't deserve that," Sam said sadly.

Glenn turned to Drina, "Should I call her? I'd like to let her know I kicked Sharon out. I think she'd want to hear that."

"Not tonight I wouldn't. She's pretty upset. I think we should respect her wish to be alone right now. She's had a rough day," she paused, "You do know she's looking for her son, right? She said the Poetry of Pain was inspired by a *60 Minutes* report just as a cover because she felt so ashamed ."

Glenn jumped in, "I assumed from her poetry that she was but when I try to get close to her, she pushes me away." He swallowed hard.

Drina patted his arm, "Give her time, Glenn, give her time."

"You sound like Sam."

❧❧❧❧❧

Connie trudged home, the sobs came as she walked along the narrow, cracked sidewalks lined with massive oak trees. Connie, prostate, gasped, steadied herself against one of the trees, catching her breath. Sharon was right. I abandoned Will by being a tramp on drugs, a whore. That's the truth. She spoke the truth. It's true. I'm a miserable excuse for a human being. Where my boy is now, what his life is . . . it's all my fault. Her thoughts played like a tape over and over and over again, the stabbing reality: She had abandoned her little boy.

She unlocked the door, threw her purse and her poetry folder onto the side table. She missed and they hit the floor, poetry lying like a fan in a circular fashion. She stared without seeing. Doodle came to her. She swept Doodle up into her arms and cried wetting Doodle's fur. Doodle licked her face. "I'm no good; just no good." She headed for the bedroom, put on a loose cotton gown, went to the kitchen, uncorked a bottle of wine, poured a glass, spilled half onto the kitchen counter. Doodle watched with dismay. She sobbed as she walked to the living room sofa, "Have I ever done anything right in my life?" She cursed her life. "Why did I hate my parents? Why am I such a bitch?" Doodle became frightened, trotted off to hide under the bed. Connie hardly noticed. She began to beat the coffee table with her fist, beat it like it was a drum, pounding, pounding, her arm began to throb. She ignored the pain, screamed, "Why am I alive?"

Drina on the porch, able to see Connie, worried, knocked on the door.

"Go away!" Connie commanded. "Leave!" her voice resounded, unnatural in its tone, even to her. Drina tip-toed off the porch.

Expulsed

Sharon burst into the house fuming, turned on her heels and threw the front door shut slamming it so hard that the tiny house shook. Windows rattled and a white, powdery dust drifted from the ceiling.

"Hey! Take it easy there," said Ray, trying to suppress a smirk, "Guess yer fancy writer friends pissed you off, eh?" He shook his head and brushed white dust from his shoulder.

Sharon wheeled, stomped to the end table next to his chair picked up the hideous ceramic horse head lamp she always hated and heaved it to the floor. The head did not shatter as she expected; instead, the head cracked into three pieces. A cold, dead equine eye now stared at her. You killed me it seemed to say. She stepped away.

Alarmed now, Ray shouted, "Whoa!" as he snapped forward in his recliner. "What'd you do that for?"

Sharon leaned into Ray hissed in his face, "Shut. The. Fuck. Up!"

He took no offense, instead he melted devouring the shape of her lips, the scent of her breasts.

She stormed out of the room.

God, she's so sexy when she's all pissed off and kind of brutal, he thought, savoring his erection with one hand and turning up the volume on "The Fantastic Four" with the other.

She, sitting on her bed, fists clenched, breathing heavily, mind racing. Connie is a problem. A big problem. The Bitch made me look bad tonight. All I said was . . . what did I say? She cocked her head. Only the truth. I alone spoke the truth. No one else has the balls to do it. A murmur in the room, her gaze shifted to the chorus of Glass Heads, their juicy red lips reassuring, "You did nothing wrong," said one. Then another, "It's her. Not you. Her." "She has to be dealt with, you know," added another. Each glass head sparkling with Marilyn's beauty.

"That's right. I did nothing wrong. She abandoned her kid. Druggie bitch whines about it all the time. She's the asshole not me. For all we know, she smothered him when he was a baby, or maybe drowned him in the bath tub. For all we know.

"Not to worry, you know what we always say," the Glass Heads chanted in unison, "I'm selfish, impatient, and a little insecure," Sharon joined the chorus quoting Marilyn Monroe. "I make mistakes, I'm out of control, and at times, hard to handle. But if you can't handle me at my worst, then you sure as hell," Sharon shimmied, caressed her breasts, emphasizing the last phrase, "don't deserve me at my best." Empowered. Justified. Satisfied.

❧❧❧❧❧

The next morning, Ray observed his beautiful wife as she sat at the kitchen table. She seemed down. "Are you sad?" he asked.

Sharon stared straight ahead, stirred her coffee, took a spoonful of yogurt then pushed it aside, "And why would I be anything else? Married to you?" her expression sour.

"It's those shitty writers, right? They got to you?"

Her expression told him to stop right there. He continued, "It's the money, right? I never should have complained about you buying yourself some nice stuff, okay? I'm sorry," his head fell to his chest. "I really am, babe, I want ya to be happy."

"Where did you go?" she asked softly in a voice filled with gloom.

"What? I been here all morning."

"Where did the man I married go? He was sexy, hot, hard-working! Now, look at you." Again, her voice low and slow, almost like he wasn't in the room, like she was talking to a ghost.

He sucked in his gut, thought of making a joke, bit back the urge. Kept quiet, unsure of what to say.

"What do you have to say for yourself, huh?" she pressed, this time full volume.

He gulped, at least she was actually talking to him, better than the cold treatment she usually dealt, "I, I, don't know," a sharp intake of his breath while Sharon peered over her coffee mug, "thing is," he said, "after I got laid off, I guess I kinda let myself go."

"Kinda," she blew air from her lips, recrossed her legs, looked out the window.

"I'm sorry, ba---"

"You think I like renting this dump? We used to have a nice place. I work to keep us in a dump or we'd be where? On the street?" She stood, refilled her mug, her back to him, he admired her shape, her small waist, her beautiful bottom all wrapped up in the pink silky robe. She left the kitchen, him standing there stupid, searching for answers. What to do? He followed her into the living room. He stank of beer, she stepped back. Sweat beads formed on his upper lip, "I have a plan."

"You? Plan? I doubt that," she glared at him. "You're lazy, Ray, that's why you got laid off."

"I'm gonna show you I can take care of you," he looked with longing at her tussled morning curls, her full lips, succulent. He reached out to touch her, she recoiled.

She wondered why he was acting so needy, so strangely. What was on his mind? She knew what was on her mind: Divorce. Ray was a dead-end. Time to move on.

Hitting Bottom

THE MORNING FOUND CONNIE AND an empty bottle of scotch sprawled on the living room floor. Darkness enveloped the room in the optics of misery. Thunder pierced the sky as rain sleeted against trembling windows. Connie lay ensnared by haunting dreams of her past. Dreams of drugs, dreams of the street, dreams of countless johns taking her sex as she existed in a haze of heroin. Haunting dreams, dark places. Rotting, stinking, moldering trash. Her life. She awoke suddenly coughing, choking on saliva. Her thoughts mangled, distorted, self-hatred once again tightening its grip. She struggled to sit up, slowly turned her head back and forth, wiped her dripping nose in the crook of her sleeve, reached out for the bottle. empty . . . shit . . . should be dead . . . loser . . . luckless . . . nothing matters . . . past eclipses present . . . ruin . . . all bullshit. Roughly she gulped phlegm. fucking idiot. can't make up for . . . what I did . . . she slobbered, tried to stand, fell back on her haunches, wicked guttural laughter penetrating the air, the ticking of the clock . . . life unwelcome. She pulled at her hair, violently twisted it in a knot, leaned forward and puked. War: Self versus Self. No quarter given. No amnesty. Or forgiveness. A whisper, deathlike, Will . . . where are you? She tried to conjure his image, failed, seeing only shadows, vaporous oh god oh god.

The phone, its ring hammering her brain . . . piss on it. Defeated, mired in self-loathing to the point of exactly what? How to find relief? Death or drugs? Or both? Where? A twisted plan formed in her twisted mind. A desire for relief fueling irrationality.

Next door, Salli looked out her window, her newspaper laying on the drive, soaking wet, no use going after it now. Connie's car on the drive, Salli found it unusual that she had not left for the spa by now. Maybe the storm held her up. Maybe she got a call that the spa was closed, maybe it was flooded. Salli's cell played *La Cucarocha*, she answered, "What's up, Drina?" Drina's voice breaking asked if she'd seen Connie. "No, but her car is here. Why? What's going on?" A clap of thunder. Drina updated Salli, asked her to look in on Connie, that she'd tried the previous night but Connie did not answer the door. I wonder if she will now, thought Salli. She shed her slippers for flip flops, popped open an umbrella and with cell in hand, headed for Connie's. She knocked. No answer. Door bell. No answer. Lightning glimmered. Salli picked her way through the ferns to the side of the house, stood on tiptoes, her pink flip flops oozing with mud, talked to her cell, "Yeah, I see her. She's in there all right. She's a mess and she looks weird."

Brilliant lights illuminated the ferns, surreal shades of green, yellow dancing in the wind. Lightning.

"What do you mean weird?"

"Speak up, I can't hear you, it's storming!" Salli yelled. Drina repeated her question.

"Like she's in a trance or something, weird, like I said." Salli rapped on the window. Called out. Connie lost in another world. Salli squealing with revulsion as her face is laced with a sticky cobweb. She tears it away and hurries home.

"I'm coming over. Tell me you have a key!" shouted Drina.

Horizontal lightning sizzles as its silver tentacles stab the brackish umbrella of sky. The air charged with ions, scalding vapor. Salli, now on her porch shivering, soaked to the bone, replies doubtfully, "Yes, but Connie said it's only for emergencies."

"What do you call this?" screamed Drina.

✴✴✴✴✴

Connie crawled to the sofa, grabbed hold and hoisted herself up . . . coffee . . .

✴✴✴✴✴

The friends crouching on Connie's porch, "Give me the key, Sal." Wind howling, turning Salli's umbrella inside out, shooting it up and out of reach. Salli shaking with fear stuttering, "I'm, I'm still not sure we should do this, Connie might be mad."

"Give me the key." Drina unlocks the door, pushes it open, softly calls out Connie's name. No answer. Calls again, louder. Nothing. Gusts of fresh air pour in mingling with stale, cursed air.

Connie, in the kitchen slumped over a cup of instant coffee croaking, "What are you doing here?" Eyebrows knitted, fingers trembling, the stench of urine, sweat and vomit permeate the room.

"We were worried," they chimed, tiptoeing on cat feet, into the kitchen. A strobe light pulses against kitchen walls. Thunder booming. Clouds, electrified, leering.

Connie, rigid, silent as stone.

"We, we brought bagels," offers Salli, snatching the bag from Drina, "Don't they smell good?" The only sound rain rushing to the ground below.

Drina thrusts the kitchen window down. Connie, unaware the floor is soaked. Drina, pale, drawn, stoops over Connie, whispers, "We want to help you. We're worried about you, Con." She attempts eye contact.

Connie will not look at Drina. "Don't care." Connie intones. "Leave," then breathlessly, "and leave the key." Her face, eerily striped with a pattern of light and darkness rendered by the quivering lightning. Its presence astral, looming.

Drina shivered, "But --"

"Go!" Connie pointed to the door.

Jackhammer claps of thunder crack open the sky. Defeated, Drina and Salli retreat. Connie, alone, wrapped in the shroud of futility, then darkness. Power out.

Redemption?

CONNIE STEWED IN HER OWN juices the next day, ignoring the phone, ignoring the door bell, calling in sick to work. She pulled on a pair of jeans, threw on a t-shirt. She had a plan. Determined, feeling she had no hope for a future anyway, she headed to her old haunt, the gritty side of Clearwater wherein lay the relief she sought: heroin. Twisted logic prevailed. She drove carelessly, radio silent, bitter thoughts brewing. *There's the scuzz bag* she thought as she pulled into the asphalt parking lot, her car rocking as it dipped into pot holes. Quickly, she killed the ignition, sucked a last drag of her cigarette, held it, then exhaled harshly. Marching up to Scuzz Bag, she made her needs known.

"You're gettin' nothin'. I don't know nothin' about no heroin," he said, giving Connie the evil eye as he rubbed snot off his nose with the back of his hand.

"Don't play dumb with me," she said, drawing herself up, "this isn't my first rodeo."

"Get outta here," he spat a pool of green slime.

"Look," she ordered, extending her hand, "I used to be a regular here, take the damn money and give me the damn drugs."

He shook his head no, studied the pavement. She softened her approach, lowered her voice, "I need the heroin, okay?" Shadowy figures appeared which she detected from the corner of her eye, old instincts surfacing, she sensed danger, threw a darting glance at two seedy thugs. Mean eyes leveled on her as they sucked cigarettes propping themselves on the crumbling concrete building. Connie stiffened.

"It don't work like that lady, I got cops crawling up my ass, and I don't got the means to know who's reliable. I mean sales wise."

The thugs snuffed out their cigarettes, exhaled voluminous smoke, stared, eyes locked on Connie. Hit time.

"If you know what's good for you, lady, you'd get outta here now," Scuzz Bag warned, eyes evil, challenging, sizzling with hatred.

Dejected, Connie returned to her car. *Just drive* she told herself. Winding along Gulf Blvd., she began to relax a bit, breathed in the fresh air and thought about life. Her eyes fell on the trinket which hung from her rear view mirror, a gift from Drina, a glass butterfly. Her thoughts turned to Drina and Salli, how could they ever understand what she had been, what she had done? They probably only pretended to. Bitter conclusion: they could not. Confused, she found herself driving north on Alt. 19. Unplanned, she found herself on her parents' street. Dazed, staring at the home of her childhood, she circled the block, two times, three times, the car creeping. *Dad's in there*, she thought, *but he wouldn't know me, I guess*. From what she'd overheard her mother say at the Spa, his mind was in a separate place, a different realm from that of reality. She roughly brushed away tears which ran down her face. A groaning metallic sound as the garage door opened and there was Ruth slowly getting into her car. Connie panicked, punched the gas, pulled away, grateful for her large, dark sunglasses. More tears, shocked at how thin, how frail her mother looked. She thought back on the conversation with Sam in which he had recommended forgiveness. "You were right, Sam," she moaned, "you were right."

Devastation. Nowhere to turn. A chasm. A soul abandoned. Connie drove on, the world a surreal landscape. Time, something operating on creaky hinges, rusty, cracked, ready to break. She blinked, *where am I*? The Dunedin Causeway, then Honeymoon Island, sitting in the car, staring, the gulf, a dull gray, then sparkling as clouds pushed by. She lit up, took a drag, got out of the car, immediately put the cigarette out. Regretted having done so, lit up again. Walked the short ways to the beach, plopped down on the sand, her mind ensnared. Seagulls wailed, circled searching for food. Predators.

In the background, the murmur of children's voices as they molded sand into castles. The rhythm of nature, calming, she breathed deeply, stretched out her legs, absorbed the scene, a numb expectancy gathering in her. The clouds, billowing, tracing patterns, then erasing them in the sky.

There, nearby, on a blanket, a young mother texting on her cell, her toddler carving his dream of the perfect road for his little yellow trucks and cars. He pulled himself up on his chubby legs and ambled toward the gulf, carrying with him his orange plastic bucket which swung from the white braided handle in rhythm with his steps. A sea gull swung low, crossed close to the child's face, its wings beating the air. The child, unaware, intent on filling his bucket with water with which to complete molding the sand. He squatted, scooped his bucket into the water, got too much sand, dumped it, went in deeper, scooped again, got sea weed. All this with his mother's eyes on her cell phone and Connie's eyes on him. He took one more step. This time, an abrupt drop in depth broke his balance and he toppled over into the sea. Connie on her feet, rushing, the bucket bobbing on the surface, the boy down, soundlessly gulping water. Connie, panicked, yet steady, hoisted the little boy up out of the water, held him close and patted his back. He gasped for breath, still choking on the salt water. He cried then, hard and loud, his mother looked up. The boy clasped Connie who spoke words of comfort. "There, there, you're fine. You're fine now." Connie approached her, "Here's your son. It might be nice if you watched him when he's near the water. He might have drowned." The woman stood up hastily, angry now, snatched him from Connie, "Mind your own business, he's fine." The little boy buried his face in his mother's shoulder as she held him with one arm, while peering yet again at the screen of her cell phone.

Thoroughly frustrated, Connie headed for her car. Maybe, just maybe, she wasn't the only bad mother. Some just got lucky and didn't lose their kid like she did. What really was the difference between a kid drowning because his mother wasn't watching him and a kid being taken away because the mother was unfit? She pondered this and rationalized that they were both bad mothers, only with the drowning, that would have been ruled an accident whereas Connie's loss of Will was a different story. Just then the young mother came up the path off the beach, still carrying her son and, upon seeing Connie in her car, hurried over. Connie considered making a quick getaway but she waited, curious, yet resentful of the pending intrusion.

The mother leaned in Connie's window, "I guess I was a little harsh back there. I'm sorry."

Connie nodded, unspeaking.

"Danny wants to say thank you." With that the little boy said, "tank you," his eyes sparkling with warmth. When he reached out his little hand and touched Connie's face, she responded, "You're welcome, little guy." Connie held herself together until they left, then, racked with sobs, a volcano erupted within her, shaking her to the depths of her being. These tears, not fueled by angst and fury but by a release of devastating, erosive guilt.

In some sense, she felt that having saved the toddler, she had saved Will. The math didn't add up, but somehow, deep inside her, the logic worked. Whether or not that young mother thanked her, or even realized how close she'd come to losing her little boy, Connie would always treasure the fact that she had been there, she had seen his struggle, and, yes, she saved his life. She had done something good, something of high value. Maybe she could try to do more good things, maybe there was a tiny sliver of hope that, before her life was over, she could help her own son, too. With streaming tears, she became resolved. Sitting there, so tired now, too tired to hold up her head, she let it fall back to the head rest. Her face soaked with tears, she watched as the sea grass lazily danced on the sandy knoll before her, she listened once more to the cry of the seagulls, the gentle rhythm of the soft waves lapping the shore. As the warmth of the sun penetrated, it nurtured her cold, weary soul, which now stirred with hope. She silently vowed that she would try, really try to do better, to be better. After all, what did she have to lose?

Connie drove home on auto pilot and collapsed on the bed. That morning, she awakened from a fitful sleep, spun her hair into a bun and mindlessly crept to the kitchen, lit a cigarette. Time. It was time. She could sense it in her bones. Years of blame, anger, downright hatred must end. She must make amends with her mother. She crushed the cigarette into the starfish ashtray, headed for the bathroom where she leaned over the sink and splashed cold water on her face. As she rose, Ruth's reflection greeted her: Ruth's eyes, Ruth's high cheek bones stared back at her. Connie flinched, rubbed her face briskly with the towel. Do I blame her for what I became? She considered her parents' marriage. Was it one of convenience? No. Never before had she realized the impact of this truth. They actually loved each other. Bitterness surfaced. Did they love me as much as they loved each other? No.

Connie brewed strong coffee, its aroma awakening her senses. Conflicted, one minute she called her mother a bitch for not raising William, then, alternately, she felt protective of her mother, alone, elderly, with a sick husband on her hands. Connie shook her head in puzzlement and sighed. Does hate have an expiration date? Do we stop feeling anger toward a parent when they die? Or, does the anger go on forever, until our death? She began to massage the back of her neck, and poured a cup of coffee. She thought of Professor Morrie in *Tuesdays with Morrie*, one of her favorite books -- "forgive everything."

Forgiveness, a difficult pill to swallow. Forgiveness, even Sam recommended it. Why should I forgive? she wondered. I wasn't the only one who doomed my son to adoption. What kind of grandmother is she? Connie set the coffee mug down abruptly and spilled the hot brew on her hand. She sniffed, wiped a tear with the back of her hand. Maybe she herself was to blame, not just Ruth. Maybe if she had stayed off heroin; maybe if she had not run away from home. Maybe! Connie rubbed her throbbing temples. We're both to blame she concluded. She questioned her compulsion to forgive her mother, return to the fold. Was it seeing how frail mother is? Was it the robbery? Was it father's dementia? Adding it up, Connie, moaned, "Oh, God."

White Sailor Suit

Sharon made up her mind. She would apologize to Glenn, get back in his good graces and back into the poetry group. She carefully dressed in an innocent little navy and white short set, very flattering, very Marilyn, but also casual in appearance befitting a drop-in visit to Glenn's law office. Perhaps they could sneak away for a quiet little lunch somewhere. But Glenn was cool to her and had the temerity to suggest that the apology should be delivered to Connie, not to him. As she stood stammering, Glenn shooed her out the door leaving her feeling demeaned, depressed.

She started her car, sat there in the parking lot thinking. Hadn't she put on the cute white sailor top with the matching shorts? He didn't notice any of it. Dream Man Glenn doesn't want me. He wants Connie the Bitch. The realization pounded in her head like thunder. She put her hands to her temples but the thoughts kept coming: Just like my father didn't want me, leaves for a pack of cigarettes and never comes home again. Abandoned . . . at the age of seven. And mother, Sharon mused, That pill-popping drug addict, sniveling, weak excuse for a woman. She abandoned me, too. Sharon learned early in life she couldn't count on anybody. But now, she could count on Marilyn. After all, they shared a common background, both had been wards of the state. Hadn't Marilyn said, "Sometimes I feel my whole life has been one rejection."

With James inconsiderately offing himself, she had no prospects for sex. A creeping restlessness grew within her. Lonely and rejected, she returned home, slunk to her room to talk it over with The Glass Heads. As usual, they saw it her way. "This is a drag," said one. "I'm not having fun anymore either," said another. "I need fresh mascara, I'm all clumpy." "Why does it always have to be about you?" another challenged.

Two days later returning from her night shift, Sharon sullenly pulled her car up onto the broken asphalt driveway. She waited sadly until "Candle in the Wind" finished, her favorite Elton John song. But she cheered when she saw the large box sitting on the front porch. The Amazon delivery. It had come!

"What's that thing?" Ray blurted scratching his belly, mildly curious.

"None of your concern," said Sharon haughtily as she dragged the box inside.

"Maybe it is my concern," Ray wagged his head mimicking his wife. "The damn box is huge, looks expensive. Again, I ask," he offered his hand as a maitre-d' offers a table, "What's that?"

"A mannequin, a dress form, if you must know."

"And why do we need, a mannequin? What's with you?"

Sharon glared at him and shoved the box toward him narrowly missing his TV tray.

"Hey watch it! You'll spill my beer!" he shouted, grabbing the can as it teetered.

"Really, Ray, beer at nine in the morning?"

"Hey, it's 5 o'clock somewhere," he answered, laughing at his own stale joke.

"And that would matter to me because?" Sharon crooked an eyebrow and resumed dragging the box across the floor. Once in her bedroom, she slammed the door.

Ray mimicked, "And that would matter to me because--"

"Size 10, hmmm, well, that's what they say Marilyn would be considered now, seems a bit large but whatever. She pulled an All Things Marilyn dress from her closet, laid it on the bed. The two-piece mannequin snapped together easily and Sharon pulled the filmy dress over its shoulders. "Interesting, hmmm," she put an index finger to her lips, leaned back assessing. "What do you think, Marilyns?" she asked turning to her collection of Glass Heads on the dresser.

"Nice to have a body," one said. "Me first!" said another.

"One at a time," said Sharon as she selected the nearest Glass Head and set it on the rounded hook that served as a head for the mannequin.

"How do I look?" Glass Head asked, batting its long lashes.

"You look beautiful!" said Sharon. "Let's take a selfie!"

"When's it MY turn?" "No! I go next!" the chatter became thunderous as the heads bickered. Sharon clamped her palms over her ears and screamed, "Enough!"

"What's going on in there?" hollered Ray, popping another Cheez-it into his mouth.

No answer. Ray drained his beer, tiptoed to Sharon's room, pressed his ear to the door. Nothing. Inside, Sharon, exhausted, had fallen asleep.

Ray returned to the living room and took a nap himself, but when he awakened, Sharon was gone. He thought about the strange chorus of voices he heard earlier coming from her room. What the heck? Then bitterly he thought, it used to be our bedroom until she banished me. He walked with stealth into Sharon's room which, despite the sunny morning, was as dark as a mausoleum. He flipped the light switch and his eyes swept the room. Everything Marilyn everywhere. "Kind of creepy like a wax museum," he muttered. Walls, covered with posters of Marilyn in different poses. "Wow." Next, he opened the closet and looked aghast upon the glamorous gowns hanging there, gowns that looked like the ones in the posters. He marveled at the sheer quantity of the stuff, big satiny skirts, long, black-sequined sheaths. There on the closet door, a shoe rack, dozens of strappy, high-heeled shoes, all colors. What does she do with this stuff? I rarely see her wear any of it. And the money it must have cost. Anger bubbled inside him as he thought about their large credit card debt but anger turned to skin crawling fear when he saw The Glass Heads. "This room gets freakier and freakier all the time," he said to himself.

"Oh, my God!" he blurted as he lurched back from the dresser, not wanting to look but unable to stop staring in disbelief at the grotesque collection. Each glass head bedecked with a different blonde wig but all bearing the same sneering red lips, just like Sharon's, and blue eye shadow, just like Sharon's and big, thick black eyelashes, just like Sharon's. The mannequin, eerily standing guard. My wife needs help, serious help, he thought. He crept from the room feeling ashamed, as if he had violated his wife somehow spying like this. He pulled a cold one from the fridge thinking there must be too much stress on her since I lost my job. He hung his head, feeling badly, then quickly concluded, it was not his fault. He reasoned, her mother was a crazy bitch, too. Soon as I'm back to work, I'll get her into therapy, counseling, some shit like that. He frowned, wait! She's a psychiatric nurse for crying out loud, "Physician, heal thyself."

He swilled beer and considered that maybe it was time to take action, solve their financial problems, be a man, reduce stress on his crazy wife, be a good husband. They had been happy once, right? Things could be that way again. He felt empowered. He felt strong. He felt horny. If he brought home the bacon, she would surely fry it. Get naked. Do him over and over again like they used to do in the Good Old Days. He formed a plan and marched to the threshold of Sharon's room proclaiming, as if to her, "I promise things will be better around here, babe." There on the far wall, on the dresser, a glint of a light caught his attention. It was light filtering through the eyes of one of the Glass Heads.

"Creepy shit!" he said, spitting out the words the way one spits out old, tasteless chewing gum.

"Who's Sorry Now?"

Severe thunderstorms expected. That made it even better. The old timers would stay home, fewer people in the way. Ray dressed quietly so as not to disturb Sharon in the next room. He stifled a nervous snicker, thinking how instead of heading to Walmart to pick up a few groceries, he was en route to rob the Bank of Florida on Havelin Street. The disguise? He mused. Something ordinary. He retrieved his old denim baseball hat from the hook by the back door. Good. Found his jet black oversized sunglasses in a kitchen drawer. Almost ready. A quick glance in the bathroom mirror showed no hair or eye color identification was possible. He pulled the bill of the hat down. What would the bank camera get? His mouth? Big deal. He smirked, studied his body, ordinary, could be anybody, 5'11" 190 pounds. Then he remembered. Gloves! He crept back to his bedroom, reached under the bed and pulled out a pair of well worn work gloves. Perfect.

He started to leave, was halfway out the door but suddenly dizziness overtook him as a clammy weakness filled his body. What was going on? Get a grip, he commanded himself, massaging his sweaty forehead. He paced back and forth, back and forth, gaining courage but in the process spreading chunks of dried soil onto the carpet. "Oh, shit!" he cursed and dutifully plucked crumbles of dirt from the carpet. Sharon would be so pissed if she saw that. A thought: We can get new carpet, get anything we want, take vacations; yes, this will fix everything. He started for the door, stopped, "Hmmm," stroked his jaw, nodded yes, marched to the hall closet, got his gun, dropped it into his duffle bag. Might need it. The plan? Leave the car home, far too easy to trace. Take the bus. "Good-bye, baby, wish me luck," he said as he blew a kiss toward Sharon's bedroom, thinking she was in bed asleep. He remembered to lock the front door not wanting to set Sharon off on that issue, all the while humming, "Who's Sorry Now?" He felt good, better than he'd felt in a long time. The panic attack was nothing. After all, anyone would be nervous. Yeah. He shrugged. There was a new spring in his step. He continued humming as he boarded the bus. But as he looked out the window, he had a strange feeling, it was as if he had never really seen the neighborhood before. Everything seemed surreal. Time slowed. Again he reassured himself, things would be different now. "Who's Sorry Now?"

Ray stumbled as he lunged down the steps of the bus, catching himself the last second before spilling into the street. He gripped the duffel bag as if it contained gold bullion bars, the gun inside giving him courage. "You okay?" called the bus driver, seeing his passenger struggle.

"Fine, thanks." Ray began walking, calm down, calm down, his lips moving repeating the chant. He strolled nonchalantly into the bank, three people ahead of him in line. Ray saw a pretty teller, hoped he'd get her for the robbery. That would give them a special moment together. If things didn't work out with Sharon, Ray reasoned, then this girl might have a drink with him, maybe a blooming onion, and a beer.

"Good morning," the teller said, it wasn't the pretty one.

Ray hesitated. He placed the duffel bag squarely on the counter and sang, "Who's Sorry Now?" The teller, confused, waited. Ray handed her a note and rolled his eyes toward the duffel bag. The teller got the message. There was a weapon in the bag; she would cooperate.

Catching the bus was easy, only a few passengers boarded with him. He continued humming "Who's Sorry Now?" as he sat in the back of the bus where he ripped off his outer t-shirt, hat and sunglasses and stuffed them into the duffel bag beside the stacks of cash. Very smart, very good planning. How easy was that? Maybe he'd make a regular thing of this. He began to drum out the tune on the window of the bus as he sang. Yeah, they'd all see who was sorry now and it wasn't going to be him, not this time.

"Nice to see someone happy despite this heat," offered the passenger to his right, across the aisle.

"Oh, yeah, I'm happy," he answered. Then Ray did something he rarely did these days: He smiled.

Section Three: Challenge -- Downfall

Then and Now

It was break time for Connie, time to grab a coffee and put her feet up. She plopped down onto the break room sofa. Oh, this feels good she thought to herself. Did she dare light up? Probably not. It was against Spa rules. She would have to content herself with coffee. *Gulf Bay Today* magazine's newest issue, its cover gleaming with a great shot of the gulf, caught her eye. She flipped through its pages. So ho-hum, the usual stuff, art galleries, recipes too complicated for her to cook, clothing she could not possibly afford. Then her eyes landed on a "Then and Now" feature. In it, prominent local figures were pictured as they looked in their 20s and as they looked today. Stupefied, she stared. Could it be him? My God, it was him: Drina's ex-boyfriend was Lloyd McHughes. His long curly copper-colored hair, now short, light brown. His beard and mustache now reduced to a mustache; that combined with a thirty pound weight gain and dark rimmed glasses definitely made him appear different. And the name, the name in Celeste's diary was different from this man's name. Of course, he used a fake I.D. at the brothel. That's what poor Celeste found in his wallet.

Connie's skin crawled. She began to hyperventilate. How can this be? Yet, it was. It was him, different looking now, different name now: *But it was him*. Celeste's killer. Will's father. She gasped in renewed horror. This was serious, this was scary. Thank goodness Drina had broken off the relationship; her instinct was correct. Connie's mind reeled to Solana's charge that McHughes groped her young friend. Blood pounded in Connie's brain like jack hammers and she struggled to gain control of her emotions. But she needed McHughes; he might be the key to finding Will. Surely with his high placement in the courts, he would be able to access records she was unable to see. She looked at the clock, it was time to get back to her station. She stood and though she felt shaky, she left the break room but then hurried back and grabbed the magazine. Her mind spun in circles: what should she do about McHughes? How should she handle this? And Drina, she must tell Drina about this horrible revelation. How would she take it? Drina had said she was through with him but sometimes couples hooked up again after a break-up. Drina would want nothing whatsoever to do with him now. No going back.

"I'd like the bangs cut a bit shorter this month, dear," said Mrs. Webster. "Dear?" repeated Mrs. Webster, lightly touching Connie's sleeve.

Connie snapped out of her daze and answered, "Of course." Inwardly, her mind churned -- shall I call his office or should I just show up? If I call, he can blow me off. If I show up he might be blindsided and more difficult to deal with. She also realized, she'd have to have a conversation with Drina. The sooner the better. Tonight was wine night, may as well get it over with.

Long Ago

CONNIE HAD KEPT QUIET ABOUT her discovery of Lloyd McHughes, unsure of how to proceed with telling Drina and Salli. Drina would be in shock, might blame herself for not realizing that McHughes was a pervert. This would be difficult for Connie to share because he was what he was, the damage was done but she did not want Drina to be hurt.

She prepared the coffee table with napkins, chocolates, wine goblets; she usually didn't bother with background music, but tonight, she would. It might help soothe their souls. She reflected on their kindness to her when she had telephoned each of them to apologize for the other night when she had her meltdown. They said it was okay, they had them, too. She smiled remembering their understanding, their forgiveness.

"Hey, Con!" called Drina.

"Door's open!"

Salli was soon there, too. "I brought a shiraz tonight. Ever hear of it? It was on sale at Walmart."

"Sure, we're game," said Connie, glad for a diversion, no matter how small.

After the wine was poured, sipped and judged, Connie began, "Ladies," she sat up very straight, took a deep breath, "I have news." She filled them in as quickly and delicately as she could.

Salli was the first to find her tongue, with eyes as big as saucers, she exclaimed, "*He* was the one? And, Drina, *you* dated him? Oh, my God!"

"I know," Drina said meekly, "I think I'm going to be sick." She headed for the bathroom.

Connie shook her head, "This is so bad, so awful. Poor Drina."

When Drina returned to the living room, Connie sadly looked at her friend who now trembled with a mixture of fear and relief. "To think I let that monster in my house, near my daughter. I can't believe I was that stupid!"

"You didn't know, Drina, no one knew." Salli handed her a tissue.

"He put up a good front, that's for sure," Connie said bitterly. "But you suspected something; you followed your instinct and dumped him." She put her hand over Drina's comforting her.

Drina swallowed hard, "Thanks to you guys. Remember? We talked about him and --"

"But it was you who had the courage to follow your heart and dump him. I say good for you," Connie said.

"What do we do now, Connie? We have to expose that bastard for what he is," said Drina, taking heart.

"Yeah!" yelled Salli, lifting her glass, "he's expired!"

"Expired, yes. But how?" asked Drina.

Connie did not speak, she sat transfixed with a faraway look in her eyes, a look of determination and fortitude her friends had as yet never witnessed.

"What are you going to do, Con?" asked Salli.

"Face him. That's what I'm going to do."

"We'll go with you!" shouted Salli.

"No, no, no," Connie said quietly. "This is mine and mine alone to handle."

Drina objected: "But Con, don't you think we should --"

"No. Now that's final. I appreciate your support. I'm a big girl now. Things will be settled up, but first I plan to use his power and position to find Will. Then we can expose him for the killer he is."

Drina and Salli exchanged concerned looks but they realized that Connie wanted things this way and that they should support her.

Salli stood, "Group hug!"

The Call

THE NEXT MORNING, CONNIE SAT drumming her fingers on the kitchen table as she watched the clock tick slowly away the minutes. From the county website, she had determined that the county offices opened at 8:30 am. She could call now, call McHughes, begin a dialog. But she had not planned on him being in court. She felt awkward leaving a message with his secretary.

"Your name, ma'am?"

"Connie Mitchell."

"The reason for this call?"

"Personal. It's personal."

"I'll need more than that ma'am."

"Tell him we knew each other a long time ago, had a mutual friend, Celeste. He'll remember me when you tell him Celeste."

"Yes, ma'am," said the secretary and noted Connie's number.

Connie puttered around the house, not wanting to take the call anywhere but in the privacy of her home. But the hours dragged. No call. She checked her cell repeatedly, no, she had not missed a call.

The Judge Speaks

THE PINELLAS COUNTY COURTHOUSE SAT prominently in downtown Clearwater on the Intracoastal Waterway which led to the Gulf of Mexico. Its white marble exterior and Ionic columns gave the courthouse the appearance of Federal architecture, the architecture of our forefathers, good men immersed in justice, their vehicle, the constitution. Would they shudder if they were to observe justice dispensed in Clearwater this stifling hot, humid, torpid day?

Carefully, the bailiff adjusted the witness chair, checked the microphone, filled the judge's carafe with the requisite water and ice. This time he remembered that the glass needed to be a 16-ounce glass, not the small juice glass he had erroneously set out the previous day. He cringed remembering the ridiculous tantrum Judge Bardmoor had over the small glass. All that anger over a few missing ounces of water. The bailiff shook his head in disgust. Seeing a smudge, the bailiff exhaled on the glass. Then, looking over his shoulder, he rubbed the glass against his slacks. There, ready now. His eyes swept the courtroom to be sure all was in order. Bardmoor could be such a picky bastard. He and his "poetry." Smart-assed rhymes was what they were. Nothing but smart-assed rhyming crap.

McHughes stepped out of the elevator of the third floor of the court house, laid a finger on his twitching eye to calm it. Nerves, he thought to himself, damn nerves. Panic began to spread through him like tremors of an earthquake. He nodded decorously to the opposing counsel who stood waiting outside the court room; his decorous nod returned with a rude wag of the chin as attorneys milled about the posted docket to be sure that their court schedules were in agreement with the judge's. McHughes felt a pang of relief at the line up, his case was second. Some pathetic lawyer had the bad luck to be first on Bardmoor's kill list for the day. This was no judge to fool with. No attorney in his right mind ever wanted to set off Bardmoor. The tiniest semblance of error would become an opportunity for his cutting rhetoric, or worse, his humiliating rhymes. Bardmoor's contempt for attorneys was legendary. His respect as a competent jurist, however, kept him in the game. The good people of Pinellas County reelected him five times. It was said that the public loved the way he created rhymes to punish legal eagles and their gobbledygook.

"All rise for the Honorable Henry C. Bardmoor," called out the bailiff in the musty, windowless court room.

McHughes rose, buttoned his jacket, careful to keep his eyes lowered respectfully. The less contact with Bardmoor the better. Bardmoor cleared his throat, glared at the attorneys, fanned his black robe, much like a bird of prey spreads its wings in order to frighten the enemy. He turned to his clerk and whispered. The clerk stuttered a reply, then called the first case.

Bardmoor waived off the opening statement. "Sit down, you clown. You're representing the idiot who was denied the right to pay a $4,000 fine with loose change in plastic buckets, yellow buckets, I believe? The color of the buckets is, of course, irrelevant. And now you're here because?" Bardmoor glared, shifted on the bench.

"Yes, your honor," sweated the counsel. "My client has suffered injury to his reputation through this most unfortunate--"

A fly circled the court room, zooming in and out at will. Not one hand reached out to shoo it. All occupants of the court room feared Bardmoor more than the fly. The bailiff stiffened, alarmed, began to pray pleading that the fly not cross Bardmoor's bench.

"The ONLY unfortunate thing about this case, Mr. Drinkwater, is it ended up in MY courtroom. Now, I've researched the case law, and I'm going to allow your client to pay the fine in change but it must be counted and boxed by him, no one else. And this exercise will be monitored and YOUR client will pay for the independent observer who will certify the amount is paid in full. Is that understood?"

"Yes, your honor," said the counsel as he found himself obsequiously bowing.

"Did you just bow?" snapped Bardmoor, eyes black beady satanic pools of evil.

"Aaah," choked Drinkwater, eyes darting about the court room as if someone, anyone, could help him.

"There's to be no disrespect shown in my courtroom! No sarcastic body posturing!" blasted Bardmoor parsing each word. Switchblades.

"I assure you I meant no---"

"Well, now, allow me to reconsider." The dank air still as the eye of a hurricane, all eyes riveted on Bardmoor who edged forward on the bench, hissing, "Nickels and dimes, nickels and dimes, this stupid case is a waste of my time." Judge Bardmoor cleared his throat, cocked an eyebrow, "Since your client is intent on paying his fine in loose change, let's make it loose change, very loose. Pennies! Until he's personally counted out $4,000?" The words were conciliatory but the tone was one of suppressed rage.

"Got it," whispered Drinkwater as the air rippled with the sound of muffled laughter.

Bardmoor's gavel came down hard, meaning he was ready for the next case to be called.

McHughes tugged at his shirt collar, experiencing a choking sensation, dreading the guillotine. He shuddered inwardly as his case was called. Slowly he rose.

Bardmoor warned, "I haven't got all day, let's move it, groove it, prove it."

McHughes' face went blank as his mouth dropped open, unwillingly, a sigh escaped. Reaching for his case file, his grasp unsteady, fingers trembling, he dropped the file to the floor. The documents slid across the terrazzo tile much like stones skipping water. McHughes gasped, apologized, "I'm sorry, your honor, so sorry." He stooped to gather the papers up.

"That's right! Drop the file. Are you a clumsy imbecile?"

McHughes sighed, louder this time. The court heard it.

"Did you sigh? Are you going to cry? Look me in the eye. Oh, fie!"

McHughes' face reddened, eyes agate. In this high-profile case, he needed Bardmoor's support. Inadvertently, he wound him up. He gulped, knowing from experience that this was just the beginning of the agony. The opposing counsel, Josh Spickler licked his lips, glared at McHughes. The unspoken message: "You ass! You pissed off Bardmoor!"

McHughes, flushed, felt as if his neck tie was suffocating him. He began to reach for the knot to loosen it, thought better of it, waited quietly for what would come next.

"Continue!" boomed Bardmoor. His eyes reflected the hostility he felt toward McHughes whom he considered to be a spoiled, spineless Ivy League brat. Amongst colleagues, Bardmoor referred to McHughes as The Bent Spoon. These nicknames gave Bardmoor a release from the tension of the bench, made the job almost fun. Some of his pet names for attorneys were Lockjaw, Mighty Mouth, T & A, Wide Girth, the list as long as the line of pathetic souls who crossed his path.

"Yes, your honor," McHughes began, "we have before us in this case a unique situa--"

"Spare me the semantics, get to it!" Bardmoor lifted his water glass, leveled a threatening look at the bailiff. (Better be cold water.)

"Yes, your honor," said McHughes, making eye contact with Bardmoor for the first time that morning.

"Did you just wink at me?" challenged Bardmoor.

"I, uh, wink? No, your honor. I have a twitch." McHughes reached his finger inside his glasses, touched the corner of his eye to demonstrate.

"A twitch. I see. And would this *twitch* have anything at all, anything in the entire universe to do with this case?" Bardmoor barked.

Above, ceiling fans rotated in synchronized fashion as a fluorescent light began to flicker indicating a change of bulb or ballast was necessary. The bailiff's eyes drifted upward, fearfully. His pulse accelerated, he began to blink repeatedly but, mercifully, Bardmoor appeared oblivious to the oscillation of the lighting.

Spickler, feeling confident, seeing his opponent's weak start, "May I speak, your honor?"

"Feel free," said Bardmoor waving his hand in the air, staring down at Spickler AKA Spitball, a money-grubbing defense attorney, one avowed to avoid truth at all costs.

"This case is definitely not unique as Mr.--"

"Stop right there," said Bardmoor raising his hand as if directing traffic.

"Your case is loose. It is obtuse. I deny you both. For I am loathe to sit. Through this unorganized abyss. Get the facts. Then I will act!"

End of story. Attorneys slaughtered. Down for the count. Finished for the day. Nothing to report. Diminished losers. Bardmoor moves the docket. Attorneys must reschedule the hearing.

The court room cleared.

Bardmoor burned the bailiff, "You idiot! This water, is *tepid*. Do you think I can drink *tepid* water?"

"But there's ice in the --" whimpered the bailiff who stopped mid-sentence. His eyes grew large. The judge followed the bailiff's gaze to the rim of his water glass, there, on the rim, a large black fly strutted oblivious to the powerful being to whom it belonged.

"Get out of my sight!" ordered Bardmoor, pointing his index finger to the door as he raised his long, black robed arm of the law. The bailiff, stoop shouldered, shuffled out of the hallowed court room located in the hallowed hall of justice.

"You got him going, dumb ass, thanks a lot," charged Spickler as he and McHughes raced to the Clerk's Office.

"Shut the fuck up. The previous case is what wound him up, not me. And you know it."

McHughes arranged his face to reflect calm and confidence as he stepped into the empty elevator to return to his office where he knew a drubbing awaited him. A dog with his tail between his legs, beaten once again by the damned nutcase Bardmoor. As the elevator climbed, it was McHughes' turn to bellow, and bellow he did, "Bastard!" his repetitive song with one lyric. His eye began to quiver, the twitch becoming quite obnoxious. "Fuck!" McHughes screamed at the walls of the elevator, "Just, fuck!" Two floors later, in strutted Cynthia, the hot new typist in the clerical pool. McHughes inhaled her scent, drank in with quick, piercing glances her breasts, her silken throat.

"Hi," he said, grinning ear to ear. The master in control now.

The Boss Speaks

McHughes had barely removed his suit jacket when he got the call.

"Mr. McHughes? The Prosecutor requests your immediate presence in his office."

As Chief Assistant Prosecutor, McHughes reported directly to Joseph Paulson, a man with whom he had no traction and a man whose temper was legendary. Paulson had come up the hard way in life earning both his college and law school degrees at night while he worked days in an automobile factory laboriously and monotonously installing the doors on the new Buicks. He couldn't look at a Buick without feeling shoulder pain.

"Of course," McHughes said, choking on his own spit, his blood running cold. Meetings with the prosecutor could be something akin to the Spanish Inquisition. Dolefully, he prepared to drag himself to his beheading. He shuddered, disarmed with the knowledge he had angered Bardmoor. The case had been kicked back on the docket and that was never a good thing. Witnesses had a way of disappearing the longer it took to get a case heard. McHughes' head would roll, there was no question about that, only how far and for how long.

"Sit down, McHughes," Paulson spit out the words like they were rotted meat.

"Yes, sir."

"Tell me your version of what just happened to our highest-profile case!"

McHughes took a second to gather his courage. He looked hopelessly about the cave like room. The drapes, perpetually drawn, dust balls clung to the nubs of its textured dull grey fabric. Never, never opened to the light of day. Paulson feared assassination was the rumor. Suddenly McHughes was amazed by the inanity of this. He stifled the desire to laugh. He looked into Paulson's eyes and saw the hatred. Quickly, he dropped his head to his chest to avoid further eye contact. He noted Paulson's skin a sickly blue tinge, pocked, a nightmare glowing beneath the fluorescent lights. Why haven't I noticed that before? he wondered.

"I'm waiting . . ."

"Well, I, I dropped the file, and . . ."

"You dropped the case file," Paulson repeated, frowning, then the scream, "Tell me what happened!" Paulson leaned over, clenched his fists then pounded the desk like a mad man. McHughes bit his upper lip, shifted in his chair, inhaled sharply, face reddening. Calm, stay calm, use your indoor voice.

"I told you, I dropped the file and it set Bardmoor off like a firecracker."

Paulson rose, circled McHughes' chair, then leaned in and whispered, "Don't get colorful with me, save your similes, counselor."

"It -- it was an accident," McHughes said barely under his breath.

Paulson, "And then?" still a whisper.

Bullets of sweat poured onto McHughes' crisp 100% pima cotton shirt. Whispering was scary, worse than the screaming.

"I picked it up and he started on those rhymes. You know he's a nut job!" McHughes said, attempting to deflect the damage.

"A nut job the public loves, votes for every damn time . . ." Paulson screamed, then took a few steps away from McHughes. McHughes breathed a sigh of relief. Too soon.

Paulson hopped back on one foot, aimed the other full force into his metal file cabinet which sat six inches away from McHughes. "Get out of my office, you dumb ass! Get out of my sight!" Paulson screamed, breathing hard as he repeatedly kicked the file cabinet which bore many dents from previous occasions.

McHughes rose, "Am I, am I?" he could barely force his voice to work. He began to back out the door, careful to face Paulson, as one does with an emperor, or a king.

Paulson turned, wiped his upper lip with the back of his hand. "Fired? How the hell do I fire the governor's nephew? You tell me."

Though McHughes was an expert attorney and Paulson knew it, he hated McHughes, considered him a snake, a candy-ass, a sneaky bastard. He continued his tirade, "And your election? It's a freaking farce, McHughes, a freaking farce. You can't handle Bardmoor, how the hell do you plan to handle this entire operation here? Hell, I'm going to be a federal judge; we'll see where you end up."

McHughes thought the day would never end. As usual, his staff attorneys were in and out of his office conferring with him regarding their cases. No one suspected he had been burned by both Bardmoor and Paulson. McHughes held his head high. Pride. Privacy. Endurance. His style carried him. It wasn't until after lunch that he found himself trembling, his nerves getting the best of him. He shut his office door, loosened his tie, opened his desk drawer, extracted a flask, took one swig, then another. He stood at the oversized window of his corner office which overlooked the Intracoastal Waterway of the Gulf of Mexico. Tourists' cars skittered across the causeway bridge and hundreds of tourists and locals dressed in "Salt Life" t-shirts and gaily printed Tommy Bahamas strolled along on the Beach Walk. He felt a pang of envy for their carefree lives. Usually referring to them as "simpletons," today he would not mind being in their ranks. Pizza, grouper sandwiches, their only goal. Sun tans. Easy. He clenched his teeth, let down his guard thinking, *Bastards! I drop a file, the judge goes off in his world of insane rhyme bullshit and I'm screwed by Paulson.* Then, with lightning speed, his thoughts turned to the media. Were any present in the court room? They loved nothing more than quoting Bardmoor, always good copy. "Oh, God," he groaned.

A knock on his door. McHughes called out, "Give me a minute." He popped a mint into his mouth. Camouflage. Later, he promised, he would get shit-faced but good.

The Visit

McHughes' secretary Alice knocked again.

"Come in!" McHughes growled.

Guardedly she said, "Here are your calls," and handed McHughes a small stack. He snatched the stack of goldenrod message slips from her hand. "Hold all calls," he hissed. Pacing his office, he tossed the message slips onto his desk, "To hell with them." One drifted to the floor. He stooped to get it. His head pounded. He massaged his temples, hung over from last night's binge. His eyes fixed on the name Celeste, right there on the message slip. What the hell? Agitation with Bardmoor was quickly put on the back burner. The whore had called. How could this be? Why now? Where did she come from after all these years? How did she find him? What was the connection? Panic escalated: Would he succumb to what was most certainly blackmail? He pictured the headlines proclaiming his sordid past. But the whore had no proof and she probably only wanted money. Yes, that was it. He could buy her off. Shut her up with a quick ten grand. The election. That's what brought her in. She'd want more than ten grand, but, no matter. Another idea came to him. Play dumb, pretend to think she's here soliciting me. Whatever it took . . . His thoughts turned to how to handle this woman. He wanted to go home, get out of this place but word would have spread by now that Bardmoor clipped his wings; he would appear cowardly if he left for the day. No, he must not leave. But he could self-medicate, and so he did. He knocked back two glasses of rum, sucked mints.

Again, an interruption, Alice announcing McHughes' brother was calling.

"Fuck it, just fuck it!" McHughes said.

"Yes, sir!" said Alice.

"Not you! Not you! Put him through."

It was a Let's Grind Your Nose Into It phone call just as McHughes expected. "You are so funny, you should get yourself a job on Saturday Night Live," said McHughes as Bryce needled him about Bardmoor.

"You never did like poetry!" Bryce added, laughing with glee.

"I've got work to do, see ya," said McHughes.

"Come on, Lloyd, where's your sense of humor?"

"I'm hanging up now," said McHughes, thinking: What a bastard! Mr. Fucking Perfect.

Connie could only wait so long -- he was not calling back. Big surprise. Well, she had a surprise for him, too. She took a deep breath, grabbed her purse and car keys and headed for the courthouse in Clearwater. She knew the way well having been arraigned there for prostitution on several distasteful occasions. My, how times had changed. She would now enter the court house with an agenda of her own: Get McHughes to help her locate her son. She reasoned that, with his connections, it should be a quick and efficient search. She wanted nothing else from him. Nothing.

Traffic crawled, the 3:30 pm early rush hour drag. She had plenty of time, it was her day off. There was no turning back: she would deal with the dirty bastard. He could intimidate her no more. Never again. She squared her shoulders, felt her jaw tighten in anticipation of a nasty encounter. She would demand to see him, be heard.

McHughes paced, should he call the whore or not? He stood before his expansive bank of windows overlooking the parking lot. Did he expect to see her? Sickeningly, he realized he was looking right at her. Yes. She was walking determinedly up to the court house. He would know her anywhere. Still a knockout. Her beauty unmarred by time. He wondered briefly what her life was about now, then shrugged it off. A whore is a whore is a whore.

Connie's heart pounded as the elevator whizzed her to the 7th floor whereupon she was greeted by McHughes' secretary. McHughes feared she might make a scene; he stepped out of his office and greeted her, feigning a hospitable attitude as he ushered her into his office. But once his door was closed, all hell broke loose.

"You've got your nerve coming here! You're crazy if you think I would be interested in any relationship with you."

"Don't flatter yourself!" said Connie putting up her hand, taking a seat which he did not offer.

"Now sit down and listen to me. I am here for one reason and one reason alone."

A diary. Was she bluffing? Did that punk kid keep a diary? McHughes strained his mind. Did she ever mention such a thing? It was so long ago. With a sharp intake of breath, he realized it was possible, yes. Possible but probable? Could he take a chance that it was a lie concocted by the Whore to control him, intimidate him? Bullshit. Plotting, what to do, what to do? This can be controlled, he reasoned. Think logically. Hold on, an idea formed in his mind. A simple idea he believed would solve the Whore problem. With that he knocked back two glasses of rum.

Reflecting, he thought about Connie. Back then she was sexy in a filthy, forbidden kind of way; now, though still sexy as hell, she seemed well, almost classy. Her classy? Right. Sure. He sipped his rum and coke and allowed himself to slip back in time when he was 28 years old, a senior at the prestigious Stetson Law School. His elite parents filled with pride that he had finally gotten his act together, after fooling around for how many years? Yes, law school was the best solution to the problem of Whatever Can Lloyd

Do With His Life? His older brother, Bryce, already in private practice making big bucks.

McHughes drained his glass. Piss on those people, he thought, the entire lot, top-down, all of them. Mother dear, a bitch, capable of loving only her first born. Father, the wimp who never once challenged her. Bryce, arrogant fucking Bryce. McHughes' jaw tightened; he brooded, chewed his mustache. Ha! he thought, he got his revenge on them all right, frequently visiting the unsavory underbelly of Clearwater, those ruddy streets where the prostitutes plied their trade, young, hot women anxious to earn money. Pimps on alert to cut a deal for any type of sexual activity, anything. He leaned back in his chair and considered that it seemed a lifetime ago that he had met Connie. Ironically, he had not met her on the streets but at a party thrown by of all people, his former girlfriend Delores Watts.

McHughes poured himself another drink, he'd do without the ice, foregoing the effort of going to the kitchen. He guzzled. Right, a law school party. His mind replayed the scene. Sexual desire burned in his groin as he reflected on the tall, buxom, blonde beauty. The joy of desire was momentary -- he frowned, his face a haven for hatred for the present-day Connie, a woman demanding what? Exactly what did the Whore want? He snapped to attention, rocked forward suddenly in his chair: "Get outta here!" he bellowed at Miss Snickers who had crept into the room hoping to be fed. It had been days. She gave a tentative meow, crouching on the carpet, then a yelp as his loafer crashed into her hind quarters. "I said get out! I don't need more fucking shit to deal with. Goddamn it!" he screamed, arteries pumping blood into his neck, turning it crimson. Desperately, he tried to collect himself: Oh, yes, Delores had thrown a party.

"Come with me for a minute," she said.

"Delores, I hope you're not angry over . . . " he intoned.

"No, no, no, we're fine. Listen, you know how I did that internship for the Clearwater Police in the Greenwood area? Well, I met this woman, and she's so cool. She actually is a good writer, writes poetry."

"Wait," he stopped, took her elbow, "didn't you work with prostitutes in that internship?"

"Yes. That's what I'm trying to tell you, a poet-prostitute."

"Oh, my God," groaned McHughes, "what the hell do I care?" Then he saw her.

"Connie, this is my friend Lloyd McHughes."

"Lloyd, Connie Mitchell."

McHughes leveled his eyes on Connie, lifted his chin, inhaled as he bit down on his upper lip and took in the fringes of his mustache. "Hi, nice to meet you," he said taking in her raw sensuous beauty. Big white breasts, short black skirt, so young. Old enough he supposed, not his problem. His gaze froze as he extended his hand, consumed with desire for the sexiest woman he'd ever encountered. Connie leaned in, took his hand, smiled. Looking into her misty hazel eyes, he was hooked. There would be no escape. Nor did he wish one.

"Can I get you a drink?"

"Chevas. I like Chevas," she repeated.

Perfect thought Delores, now it was his turn to be manipulated. Connie will extract her toll from his phony entitled ass. She nodded sweetly to the couple, "Excuse me a moment," then turned to make her way across the room to the other guests. Mission accomplished. McHughes, her heart throb for the past three years of law school, had made many promises, then one day, without warning, had said the damaging words that he "wanted something different." There's "something different for you, you bastard," Delores thought, she, a diminutive brunette, highly educated, destined for success as opposed to Connie, a tall blonde under-aged prostitute hooked on heroin. She smiled at them across the room. Rot in hell. Little did he know then what she was up to. It was only now, years later, he saw the sabotage and his own vulnerability. It was all her fault, vengeful bitch.

He drank the booze as if it was water, licked his lips. Connie's breasts, he had never seen a woman sport them, exhibit them with such ease. How could an uneducated nothing like her have so much self-assurance? Revulsion, commingled with titillation, desire for the Whore had gripped him in his youth. It wasn't his fault. He stroked his member, cursing as he did so, sweating profusely, then the release. Bitches, all of them, bitches.

His thoughts moved ahead like a fast train: Celeste. He had forsaken Connie for Celeste. Why? Her childlike innocence captivated him. She was like a doll, exactly like a doll. Too bad she died like that, he thought, but she should not have rushed him. She went too far, expected too much. The rodeo was over. Why didn't she get that? And now, the Whore says there's a kid.

McHughes slammed his fist on his desk. This development, coupled with Drina Alvarez walking out on him, was not good for his ambitious political plans. Not good at all. None of this was good. McHughes sat, eyes glazed, thinking, thinking, thinking.

Destruction

MᴄHᴜɢʜᴇs ᴡᴇɴᴛ ʜᴏᴍᴇ ᴅʀᴀɢɢɪɴɢ ᴛᴀɪʟ. The Whore was adamant. Where in the hell did she get her nerve? Demands. All the time: Everyone wants a piece of me he told himself as he mixed his drink of choice, sat down in the leather arm-chair whereupon the phone rang. "Go to hell!" McHughes screamed into the stale air of his cloistered home. What to do? What to do? He knocked back the rum and coke in three quick swallows, strode recklessly into the kitchen. Doomed: The ice maker would not release. McHughes, enraged, grabbed the first thing he saw which was the $500 Vitamix blender his parents had given him for Christmas. Whoosh! He yanked it off the shining granite counter and heaved it into the door of his Sub-Zero fridge whereupon, it fell with a clunk. He kicked it aside and settled for warm coke with the rum.

Miss Snickers wisely remained hidden behind an arm-chair in the living room. This, her refuge.

McHughes, Boss Man, Decision Maker, being dictated to by a Whore. The nerve. His breath came quickly and he realized he was an inch away from hyperventilating. He retreated to his office, leaned back in his leather chair and waited for the rum to course through his veins. Her damn son, such a pile of bull shit. Her damn refusal to take a check, right there, on the spot, he had generously offered a cash settlement. What the fuck! What was her agenda? McHughes face screwed into intense analysis, his eyes turned to narrow slits. Did his opponent in the election dig her up? How had she happened to materialize in the middle of this election process? Something didn't add up here. Feeling pinioned, McHughes purposefully began to calm himself; he needed to think. She, a problem. He, a problem solver. He would win. Like always. She would lose. That simple.

The next morning, McHughes' confidence had returned. He'd show that Whore what was what. Wants to find some punk-assed kid she claims is his. Bull shit. Just a line to get into his business, his life.

He walked into his office, determined to do the business of the people, he picked up a case file and attempted to focus, take a prudent course of action. Get back to work. But paranoia began to set in. Would she call today? Would she show up? Somehow, his confidence began to fail him. He stood, scanned the parking lot, cursed himself for not taking note of the car she drove yesterday. That would have been a clue; how did he not think of that? He rubbed his temples, a throbbing headache took hold. "Oh, shit."

A harsh knock on the door, more akin to pounding than knocking.

McHughes, pissed, "Come in!"

The door swung open and there stood Jimmy Mac, Cyber Division Chief, not looking any too happy. Here we go, thought McHughes, another pain-in-the-ass confrontation. Mac, thoroughly incensed over case assignments: Seems Alisa Chambeau, a hot young assistant prosecutor McHughes just hired got the assignment for a high-profile drug case involving cyber fraud, Mac's bailiwick.

"How in the world did a rookie know-nothing-new-hire get this assignment?" Mac demanded.

McHughes smugly answered, "Get over it! I have bigger fish to fry."

After more harsh words with McHughes, Mac angrily returned to his office, said to his associate, "This guy wants to be prosecutor? He's got his head up his ass half the time."

The associate replied, "Yeah, or someone else's."

Raw Eggs

Sharon Fuller rarely saw much of her husband during the week which was fine with her. She had long since their marriage twelve years ago given up on him. Initially, Ray was a brawny construction worker with high hopes and big dreams but as the years went by, he grew tired of the long hours and low pay and constantly complained to Sharon that the crew bosses were idiots. Fed up with his nightly drunken temper tantrums, Sharon requested the night nursing shift. Usually when her shift ended, she headed straight home. This morning, she decided to stop off at a mom and pop breakfast joint on U. S. 19. It was still quite early and none of the regulars would be there. Maybe it would cheer her up to have a bite out and delay seeing Ray, especially after the rough night at the hospital.

Dust billowed up from the dirt and gravel parking lot as Sharon pulled in. Angry, she bit her lower lip. Old biddies!. How dare they make those remarks? Those snotty, mean comments? I hate them all.

Turns out there was gossip, lots and lots of gossip spreading through the ranks at the hospital since James had committed suicide. Sharon observed as she relieved the day nurse each evening just the slightest curling of the nurse's upper lip, and the narrow, sidelong glances. Snippets of the gossip had made their way to Sharon but she told herself they could prove nothing. What's wrong with having a little fun on the job anyway? Marilyn had sex with all her leading men. They're all a bunch of jealous, ugly old biddies. Then another thought occurred to her. Duh, he was in for suicide watch -- he committed suicide --big surprise. Why blame me? Bitches. Bitches everywhere I go, like Connie the Bitch.

"May I take your order?" the waitress asked.

"Yes. I would like a glass of warm milk and two raw eggs," said Sharon.

"Yes, ma'am."

"Please do not call me ma'am. I'm not old," scolded Sharon raising her eyebrows.

"I'm sorry." Then in an effort to be friendly the waitress asked, "Your order, is this a new diet thing? Because I'd love to drop a few pounds." She frowned and patted her stomach.

"New, goodness, no! This is tried-and-true. The Marilyn Monroe diet. She eats this way and you know how gorgeous she is. She also eats a lot of broiled meat and raw carrots."

"Well, thanks," said the waitress, somewhat confused. Marilyn Monroe is dead, this crazy customer talks like she's alive or something. Wow.

Sharon cracked the eggs into the milk and gave it a good stir with her fork. She took a long pull of the silky liquid. Her mind working: In fact, I made the last months of James' life exciting. Yes, I did that for him. I'm proud of myself. She raised her chin haughtily, after all, sex is part of nature, I go along with nature. That's what Marilyn says.

But soon breakfast was over and Sharon unhappily went home. Ray was waiting.

"What're you grinning about?" she asked with disgust as she tossed her purse and car keys onto the side table.

"You'll see, step this way madam," he bowed and directed her with a sweep of his arm toward the kitchen.

Sharon cringed, "I'm in no mood for this, Ray--"

"Please," he pleaded, "you've got to see this."

Sharon reluctantly followed him into the kitchen. Her eyes grew large as she saw stacks and stacks of cash sitting on the table.

"Feast your eyes!" he proclaimed, proudly tossing piles of money into the air.

Sharon took a step back, aghast, "What did you do?" her voice barely a whisper.

"Does it matter? Look! We're rich! Isn't that what you want? To be rich? To get out of this dump? Get nice things for yourself, more Marilyn stuff. Quit your stupid job--"

Sharon backed away, shaking her head, "No, no, no," fearing the worst. Her fear quickly validated by the incessant blare of the doorbell and the visual specter of the squad car sitting curbside.

"Jesus, Ray."

The Better Half

"Sɪᴛ ᴅᴏᴡɴ, Mʀs. Fᴜʟʟᴇʀ, ᴛʜᴀɴᴋ you for coming," said the gracious Chief Assistant Prosecutor, the handsome Lloyd McHughes, as he offered Sharon a chair. As he stepped away to close the door of his office, he wondered how such a gorgeous woman could be married to Ray Fuller. He pulled up a chair next to Sharon's rather than sitting behind his desk. Sharon, somewhat nervous, fidgeted a bit, then crossed her legs demurely, her micro skirt inching higher by the minute. She spoke breathlessly, "I had no idea he was going to do this! He's been laid off from his job and--"

"You are not under investigation, Mrs. Fuller," McHughes confirmed. "The reason you are here is we were hoping you might be able to convince your husband that it's ill advised he represent himself as counsel."

"I see," she said as she leaned in. "He isn't remotely capable of doing that."

McHughes savored her body language. "I'm glad you see it our way--"

"Oh, I do! I do see it your way," she exclaimed as she adjusted the bow on her deeply cut blouse.

Their eyes locked. "He insists upon representing himself despite our efforts to secure him court-appointed counsel, to which . . . " McHughes paused as Sharon bent to dust a speck of lint off her shiny red spikes, breasts tantalizing. McHughes gulped, "I might add, he is entitled to by law."

Sharon sighed helplessly. "I'll talk to him, I promise, but would you mind if I ask you a question?"

"Of course not."

"How was it that Ray was arrested so quickly? I mean, it was right away!" She tossed her head, "Just curious is all."

McHughes suppressed a smile, lowered his eyes, "We traced him from his cell phone, he left it on the bus."

"I see," Sharon said quietly while raging inwardly *It sounds like that dumb ass. I never got a chance to spend a dime.*

"I'll be in touch, Mrs. Fuller," the Chief Assistant Prosecutor said warmly as he ushered her out. He closed the door behind her and sat down to think about the glamorous Mrs. Fuller. A player if ever he saw one. Might be useful. Entering Sharon's name into the criminal justice system files, he saw she was clean. Good, he thought. However, her traffic record was ablaze with speeding tickets and reckless driving citations. Her car insurance must be off the roof he mused, grinning. She drove her car the way she drove sex, full throttle. He liked that. Though older than his usual prey, she was a hot one. A devil. He liked it. They were evenly matched. He could sense it. His blood pressure rose, he felt his member harden. Not here, not now, he thought reaching for a glass of water. He focused: Maybe it was time for a little wheeling and dealing. Maybe the husband could be coerced into putting the fear of God into Connie Mitchell and maybe Mrs. Fuller might be grateful when her husband's case was dismissed for lack of evidence, evidence somehow misplaced, or somehow erroneously destroyed. This could be arranged.

Heads turned as Sharon haughtily strolled out of the office. The clericals chattered.

"Who is that?"

"She's that duh -- I Think I'll Leave My Cell On The Bus guy's wife."

"Who?"

"That big guy they brought in for the bank robbery, Fuller."

"Figures McHughes would call her in."

"Yeah, if she weighed 400 pounds, he wouldn't go near the case"

"Got that right!"

"For sure!"

As McHughes calculated things, second thoughts rose in his mind, maybe Mrs. Fuller would not be so grateful, maybe she would prefer her husband be locked away. He stood, sauntered over to the corner window, put his hands in his pockets, and rocked to and fro' on his heels watching with pleasure as the lovely Mrs. Fuller strutted her stuff in the parking lot. What a swing she had to her gait. My, oh my. He would have to think hard of an enticement, some-thing to get her on his side. He intended to use Ray and to use her, just in different ways. He would think of some-thing. He was confident of that. These were light weights, the Fullers.

Sharon, in her car brooding, finished with posturing. Hatred boiling. Idiot. Everything Ray touches turns to ashes. I hope they jail his ass for a long time, a good long time. Give me time to get a divorce, be free. Maybe hook up with a heavy hitter like this McHughes.

Her eyes scanned the courthouse; there, slightly vis-ible, in the corner window, she saw McHughes. I never miss, she thought smugly. With that thought, Glenn's handsome face flashed before her as fleeting as a butterfly. He'll come around, too. They always do. She triggered the ignition, tromped on the gas and sped out of the court house parking lot.

The Other Half

NOT WASTING ANY TIME AFTER meeting with Sharon, McHughes met with Ray in the interview room adjacent to the holding cell at the jail. It was unusual for the Chief Assistant to show up at the jail like this but jail personnel assumed that since McHughes was running for office, he was trying to project the image of Super Prosecutor with every case. This made sense but was not true.

McHughes extended his hand to Ray, "Mr. Fuller, I'm Chief Assistant Prosecutor, Lloyd McHughes. Have a seat."

Begrudgingly, Ray sat down. He missed home. He missed Sharon. Even her anger was better than this. Depressed, he told himself a guy can't get a break anymore. Shit. He looked at McHughes and wondered what the hot shot wanted.

"I met with your wife. We spoke about the possibility of your agreeing to court-appointed counsel," McHughes said, then turned to the guard, "No need. I've got this under control." Once they were alone, McHughes continued, "Here's the thing, I'm betting that you're worried, very worried about leaving your pretty wife alone with no one to look after her. After all," McHughes feigned empathy, "a jail sentence can be as hard on the family as it is on the felon."

Ray bristled, "Felon? Who you calling a felon?"

McHughes sighed, "Look, we have the duffel bag --"

"I found that on the bus, I don't know nothing about the money."

"We have the gun with your prints on it."

"Gun? I don't know nothing about a gun."

"Mr. Fuller, would you like this case to . . . " McHughes paused for dramatic effect, "disappear?"

"Hell, yes, I would like to see this case--"

"Keep your voice down," McHughes cautioned.

"There's a little problem that needs your fixing. I think you've got the talent to fix it for me." McHughes waited, gauging Ray's reaction. "How would you feel about that, Mr. Fuller?"

"Ah," Ray said, stalling for time, unsure of what was being suggested. "I, uh, I'd be interested, sure." He inched forward in his seat, thought, Is this some sort of scam? Did Sharon put this guy up to something? He leveled his eyes on McHughes as McHughes moved in for the kill.

"Here's the deal," McHughes said quickly, wishing desperately to conclude the meeting, "you do something for me and certain evidence against you, well, it disappears. Your case folds, you go home to your lovely wife."

Ray nervously reasoned he had nothing to lose. May as well see where cooperating with this guy might get him.

He wanted, above all, to be with Sharon, not stuck in a jail cell for God knows how long. "I'm in. Anything you want."

McHughes stood, offered his hand, "Thank you, Mr. Fuller, I'll be in touch."

The hook was set, Fuller was in. McHughes reasoned Fuller was dumb enough to be manipulated, crude enough to intimidate Connie Mitchell, and unprincipled enough to make a good partner in crime.

McHughes was back in his office a short time when there was a quick knock on his door, and Jimmy Mac, chief of the Cyber Crimes Division, popped in. "Got a minute, Lloyd?"

"Come on in," McHughes said, anticipating the question to follow.

"I heard you stopped off at the jail this morning to talk to Fuller. Just wondered if there was something going on that maybe we in Cyber Crimes needed to know? Maybe this was more than a simple bank robbery? Is there more?" His eyes drilled McHughes whom he instinctively disliked, distrusted.

"No." McHughes said bitterly. He stood, narrowed his eyes as they met Jimmy Mac's. "Are we done now? I have work to do."

Hiding the Truth

Wine night at Salli's and the tiny house pulsated with Latino music. Connie and Drina stood on the front porch, doorbell unanswered, peering into the front window and laughing as they saw Salli, unaware of their presence, dancing the guacamole, salsa and chips into the living room.

Drina asked, "Connie, anything new on you-know-who? What's happening?"

"Nothing much yet," Connie deferred. She called out, "Knock, knock," as she opened Salli's door. She had given considerable thought about the wisdom of sharing with her friends the fact that she had confronted McHughes. She felt a pang of guilt keeping it a secret but promised herself, it was just for now, just until something concrete occurred. She knew, at the bottom of her heart, that it was the persistence of shame for her past which made her secretive, even now, even with these close friends. The evening looked so promising that she hated to spoil it talking about McHughes.

"Oh, hi," yelled Salli, "this is the Samba!"

"My, aren't we happy tonight?" said Connie as she slipped the bottle of wine into Salli's hands.

"Yes, we are!" Salli exclaimed. "Bill's out with the boys having beers, and I've got my BFF's here for the evening. Ole'!" she snapped her fingers, whirled.

Drina pressed her palms over her ears, "Wow! You're wired! And the music's too loud!"

"Oh, sorry," said Salli as she exaggeratedly wiggled over to the CD player.

Hardly able to keep a straight face, Drina asked, "What's with you tonight?"

Connie cupped her hands around her mouth and in a Vaudeville announcer's voice blasted, "You heard her, Bill's out, she's thrilled to have the house to herself."

"Yeah," Salli iterated, "you know living with Bill, I don't get much me time."

"Right. Like I do living with a teenager," Drina rolled her eyes.

"I bet Solana's gone more than Bill is!" Salli argued.

Connie made her way to the kitchen, "Okay, ladies, enough, time to uncork."

Drina followed her lead, then changing the subject, "I love your kitchen wall plaques. They're so funny."

Connie read, KITCHEN CLOSED, CHEF QUIT. IF YOU'RE IN THE KITCHEN, WHY ARE YOU STANDING THERE? CHOP SOMETHING!"

"I take it you dislike cooking?" asked Drina.

Salli wrinkled her nose, "I don't like cooking, I like dancing!"

They filled their glasses, moved to the living room, sat on the floor encircling the coffee table.

"Well," said Connie taking a chip and dipping into the salsa, "how's your dance class going?"

"Dance class?" asked Drina, pretending she'd forgotten about it.

Salli takes the bait. "Don't you remember?" she said as she pushed herself up onto her knees, "the one I signed up for a month ago . . . the one at the Largo Community Center? It's awesome and I meet cool people," her eyes bugged out.

"Such as?" asked Connie, throwing Drina a glance, detecting there was something more to the story.

"Well, since you asked," Salli rolled her eyes flirtatiously at her friends, "I met someone."

"And does this someone have a name you care to share?" asked Drina.

"Miguel," said Salli breathlessly, "his name is Miguel. Oh, my God, he's so, so exotic! So gorgeous!"

"Whoa, slow down, Sal," warned Connie. "What's going on?"

"Nothing . . . yet," said Salli, tossing her hair.

"Now hold up," Drina said. She set her glass down, "You sound like a love smitten school girl. YOU," she pointed her finger at Salli, "are married to a good guy, from what I can see."

"Yeah, he's good. Good and boring," Salli sulked. Her mood shifting by the minute.

Connie threw Drina a warning glance and said, "So tell us about this guy, this Latin lover Miguel."

"I'm not sure I want to talk about him anymore. I can see you both disapprove." Salli pouted took a gulp of wine.

"Oh, don't be angry," said Drina. "Come on, tell us, we're not judging you. We're your friends."

"Well," began Salli. She had their attention and savored it. For once, Salli felt as if she were the center of things rather than on the sidelines.

Connie studied Salli as she relived her evening with Miguel. Then, when Salli finished, Connie leaned in, asked gently, "Did something happen with Miguel other than the sexy dance?"

"A kiss," said an enraptured Salli, "a long, delicious, lingering kiss."

❧❧❧❧❧

Connie, home now, slumped on the sofa and considered the evening as her thoughts fired warning flares for Salli's obvious infatuation. An infatuation which Connie believed could destroy her marriage. Sure she's bored. But that's no reason to leave a good guy, is it? Connie sighed, maybe it was. She recalled several of her clients' comments:

"I don't know why I bother with a new hair color, my husband won't notice!"

"Someday, I'm just going to let myself go. Men are bald, paunchy and they don't care, why should I?"

"We go out to dinner and struggle to make conversation. It's all been said already."

She thought about idealization and its destructive qualities. Hmmm . . . Things can appear to be perfect, but in reality when I talk to married women, they're dissatisfied. She kicked off her flip flops, laid on her back clutching the sea foam green pillow to her chest. She thought of Glenn, then pushed the vision of him out of her mind. Relationships: Do they have to become routine, boring, deadly? That's why people cheat. How many of the johns were married men? She wasn't sure. She was so young, so strung out she never cared about anything except the cash they tendered. Were my parents bored? Good question. Marriage: Forever was a very long time.

She grew tired, turned on her side, closed her eyes. Let it go. And from deep within, a feeling of self-nurturance passed through her. She was safe, not involved with anyone, might never be. Self-reliance yielding peace. Her one resolve, finding Will, the other, seeing Ruth, apologizing to her mother, seeking forgiveness and seeking to forgive.

But early the next morning, a rap on her door.   Salli in tears.

"What's going on?" asked Connie, nervously.

"I went out last night after you and Drina left," Salli said. "I went to the Latin Club. I just wanted to see Miguel for a little bit, you know?"

"And?" Connie ushered her friend in, gestured to the sofa.

Salli's mood flipped from guilt to anger, "Something bad happened."

"What, pray tell?" asked Connie raising her eyebrows but pretty sure she knew.

"He has a girlfriend behind my back; I saw them. I saw him kiss her, and I heard him say the same stuff to her he says to me!"

"Oh, honey," said Connie.

"Yeah, and I bought all those new clothes, ran up my charge card so I'd look good for him. And her? She wears cheap teenybopper clothes!"

"Well, how old do you think she is?" asked Connie.

"I don't know, 16-17."

It was a struggle, but Connie did not laugh, instead she said, "This was a lucky break for you, Sal. I know it hurts but it's better to see who he is now, rather than later. Wouldn't you agree?"

Salli sighed. "Yeah, I guess. Well," she brightened, "it all kind of made me horny so Bill got some action he enjoyed!"

"Oh, you are something!" Connie said and reached out to hug Salli.

Reunion

Ruth sat pondering life in her White Garden. It had been a difficult day at the Morgan Memory Care Center where William was now housed. It had been torturous admitting him to the facility but Ruth understood that it was for William's good, for his protection. But Ruth now felt loneliness deeper than she had ever experienced. She reflected on the burden of illness on life, how it strangled out the joy of living. Though Alzheimer's had a genetic component, there had been none traced in William's family tree. "Circumstance, random circumstance," the doctors told her. She sighed and looked at the decaying white rose petals strewn on the lanai. She should sweep them she thought but somehow the feeling of desolation disarmed her.

Ennui set in and encroached with a frightening negative effect. She was alone in life and questioned her past decisions: Should I have adopted Will? Should I have sought help sooner for William's care taking, spent time with my daughter and my grandson ? Where were they now? Were they even alive? She lowered her head and prayed, feeling utterly alone. A pair of cardinals fluttered their wings and landed on the lanai nibbling the bird seed Ruth had scattered for them that morning. Their chirping, such a pleasant sound, cheered her up a bit. How adroit they were, how quickly they moved. When they hopped, it almost appeared as if they were floating on air. Weightless. Ruth watched as the pair flew up to the bougainvillea covered trellis, blooming its sumptuous fuchsia color. The one color Ruth allowed in her white garden. They nestled there quietly.

A soft voice, a voice from the past. "Mom?"

Ruth's heart stopped. She turned to see her daughter standing before her not ten feet away on the side of the lanai. Ruth blinked repeatedly, trying to focus, she wondered if she imagined her daughter's presence. "Can it be?" A visible wave of nostalgia filled her face.

Forgetting the speech she had rehearsed, Connie stammered "I'm sorry, Mom. I'm so sorry."

Ruth rose to greet her daughter. "Come to me, my darling girl," she said, weak from the shock, yet exhilarated by the sudden realization that her daughter was home. She led Connie to the two-seated glider they had shared for many a story time in Connie's youth. Connie, ashamed, sobbed while Ruth held her in her arms. The embrace said it all: love and forgiveness. Reunion. Mother and daughter.

Wine Night Update

Drina and Salli sat spellbound as Connie related her news about having visited her mother. Salli's eyes, as big as saucers, asked a myriad of questions; Drina quietly listening, gauging the effect this would have on Connie's well being, hoping and believing that the reunion was for the best. Connie found herself crying softly at the end of the story -- she realized how important it was that she had swallowed her pride and gone to her mother who needed her now, more than ever. It was obvious to Connie that the stress of the situation had taken its toll on Ruth; therefore, Connie's concern for her mother's health equaled her concern for her father's. She bitterly condemned herself for her youthful insensitivity to her father's condition, a condition much worse than she had ever imagined. "I feel so bad, you guys, I was a selfish fool, a teenage monster. So uncaring."

"No! We were all like that. It's normal to be selfish when you're a teenager," said Salli, then added, "I think I still am." This made Connie and Drina laugh.

"That was then, this is now," Drina said. "You went to her, you comforted her, you'll be there for her. What about your father though? Will you go to see him, too?"

"Yes, just not yet; I asked mother for a little time before I go with her to the memory care facility." Connie shook her head, tearing up again. "It's so awful. Mother said not to be surprised if he doesn't know me. It's been a long time, and he isn't well in the head, you know," she sighed. "I missed out on my father's life, the part where he would have known me." Connie wept. "I didn't get to know him, not really. What if I never get to know my son either?"

Drina and Salli commiserated with Connie, empathic to her suffering, trying to alleviate the guilt eroding her heart. They were careful not to press her about Lloyd McHughes. She was on overload and they could see that. For Salli's part, she appreciated that Connie made no mention of Miguel. That subject was closed.

More than ever, Connie wanted to find Will. Where was he? Why had all her efforts to find him failed? It was as if he vanished off the face of the earth. She desperately wanted him to meet her parents, despite her father's condition, just at least meet him. Know his grandfather a little bit before it was too late. Was it too late now? And mother, Will's grandmother. Would Will remember her? There was still time to build a semblance of a relationship, wasn't there? So many years lost. Connie reproached herself: Why was I so cold-hearted?

A Father Remembers

THE VISIT TO THE MORGAN Memory Care Center came up faster than Connie had bargained for. Ruth, having received a call from the caretaker explaining that William was particularly agitated that day and she needed to come in earlier than her usual visiting hours. Ruth's presence calmed him well beyond the atypical antipsychotic drugs they administered. Patients with at least one family member, someone they recognized, fared better than those who recognized no one, lost in the fog of forgetfulness, that desolate uninhabited plain of forlorn emptiness.

It was with heavy hearts mother and daughter walked, arm in arm, into the facility. Connie felt chilled. Why do they keep it so cold in here? What kind of elevator music is that to play for people? This is funereal in here. Too quiet. Creepy. Her skin crawled. Where's my dad?

The security door to William's room was difficult for Ruth, "I've got it, mom," said Connie holding it for her mother as she glanced nervously about the room. An arm chair. A bed. A window. A bathroom. Quiet earth tones, everything gauged to be calming, light blue accents. Room darkening shades at half-mast, too much sun pouring in from the east. "Where is he?" asked Connie.

"He'll be here any minute now; he's probably in physical therapy," Ruth answered. "His throat tightens you know; he can barely swallow the fluids they give him."

Connie grimaced. This would be worse than she thought. Minutes passed like hours but ten minutes later, an attendant approached with an old man.

Connie studied the man, "Daddy?"

His eyes downcast at first, lifted at the sound of her voice. "Constance," he called, shuffling toward her, eyes gleaming, a bit of drool escaping the side of his lips, in anticipation of his child. His clasp cool but firm.

"Daddy," Connie whispered, whimpered, as they embraced. The attendant smiled, turned and left the family to their reunion.

Sam-I-Am

ANOTHER EVENING OF FISHING AT the pier. Sam baited his hook, cast his line, Will waited, somewhat pensive. Tourists leaned anxiously over the railing of the pier hoping to see the legendary manatees, and in doing so missed a pod of dolphins in the distance riding the waves as the setting sun cooled the earth and a slight breeze stirred. Will's mind was not on manatees or dolphins, nor fishing. "Sam, you never really talk about the war."

"Oh, well now," Sam kept his gaze steady ahead, "that's not something I relish remembering."

"I mean, I know your leg got hurt but I don't know how. Did a grenade go off or something?"

"Yeah. There was an explosion. Big. Threw me a ways."

"And?"

"And?" There was an edge to Sam's voice.

Better back off but curiosity prevailed. Will cast his line, paused, "Did you have other injuries besides your leg?"

"Not to the eye."

"What?"

"I mean to look at me, other than the leg."

"But something else was hurt?"

"You could say that."

"Well, the way I see it, Sam, we have a lot in common."

"That right?"

"Once I turn 18 this fall, I'm officially homeless. Me and Sam-I-Am, homeless."

"Why's that?" Sam questioned.

"I'm in the foster care system and once you turn 18, you're out."

Sam nodded, "Why'd you call me Sam-I-Am?" Thoughts danced at the edge of his mind.

Nurse Ratched

Wow, THOUGHT SHARON AS THE new young hot patient, Alan Wilson, was admitted. What's his story? She smiled and introduced herself. Carefully, she kept her demeanor professional since Nurse Ratched was keenly observing her from the corner of the ward. As it turned out, Mr. Wilson was admitted for observation, anxiety attacks, might not be staying long. Sharon took note. If she wanted any action, and she most certainly did, she would have to move fast.

The trap is set Nurse Ratched said to herself primly. That little cupcake is toying with the men. She is unfit to be a nurse in this facility. How well Nurse Ratched remembered the story of that pathetic young man, what was his name? Hung himself. Cupcake had plenty to do with it, Nurse Ratched reasoned. This time, she would be caught.

Sharon took the bait slipping seductively into Mr. Wilson's room that very night wearing a revealing All Things Marilyn gown from "Some Like It Hot."

"Are you stressed?" she cooed. "Would you like me to *entertain* you?" She began to slowly gyrate her hips and shimmy as she became Marilyn Monroe singing, "I Want to Be Loved by You and Nobody Else but You." Mr. Wilson, a delighted observer. But the mood of the private party was broken when Nurse Ratched sprang from out of nowhere. Boom: Cupcake fired. Out. Out of a job. Out of a paycheck. Out of a source for quick, fun sex. Out of everything, including the Poetry Group. What was left? Anything? Oh, yes, Ray. He would be waiting for her. McHughes had sprung him out of jail quickly, as promised.

Sharon drove home in a trance. Life surreal. She slunk in the house. Thankfully, Ray was asleep. The thought of having to deal with him sickened her. Her stomach wrenched. She tiptoed to her room, quietly closed the door so as not to awaken Ray. She sat on the bed.

"What do we do now? We're out of money," said Glass Head.

"I don't know," Sharon whimpered. She looked wistfully at the poster of beautiful Marilyn. "What would Marilyn do?"

"She'd do Lloyd Baby. He'll give you some dough," said another Glass Head.

"Good thinking," said Sharon, cheering up. "Who needs work anyway? Bunch of nutcases and losers."

Dinner with Sam-I-Am

Shyly, Sam rapped on Connie's door. "Am I early?"

"Come on in," she called from the kitchen alcove as she pulled a roaster from the oven. She greeted Sam with a hug invited him to sit. This was something she'd wanted to do for a while now, have Sam in her home, give the man a good home-cooked dinner.

"Sure smells good in here, little lady," said Sam savoring the aroma.

"I'm not a bad cook," Connie half-boasted, "so I think we'll have a good dinner. I made us pot roast, potatoes, and carrots." She set the table with her Corning blue patterned dishes.

Sam sat down at the little table cautiously avoiding bumping the plates and silverware. His eyes danced on the cloth napkins. It had been a very long time since he'd used one of those.

"Have you been doing much writing?" he asked.

"Oh, some," answered Connie as she set a butter dish and bread on the table.

Sam's eyes strayed to a small corner of books on the kitchen counter held upright by a parrot book end. He saw a frayed and faded "Dr. Seuss" book. He read the title aloud, "Green Eggs and Ham."

"Yes," said Connie quietly.

"May I?" asked Sam as he reached for the book.

Connie nodded yes and Sam thought he saw her flinch, just barely. He thumbed through the worn pages, read a verse or two, chuckled. Then his eyes rested on the words, "Sam-I-Am". He grew thoughtful, "You kept this book all these years, must be special."

"It was my son's favorite book," she wiped a tear. "He walked around reciting, 'Sam-I-Am, I like green eggs and ham.' Once I put green food coloring into his scrambled eggs. He loved it!" She grasped the lovely cloth napkin and wept into it.

"I see," said Sam patting her shoulder, "I'm beginning to see." Here it was, simply an intuitive feeling that Connie and Will were mother and son. What if he was wrong? He would arouse hope where there was none. What should he do? Sam pondered this realizing he needed time, time to think. Gather any other proof he could find. He would say nothing until then.

The Wright Brothers

Sam was anxious for Will to report to work for two reasons: The shop was on overload with bike repairs and secondly, Sam decided he might talk a little about two famous brothers who owned a bike shop once.

"Here you are, thought you'd never get here, boy," said Sam, not unkindly.

"Sorry, Sam, I know I'm a little late."

"Yeah."

"What do you want me to do first?" Will looked at the cluttered shop. "Looks like a lot of people need their bikes fixed all at once!"

"Aaah, feast or famine. Feast or famine. Grab that green oversized two-wheeler, start there, Will. Good."

"You got it," said Will, relieved Sam didn't seem angry.

"Ever hear of the Wright brothers?"

"Yeah, sure. Who hasn't?" Will wondered why Sam brought that up.

"Tell me what you know."

"They built an airplane, flew it. They were famous pioneers of flight," said Will racking his brain for more facts in case Sam quizzed him further.

"They changed the world in 1903," Sam said. "Wilbur and Orville Wright changed the world. Did you know their work on bicycles helped them to create a viable air plane?"

"Now that you mention it --"

"Do you remember their beginnings? They opened their own bike shop in Dayton, Ohio, created their own bike models, were very successful."

"Okay," said Will, wondering why Sam was going on about them so much today.

"I can see you think I'm crazy," said Sam.

"No. No, it's interesting," Will lied.

"Yeah. You know, it's what we do, we work in a bike shop."

"Right."

"We do honorable, good work. Remember that boy, there's no shame in good, hard work."

"Sam, what's up with you? Why are you telling me this?"

Sam got to his feet, began to pace, then he approached Will. Putting his hand on Will's shoulder, he said, "I know you've been hoping to go to college but if you can't, there's honor in manual labor. Yeah. Never be ashamed of that."

"Okay," said Will, feeling a little embarrassed wondering if he was that transparent to everyone who knew him or just to Sam. He decided only Sam-I-Am could read him like a book, understand his innermost struggles to belong. No one else cared. Well, maybe Liz did a little. Was she the reason he wanted to go to college? he asked himself. Partially, yes.

The front door bell alerted Sam that a customer was in the showroom. "I'll be right back," he said to Will.

Will nodded, his hands busy maintaining the bike but his mind working vigorously.

The greater reason for his wish to attend college was he felt unmoored, untethered, unconnected. At least college would give purpose and hope to life. Educated people usually got pretty good jobs. He sighed remembering that the Maloney's had made it clear that they preferred a younger foster now for their son. Will was simply too old. Nothing personal they assured him. Nothing personal. For sure.

The Question Game

WINE NIGHT. SALLI CAME IN carrying a small bowl and wearing a big smile.

"Hi, Sal," said Connie. "What you got there?"

"Questions." Salli answered, coyly.

"Questions? Questions about what?" asked Connie.

"Us. We answer questions we pull from the bowl. I saw it on TV."

Drina strolled in, "I'm game!" She handed Connie a bottle of cabernet sauvignon.

Connie went to the kitchen for glasses. She felt apprehensive somehow about playing the game, wondering what it would involve. She set dark chocolates onto a plate and returned to the living room.

Drina poured and the ladies cried, "Cheers!"

Salli, excited, said, "Let's begin." She reached into the bowl, pulled out a slip of folded paper: "First question: What makes you happy?" She turned to Drina.

Drina took a sip of her wine, "This. Us talking, being together, this makes me happy."

"Aw, that's so sweet!" Connie teased. "Just for that, have a chocolate." She passed the plate.

"Your turn to pull a question, Connie," Salli said.

Connie hesitated, then answered, "Poetry. Poetry makes me happy."

Salli giggled. "You know what, or should I say who makes me happy? Curious George!"

"What?" asked Connie.

"Curious George, he's adorable. He makes me laugh and also they teach things on that program, you know," Salli said defensively.

"OMG!" said Drina. "You're kidding."

"I'm not kidding. You should watch it sometime."

"Okay, what else, Sal? You look like you have more to say," said Connie.

"I like pulling Bill's chain. He's easy prey, if you know what I mean," she edged forward on the sofa. "I tell him stuff. Like yesterday, I told him I went on Groupon and bought us a trip to Reykjavik, Iceland. He believed it!" He was so upset. "I think it's funny!"

They broke out in laughter.

"See, it's a good game, isn't it? Want the next question?" asked Salli.

"Let me choose one," said Connie. She pulled a strip of paper from the bowl, "What do people do that really makes you mad?"

Without hesitation, Drina answered, "Lie. I hate liars."

"People who think they're better than me make me mad," said Salli.

"People who are late for their hair appointments. They mess up my work schedule."

"Next question," said Salli. "If you could change something in your past, what would it be?"

Drina looked worried, drilled Salli with her eyes which said, "You're an idiot."

"Oh, we don't have to do that one," said Salli, beginning to get the idea.

"It's okay," said Connie. "You know I would do everything differently."

Drina comforted her, "But you wouldn't have a son, Connie."

"Like I know where he is," Connie snapped. Then, "I'm sorry."

"It's okay, Con," said Drina. "What would I do differently? I wouldn't have married Tom," she sighed, "but then, I wouldn't have Solana, would I?"

Salli said, "I guess I would have married Bill, but I'm not sure about that sometimes."

"Let's lighten this up!" said Drina. "Can I ask one that's not in the bowl? How about a favorite childhood memory?"

Salli spoke first, "You guys remember my mom died when I was ten so I don't really remember too much about her but I do remember the day we were baking chocolate cake, my favorite, and I lifted the beaters up out of the bowl while they were still running and the batter splattered all over the kitchen! I thought she'd be mad but she wasn't. She laughed! I still remember crawling around on the floor wiping up tiny spots of batter while she scrubbed the walls."

"Wow!" said Connie.

"What a nice mom!" said Drina.

"I'll say," said Connie. "I remember when I was little, my dad took me for a walk, bought me ice cream cone but within five minutes I dropped it on the sidewalk. When I cried, he took me right back to the ice cream shop and bought me a new cone."

"Aw, that's sweet," said Salli.

"Really? Talk about being spoiled!" said Drina, teasing. "You know what my memory is? When I was about four, I stuck my head between the spindles of the stair railing and could not get it out! My parents had to call the fire department!"

Connie began to tear up thinking of Will who was four when DCF removed him.

"What's wrong?" Drina and Salli asked, almost in unison.

"I'm sorry, did I say something that upset you?" asked Drina.

"Course not," Connie stifled her tears. "I was just thinking."

"We understand," said Drina.

Salli nodded soberly in agreement. She wondered if the game was not such a good idea. It seemed that Connie's guilt and worry about her son overshadowed a great deal of her life. Salli wished things could be better for her friend. She decided that this was not a good time to tell the girls that she was pregnant. She herself was not sure how she felt about the pregnancy. Could she cope with working and parenting? It was all on her: working and keeping house, fixing meals, even if they were simple meals, they still took time and effort. Bill was not much help. She wished her mother was alive. She would have helped her. She wished a lot of things but most did not come true.

Salli's Suggestion

ROBOT LIKE, SALLI ASKED, "DID you find everything you need?"

"Yes, thank you," the customer said, unloading her purchases on the conveyor.

This was Salli's day, scan, scan, scan all day long and bag the multiplicity of items the Walmart shoppers purchased. Waiting next in line, she saw one of her favorite customers. It was a case of mutual admiration. Will chose Salli's line any time she was on duty; indeed, he looked for Salli, enjoying the warmth of her personality. He laid the soda, candy, and chips on the conveyor and smiled hello shyly. He noticed she looked tired, a bit worn today.

"How are you?" Salli asked, happy to see Will.

"I guess okay," answered Will.

"So," she began, "soon you'll be graduating. Any plans for college?" she scanned the candy, waiting for a reply which was slow in coming.

"Not really," Will shrugged.

"What? A smart guy like you, come on!" Salli probed, "What do your parents have to say about this?"

His voice low, "I don't really have parents; I'm in foster care."

Salli hesitated, taking this in, "You know, I saw a program on how kids are locating their parents," Salli slowly loaded his bag, buying time.

"Nah, I'm not into that."

"Well, think about it," Salli maintained her enthusiasm. "You know YouTube, all those sites, make a video of yourself. You'll get lots of hits and then maybe--"

Salli's manager approached, "You have a customer waiting, I believe," he raised his eyebrows and jerked his head toward the pile of groceries sitting on the conveyor.

"Yes, ma'am," said Salli deferentially, reluctantly handing Will his bag.

"I'll see ya, thanks," said Will sauntering off.

"Sorry!" Salli called after him, feeling contrite. She turned to her next customer, "Did you find everything you need?"

The customer answered that yes, she had, in fact, she had found too much. The customer laughed at her own joke. Salli feigned laughter having heard the comment hundreds of times before. She sighed and stole a glance at her watch. How many hours till the end of her shift? Too many. Always too many. Sadly she thought to herself how she had miscarried the baby before she even got a chance to tell Connie and Drina she was pregnant. She felt badly about the miscarriage, yet somehow relieved to be pregnant no longer. The relief caused guilt.

"Have a good day," she said to her customer.

"Hello, did you find everything you need?" she asked the next person in line. Deep inside she wondered, would she ever want a child? Was there something wrong with her that she felt such confusion over an issue seemingly so simple. People had kids all the time. She resolved to talk it over with Connie and Drina. Talking with them always helped her to sort things out.

Finally, Salli's shift ended and she dragged herself home where she kicked off her shoes and sank into the sofa.

"How's it going?" asked Bill softly.

Without looking up, she said, "Oh, I don't know."

"I've got something for you," he said. "Maybe this will cheer you up." He held out a large bouquet of flowers, mixed colors of red and white carnations, even a few miniature sunflowers, her favorite.

Tears welled up and she brushed them away with the back of one hand as the other reached out for the flowers with the other. "Thank you."

Bill eased down onto the sofa next to his wife. "I know this has all been rough on you, hon, I'm sorry. We can try again, you know," he said encouragingly.

"That's just it," Salli whimpered, "I'm not sure I want to try. We weren't trying this time, you know. It . . . this came out of nowhere! The baby I mean."

She began to laugh hearing her own words. Bill watched patiently as her laughter turned to tears.

"Want to talk about it?" he asked gently.

"No. Just hold me," said Salli.

They huddled together. He, gently rocking her in his arms. She, dissolving into the tenderness of the moment.

"I love you, hon."

"I love you, too."

Will's Post

Will got home, plopped on his bed, set the chips and soda on the bedside table, put up his feet, thought about what Salli said.

Tommy's freckled, smiling face appeared in the doorway, "Can I have some chips, Will?"

Will smiled in return, "Sure, buddy, help yourself."

Tommy took a handful, "Thanks! See you later!"

"Okay, buddy," said Will.

Will picked up his cell phone and touched the video icon, steadily holding the phone for a head shot as he spoke. He stated his name, age, location and simply that he was searching for his parents. End of story. He uploaded to several sites, including Find Your Parent. Done deal by 8:00 pm. A tiny flicker of hope burned in Will's heart . . . maybe his parents would find him, have reasons, good reasons for not keeping him. Maybe they would be nice people. Maybe they could not help it when they gave him up? Maybe only one parent was out there anyway. Maybe the other one skipped town or was dead already. Time would tell.

The Journal

School was a mixed bag for Will. Not one to put much effort into his studies, Will was saved by his innate ability to listen to a lecture, grasp the tenets and without much studying, do well on exams. Content to cruise with Bs and Cs, he rarely turned in homework. What was the point? A quiet rebel, he bucked the system whenever he could. Being an outsider had its own brand of success. Hacking the school district's server then watching the grades in free fall gave Will a delicious sense of power, rebellion. Rebellion against the smug cliques, the hot-shot jocks, all the spoiled brats driving nice cars mommy and daddy gave them, all heading for fancy colleges. Ass holes. And though stocky and strong, Will shunned athletics, never feeling an affinity for the people connected with school sports, nor anything connected to the high school. Connected. Isn't that what every adolescent wanted to feel? Until Sam came along, Will felt connected to nothing and to no one; however, there was one exception, his English teacher Mrs. Schultz. Somehow, she was different, accepting and warm.

The assignment early that Tuesday morning, write a journal on the topic of disappointment. Will wrote:

If there was one thing I would say is a disappointment in my life, I would have to say that I never got to know my parents. I have no memory of my father. I can remember my mother in bits and pieces but I was pretty young when she gave me up. I have never understood why she did that. I must have behaved badly or something. Maybe she got sick and died. I don't know, probably never will. But I do remember a nice older couple the Stover's who adopted me. We lived out of state for a few years but then, shortly after we moved back here to Florida, they were killed in a terrible auto accident. Again, I was alone. Story of my life. Since then, I have lived in a series of foster homes, some good, some not so good. Then the Maloney's came along, the family I'm with now. Nice people, really nice people but when I turn 18 this fall, they want me to go. I thought they'd keep me if they could afford to. I try not to eat too much, be a burden. I told them that if I went to college and lived with them, they would still qualify for foster parent reimbursement, but they said in a roundabout way that they want a younger foster kid, not an older kid like me. I get that.

Recently I made a new friend, Sam, a Vietnam War vet. He's been on his own for a long time and he survived. He even got me a part time job at the bike shop where he works. He's kind of like a dad to me, I like him, respect him. Someone was saying the other

day that people can track down their parents but I figure if they didn't want me then, why would they now? Besides I have Sam to talk to anyway and that's cool.

Will stuffed his backpack with a few books he might or might not open, tossed in his English journal, not sure why. Later that day when things were quiet at the bike shop, he found himself pulling out the journal and handing it to Sam.

"Sam-I-Am . . . I wanted you to see this. I got an "A" on it, some of it's about you."

"Me? Let me see what you've got there, yeah," Sam extended his hand, sat down read through the entry. "This is sure something," he nodded, "yeah."

Their eyes locked, no conversation, just two friends working together in the bike shop, one began to oil a bike chain, another to sweep the floor. Home.

Then, studying Will's young face, Sam offered, "You'll be all right boy, you will."

Walt Whitman

WILL WAS CURIOUS. SAM SPOKE about some old poet, Walt Whitiker or Whitman, was it? Today his modern lit class had library time. The students were directed to the Modern Lit section of the library by their teacher, Mrs. Schultz, who was insistent on students getting their hands on real books, forget the web for a change. Will had been in the school library, maybe once before in ninth grade. It always seemed to him the library took up a lot of space in the building for nothing. He lingered in the stacks, feigning interest, then, when Ms. Schultz's back was turned, he headed straight for the poetry section, the W's. What was that poet's name? Here, he thought, this is it.

He pulled the hard cover book from the shelf, "Walt Whitman, the Complete Poems" and thought, Wow, this is huge. This guy wrote all this stuff? Will sat down at a table in a quiet corner and studied the volume. He learned that Whitman and he shared a common denominator, that of being unattached. He rather liked that. Understanding better why Sam was so hooked on the guy. Will read passages about the sea, about Manhattan, about the ravages of war. Then his eyes settled on, "Thanks in Old Age" and realized that as Whitman looked back with thanks for the blessings and acceptance for the losses in his life, so did Sam. The management of the past, placing the memories into little file drawers was important to old people, Will reasoned. This was Sam. The bell rang and Will reluctantly returned Whitman to the shelf, the book so new, it didn't seem like anyone else in the building was interested in Whitman's poetry, what a shame.

Salli Tells All

SALLI PACED HER KITCHEN, PULLED open a drawer, briefly looked inside, snapped it shut, opened the fridge, briefly looked inside, snapped it shut.

"Looking for something?" asked Bill.

"I don't know."

"Isn't it wine night at Connie's?"

"Yeah."

"So . . . aren't you going?"

"I don't know."

Bill tenderly wrapped his arms around his wife, "Go see your friends, it'll do you good."

"What if they get mad at me?"

"Why would they do that?"

"I didn't even tell them I was pregnant, and now the baby's gone." She began to whimper.

"If they're angry you didn't tell them about the pregnancy, then they're not your friends. But they won't be angry. You'll see." Bill held Salli's hand and walked her to the door, "Honey, you forgot something," he pointed to the bottle of merlot sitting on the counter.

Salli grabbed the bottle and slowly walked to Connie's. "Knock, knock," she called softly.

"Come in, Sal," Connie answered from the kitchen.

Salli took a deep breath and walked in. She watched as Connie pulled large Greek olives from a container and laid them on a plate, alongside wedges of feta cheese and toasted pita.

"That looks good," Salli said, trying to inject enthusiasm into her voice.

"You bet! I went into Tarpon Springs today and got us all set up for a delicious Greek platter. I mean look at this!" Connie turned to show Salli. "Hey, why the long face?"

Before Salli could answer, Drina strolled in. "Yum!" she said, seeing the food. "By any chance, Con, did you buy ouzo?"

"Oh," Connie moaned, "I didn't think of that. Sorry!"

The women proceeded to the living room. "Get comfy," said Connie, keeping her eyes on Salli who stood awkwardly by the side of the sofa.

Drina sat down and looked up at Salli with concern, "Have a seat, Sal." She patted the sofa and reluctantly, Salli sat down.

Connie gently touched Salli's arm, "What's wrong, honey? You're stressed about something."

Salli began to cry, and between sobs, told her friends about the pregnancy and miscarriage. Doodle sensed Salli's grief, hopped up onto her lap and began to lick her hands.

Salli clung to Doodle and continued, "It all happened so fast, and I was going to tell you guys I was pregnant the night we played games, remember? The question game? I had one in the bowl about pregnancy. That was going to be my way of sharing. But then I decided I didn't want to talk about it that night after all." She lowered her head, avoiding looking at Connie, not wanting to bring up how Connie had been emotional that night about losing her son. "And then, I lost the baby. I wasn't pregnant very long, not long at all."

The women dissolved into tears. Connie passed tissues.

"How are you feeling? I mean, are you all right? Have you seen a doctor?" asked Drina.

"I'm tired, but I'm fine. The worst part is," she hesitated at first and then the words rushed out in a torrent: "I wasn't sure how I felt about the pregnancy, it wasn't planned. In one way, I was happy about it. Bill sure seemed happy. But, I was scared. I mean, I don't know how to take care of a baby. Then, just as suddenly, I lost it and I feel terrible about it, but at the same time, I feel kind of relieved. It's crazy." She shook head.

"No. It's not crazy. You've been through a lot in a very short time," said Drina.

"I just kept thinking, will I have any time for myself taking care of a kid and working at Walmart? I know it sounds selfish but . . . " she stopped, feeling ashamed of herself.

"These are natural concerns," said Connie.

"Yes, they are; I felt like that too when I found out I was pregnant with Solana," said Drina.

"I hate my job!" Salli blurted vehemently.

"What? What's that got to do with this?" asked Drina.

"Everything! Don't you see?" Salli began to cry again.

"Now wait a minute!" Drina held up her hand, "Let me think. I'm confused." She looked at Connie to see if she understood the connection.

"I'll never be able to quit my crappy job if we have to support a baby!" said Salli.

"So you want to stay home, not work?" asked Connie.

"No! That would be boring!"

"Well, what do you want, Sal?" asked Drina.

"I don't know."

"Okay. Hold up here," said Drina. "What if you had a job you liked?"

"That'd be different. But what am I any good at besides cashiering?"

There was silence in the room for a moment, then Connie spoke, "Gardening. You're good at gardening."

"So?" asked Salli, glumly.

"I have an idea. I should have thought of this before -- you are the best gardener in this town. *You* could be a Master Gardener. One of my clients is and I bet she'd help you to learn the ropes. I know there's a certification process, but you can do that," said Connie.

"What does a Master Gardener do?" asked Salli, feeling a bit hopeful.

"You would be *paid* to plan gardens for private homes and for commercial properties," said Connie. "You could quit your job at Walmart."

Salli's eyes grew large. It was true. Gardening was her favorite activity and she was good at it. Everything she planted thrived. Her yard was stunning. She was already the neighborhood consultant. Her bookshelves were filled with gardening books she studied.

"It's a natural for you," said Drina, warming to the idea. "Here's the thing, if you enjoy your job, you enjoy your life. Think about it, we spend more time at work than we do at home. Whether you have a child in the future or not, you owe it to yourself to explore this option."

Salli was aghast at the depth of understanding her friends offered. She felt utterly amazed with the wisdom of their counsel.

"I hope I'm as smart as you guys when I'm your age," said Salli.

"Wow! Thanks a lot. Way to make us feel old, Sal!" Connie teased.

"Yeah. Thanks a heap," said Drina, glad for the levity of the moment.

"I'm sorry; I didn't mean--"

"We know!" said Drina laughing at Salli's embarrassment.

Salli swallowed hard, stood, wiped one last tear, "Group hug!"

Later, as Connie rinsed wine goblets and stacked snack plates in the sink, she thought about Salli's life. Perhaps, she wondered, was Salli strongly attracted to Miguel, falling for his lies, simply because she felt empty inside? A dead-end job. Endless housework. Bill attached to every sports broadcast on the television. Salli was young; she needed more. She was struggling with self-validation. Connie thought about her job versus Salli's, the sense of satisfaction she felt when she created a new look for one of her clients. Of course, it was nothing anywhere near the feeling she had when she created a poem but, nonetheless, a feeling of completion. The time spent with Glenn had expanded Connie's love of writing nature poetry. The walks with Glenn became a regular thing and Connie realized that the very act of walking along helped to ease the tension between them, a tension she knew she created. It was obvious that Glenn cared deeply for her. She listened attentively as he shared his feelings about life, about friendships, such as his with Sam, how meaningful it was. She liked what she heard but kept the barriers up because becoming involved before finding her son seemed disloyal, off center, not right. Will had to come first.

Thus as Glenn shot more and more nature scenes, she helping direct the shots, an impressive collection came into being. A collection which Glenn happily shared with Connie bestowing upon her many large-size prints, some of which she framed, some she simply admired. It was these prints which inspired Connie to write her nature poems. She now examined the latest of these poems:

Jacaranda

jacaranda branches
  touch the sky
  tinting blue amethyst, by and by
  lavender silk airily bends
  to the luring call
  the sigh of the wind
  parachutes, purple
  cascade to the ground
  nestle in dew make no sound
  yet high above, reluctant to fall
  some silken blossoms refuse the call

  the pirouette of Spanish moss
  drapes the scene, no time is lost
  floating wisps and lacey dreams
  veils of gray and veils of green

  the seed pods, brown,
  shake tiny castanets
  completing the lovely minuet

Doodle's tiny barks interrupted Connie, "Oh, you! Treat time, right?" Connie reached into the doggy treat canister and pulled out a liver treat. "There you go, sweetie." Doodle trotted off happily to the corner of the kitchen. Connie watched lovingly and thought -- If only happiness could be that easily attained for people. She made a mental note to speak with her client regarding Master Gardener certification. Salli could Google it she knew, but getting some inside information and perhaps even a mentor for Salli would be wonderful. Connie smiled remembering the special night when Salli had her and Drina over to watch her night blooming cereus flower open, an event of special significance since it opened only one night each year. Salli had been thrilled, more alive than Connie had ever seen her. Truly, her passion was for gardening. Connie would help her to fulfill that passion.

She also resolved that she and Drina would help Salli to work through her feelings about the pregnancy and the miscarriage. This subject would be painful for Salli, but she must deal with it in time. For now, they would allow Salli the comfort of denial.

Section Four: Sam And The Killer

No Denying This

Nine o'clock in the evening. The only sound in McHughes' house, the tapping of computer keys. McHughes surfing the web, combing through illicit sites for provocative conversations with the on-line chicks, everyone looking for a turn on. He smirked, guzzled his booze, pushed his plush chair back, rocked a bit, dissatisfied tonight somehow with the pickings. There were, however, a few legitimate sites he routinely visited looking for strays, one such site: Find Your Parent. He clicked and scanned the feed. What? There on the screen, looking right at him, a young version of himself. McHughes bolted upright, spilling rum and coke down his navy blue polo, mustache bristling with shards of ice, his face turning a fine shade of crimson.

"What the?" The whore did not lie. No mistake. There was a kid and it was his.

"Oh, God," he groaned, "this can't be happening, not now, not now." He gasped as bile rose in his throat, then promptly puked his rib steak dinner all over his dead aunt's desk, vintage mahogany.

The Brutal Beating

Ray was nervous. Sure, he'd had a few bar fights in his time, roughed up a few people. But a woman? And it might just come to that. Yet Ray realized he must do McHughes' bidding. "You need to send a message, put the fear of God in her," McHughes instructed. "Tell her to back off, or else. And . . . most importantly, get the diary." When Ray had questioned McHughes about the diary, McHughes assured him that she would know exactly what he was talking about.

Ray sighed. He paced the kitchen. And he wondered, where was Sharon? Probably shopping. That's all she does since she got fired. The bills are worse than before. What to do? But that's another problem he realized, shaking his head, "I gotta think what to do here." He gazed at the UPS box on the kitchen table, as yet unopened by Sharon. An idea formed. He would pretend he was a neighbor, a kind neighbor, that was it, take a delivery to the woman, something delivered by mistake to his house. He grabbed the box, tossed it onto the back seat of his car, checked his pocket for the address McHughes supplied.

"Off we go," he hummed, thinking this should be quick, easy, get McHughes off his back, get it over with. He revved the engine, pulled out confident and somewhat relieved to have the deed underway.

Salli scurried about the house tidying up. There, on the bedroom floor, Bill's soiled underwear. Why did he continue to toss it on the floor instead of walking five short steps to the hamper in the bathroom? But the pulsing salsa music made housework light. She began to dance about the bedroom singing along with the music ignoring Bill's request that she turn it down. She sang, "Something about you is thrilling me. Something about you is killing me" and thought of Miguel. Her mood turned sour thinking about how he had lied to her. "Wow. He really pissed on my parade," she hissed.

Connie finished reading the paper, drained her coffee mug, stood up and stretched. Doodle had her breakfast and napped. The doorbell. Connie looked at the stove clock. Was Glenn here already? She thought they had made a dog park date for later in the morning. She checked the mirror, fluffed her hair. But when she pulled the front door open, a stranger stood there holding a large box.

"I think this is for you, I got it by mistake," he lied.

Connie smelled a rat. "I haven't ordered anything, thanks anyway." She began to shut the door. The man put his foot in the door, pushed his way in. "Look, I gotta talk to ya about something."

Connie stared at him. What did he want? Who was he? She felt fear. Doodle sensed this, bared her teeth and growled. Ray eyed the dog, decided Doodle was not dangerous, kept talking.

"Someone we both know said you have something he wants, a diary. Plus, he said you have to back off, leave him alone. Can you do that?" He waited.

"No. I can't do that and I won't do that. Tell your friend *he* has to back off and *he* has to cooperate."

"You don't understand, lady, this guy, he, he isn't the kind to back off. You, you have to do what he says." Ray began to perspire.

"You need to leave," said Connie feigning courage.

Doodle jumped from one foot to the other, nervously, barking to no avail.

"Ah, I don't think so." Ray, fearful of disappointing McHughes and returning to prison, became aggressive. He took Connie by the shoulders, shook her, "You gotta listen, lady. Give me the thing, the diary."

"Get out of my house!" Connie commanded.

Ray did not leave. A few minutes later, Connie lay unconscious on the living room floor, Doodle barking over her incessantly. Next door, salsa music blasted.

Ray ran off empty handed, a cursory search of the house had yielded nothing, no diary. He would tell

McHughes it was her fault she got hurt. She was the one who tried to hit him with the stone statue. It wasn't his fault. A guy has to protect himself. Then he remembered the box. He groaned. It had a shipping label, he should have removed it. "I'm an idiot," he said as he raced back to Connie's where he scooped the package off the porch. From next door, the sound, *Something about you is thrilling me. Something about you is killing me.*

"Hold on there, girl," said Glenn to Buffy who was over-excited since she had heard the words dog park. "We're going to get Miss Connie and your friend Doodle in just a minute now."

Glenn hopped up onto Connie's porch and smiled hearing the salsa music from next door. That Salli was sure something, so high energy. Glenn could hear Doodle, the bark was strange, compelling. What was going on? Where was Connie? Glenn peered into the living room window. "Oh, my God!"

Stupid or Something

"I'LL BE DAMNED," SAID RAY. "That bastard. The way he talked to me -- wow! Like I'm stupid or something," Ray complained to his cell mate, bitterly reprising his brief criminal career.

Ray was pissed, super pissed, McHughes had reinstated his prosecution with one stroke of his mighty pen. "Hey, I overdid it but if that woman, if she was so easy to scare off, why didn't he do it himself?"

"Shut up, will ya?" his cell mate yelled, "I'm sick and tired of your yammering."

Ray scratched his head wondering where's Sharon? Sharon had not visited Ray since his rearrest. Without his knowledge, she visited a divorce attorney. Ray sighed, I guess she's busy shopping for Marilyn stuff. Bankrupting us. Ah, but he loved her, that gorgeous creature. Yes, she was cruel but cruelty was somehow a norm for Ray, whose battered childhood created within him a tolerance for pain, emotional and otherwise. She'll be here soon, he reasoned. His thoughts turned to the cash, the bank money sitting on the kitchen table, how proud he'd been. But her. She didn't look happy about it, didn't appreciate his effort to give them a better life. What the hell was her problem? What do women want? Go figure. They're all crazy.

"I almost pulled it off," he said with pride.

"Do I have to come over there to shut you up? Because I will!" his cell mate threatened.

"Oh, sorry," said Ray mindlessly concluding his tirade by whistling a few bars of "Who's Sorry Now?" never realizing *he* was sorry now. Again, his mood changed as his eyes swept the gray concrete walls of the cell. He should have called McHughes' bluff, should have told the police McHughes hired him to hit Connie. "No one will ever believe you, Fuller," McHughes had said. Ray believed him.

The Perfect Couple

MᴄHᴜɢʜᴇs ᴅʀᴜᴍᴍᴇᴅ ᴛʜᴇ ᴘɪᴛᴛᴇᴅ sᴜʀꜰᴀᴄᴇ of the seedy bar. Where was she? He sighed, regretting setting up the meeting in such a dump. But Toad's Crossing Tavern was off the beaten path, and that's exactly what McHughes needed: secrecy. Impatiently, he checked his cell and ordered his third rum and coke.

"Wow! Look what just walked in," said the bartender, pushing the frosty glass toward McHughes.

McHughes stood to greet the stunning, sexy Sharon Fuller. "Here you are. I was getting worried," he said and gently steered her to a dark booth in the back of the lounge.

"This place was hard to find," said Sharon breathily. "If I would have blinked I would have missed it."

"I know, I just thought that you and I deserved some privacy. This way," he eyed the greasy floor, cracked tiles, "we've got it." Changing the subject, he said, "I must say, you are looking more beautiful than ever."

The bartender interrupted, "What's the lady having?" Demurely, Sharon ordered a glass of chardonnay then turned to McHughes and smiled warmly, "You wanted to talk?"

McHughes believed that Sharon had no regard for her husband, but his wary instinct compelled him to confirm that fact before continuing. "I was wondering how you are holding up with your husband back in jail. This can't be easy for you," his face bore a false sense of empathy. "I hope," he continued, setting his drink down, "that there are no hard feelings. It was unfortunate that his release was premature, a clerical error you might say." He waited. Would she believe the lies?

His concern pleased Sharon. She felt valued, as if her feelings counted with someone. Fired from her job, kicked out of the poetry group, McHughes' consideration was the vindication she so desperately desired. Coming from a powerful man like McHughes made it all the better. She raised her hand to her heart, appeared astonished: "Why none, none whatsoever. In fact," she giggled as she leaned in, "good riddance. He's toast with me, you know."

"Good." McHughes smiled lasciviously, "How would you like to spend time with me, Mrs. Fuller?"

"I would love it, and please, call me Sharon."

McHughes raised his glass, "To us."

"To us," Sharon chimed as their glasses clinked.

"So what's next, counselor? I'm sure you must have a plan," she cooed, knowing full well the plan included sex, lots of it. He struck her as the type of man who liked his sex kittenish at the start and rough at the finish. She waited.

His eyes roamed her lips, her throat, her breasts. "I'm sure we'll think of something," he said, then he inhaled deeply and flushed as he pictured her porcelain flesh in a skimpy black leather outfit, breasts bare except for a small patch of leather covering her nipples, her hips, bearing thin black leather strips, she a temple of erotica in spiked heels carrying a naughty whip. Sweet pain. Kinky sex. The best kind.

Reading his emotions, Sharon said, "I'm sure we will," then she rose and joined him on his side of the booth. Deliciously, she stroked his member. What a woman. Maybe he would forget all about the tweens, such amateurs, go with a woman who knew how to please a man.

"There is something," he gasped. Ecstasy.

"Anything, counselor," she touched her tongue to his lips, pressed her breasts against him.

"There's a woman," he said struggling to form words, "who is in the way of our," he hesitated, "relationship."

Sharon froze. Her tone icy, "Who is she?"

McHughes explained that he was a victim, the victim of a psycho woman, a woman named Connie Mitchell who was demanding things from him, blackmailing him. He was an innocent man, a target of this opportunist. He further explained that Ray had failed to convince this woman to lay off, leave him alone. "He botched it, went too far, now she's in a coma. When she awakens, *if* she awakens," McHughes paused, raised his eyebrow, "she can do real harm to our future." McHughes' blood ran cold as he witnessed Sharon's visage abruptly change from that of a pouty-lipped ingénue to that of a force of pure evil. Was she lethal? Should he watch *his* back?

"I know her," Sharon's jaw tightened, her voice filled with resolve, "I know what to do," her lips curled with hatred, "And I will do it." Then inaudibly, "Connie the Bitch will die."

Though somewhat jolted by Sharon's intensity, McHughes was pleased. This was good. As long as Sharon's hostility was aimed at Mitchell, what did he care if she was pure evil, insane, or just plain hateful? She was in. That's what counted. She, a registered nurse, could easily gain entrance to Mitchell's room, administer the necessary drugs. End the nightmare. Shut Mitchell down, once and for all. Besides, there were other benefits, Fuller was gorgeous, her complicity desirous in so many ways. And that strength, that resolve, that passion she possessed, so natural to her, so easily forthcoming could be very interesting in the bedroom.

"I knew I could count on you. But remember, no one must know," he cautioned. "Tell no one. Just get the job done quickly. It will be assumed she died from natural causes, that her brain function shut down her heart."

"Leave it to me," Sharon said.

The Needle

THE NURSE SMILED KINDLY AND said, "Please keep your visit brief. You may speak softly to one another but please do not try to awaken the patient."

"Is she going to be okay?" asked Salli.

"Concussions are unpredictable but the CT scan did not indicate a long-term coma."

"Listen," Drina cautioned, leveling her eyes on Salli, "if she does wake up, no one say a word about her mother's stroke, okay? It was a mild one, they said she'd be okay, but still, don't say a word."

Salli nodded in agreement.

Several minutes passed before Glenn said bitterly, "I'd like to get my hands on whoever did this."

"I know, it's so hard to make sense of this. Was it a robbery gone bad? I thought thieves robbed big rich homes not humble homes. I don't get it. Sal, did you see or hear anything suspicious?" Drina asked.

At that, Salli burst into tears, "No, I was playing music, pretty loud actually and--"

"That's all right," said Drina comforting her.

Sam, heartbroken, remained silent. He would not take his eyes off Connie as if by watching her he could bring her back to health. Who would do this?

The nurse returned, requested that they leave for the day that perhaps tomorrow, Connie might be awake. Sam asked, "Mind if I stay a few more minutes?" The nurse looked upon Sam with compassion, his face haggard with worry and with the weight of his years. She agreed but cautioned him not to stay too long. Salli and Drina reached out to touch Connie's hand. Glenn whispered softly to Connie, "Get better. I love you," and kissed her cheek.

Once alone with Connie, Sam pleaded, "Wake up, little lady. You have to live to see your son. . . I think I know who he is. I didn't want to get your hopes up. But now I wish I would have told you." Tears streaming down his face, he again pleaded, "Wake up, little lady." Then, feeling spent, Sam closed his eyes and drifted off to sleep as he sat in the arm chair next to Connie's bed.

In the hallway, Nurse Fuller observed Sam: He appeared asleep, she could get past him. The ugliness of jealousy and hatred motivated her to kill Connie the Bitch. Even The Glass Heads backed this and Mannequin Marilyn most certainly backed this. In the pocket of her nurse's uniform: death in a syringe. She cautiously tiptoed past Sam and leveled hate-filled eyes onto Connie. She could not resist speaking, "Today you die, Bitch. This will end your Poetry of Pain." Connie groaned.

Sam's eyes snapped open. At first he merely saw the outline of a nurse but as his vision focused, he realized it was Sharon. "What are you doing here? You don't belong here!"

Sharon wheeled, the long flinty barrel of the needle shone, "Shut up you miserable old coot!"

Sam tried to stand, his arthritic legs stiff. "What have you got there?" he cried as he struggled with Sharon who prevailed, viciously stabbing the needle into him. Sam weakened as the killing serum pulsated in his veins; his legs buckled. Then in crushing pain, Sam clutched his heart and crumpled to the floor. As he lay dying, he envisioned his wife, how beautiful she was. How very, very beautiful. A smile formed on his lips as life slipped away.

"Old coot," Sharon spit out as she bent over his body. "No pulse. Good. Dead." Composing herself, she sedately left the hospital but as she walked through the parking lot, her thoughts centered on McHughes, how pissed he would be. She reassured herself that she had no choice but to kill the old geezer. McHughes would see that, wouldn't he? Sure he wanted Connie the Bitch dead but so did she. Next time. Impatiently, she yanked the car door open whereupon a wave of stifling heat assaulted her. She slumped behind the steering wheel, crushed, worried what McHughes' reaction would be when he learned she had failed to kill Connie. Her cell vibrated. Him. She did not pick up. Outside, birds made strangled calls as they flew overhead. She started the engine, cranked the air. Sat there, brooding.

"What went wrong? You botched it, didn't you?" demanded Mannequin Marilyn.

"I couldn't get her! That old bastard got in the way." Sharon sucked in her breath. "He won't be in the way again, I'll tell you that."

Again, the cell.

"Better take his call. Tell him! Tell him how you failed!" bellowed Mannequin Marilyn.

Grief

IT WAS SAD THAT IT took Sam's death to bring Connie and Glenn close to one another but that was the upshot of what had occurred. Bruised, both emotionally and physically, Connie collapsed into Glenn's willing arms when one day shortly after Sam's death and her release from the hospital, he impulsively stopped in at her house. This time he didn't have Sophie with him. This time there was no dog talk needed to bridge the gap between them. United in their love for Sam, they clung to one another. No longer able to contain the grief, Connie wept, all her defenses depleted. Sam, the center of kindness and understanding had trusted Glenn, she would, too.

"I can't believe he's gone," Connie cried.

"I know," Glenn said sadly.

"The funeral?"

"Friday. It's Friday. I contacted Veteran's Services and --"

"It'll be beautiful, won't it?" She stifled a sob.

"Yes," Glenn took a deep breath, "the chaplain, the Honor Guard, the special flags for his casket, his friends at the camp notified," Glenn's voice cracked as he added, "all arranged."

She nodded in gratitude, "Thank you."

"You get some rest now," Glenn said softly, then gently held her as she wept in his arms.

It was Friday, the day of Sam's funeral. Connie, forlorn, lay listening to the plaintive song of the mourning dove perched outside her bedroom window, its somber chords melding with her heart. Slowly, she dragged herself out of bed, peered out the window to see rain clouds floating disconsolately. A gloomy, dreary day unfolding, a day befitting a funeral. The phone: Drina calling to ask how she was, did she want her to pick her up? Connie declined. Salli and Bill also offered. Connie declined. She desired solitude, time to grieve for Sam, try to get a hold of herself, heal the chasm which had opened in her heart. With difficulty, she made her way to the kitchen, her body stiff and sore yet from the terrible ordeal with Ray Fuller. She sat down to the comfort of a cup of coffee to reflect upon the last night Sam had been alive. He had been sitting next to her, so close; she fervently wished she had awakened from the coma before he passed. She might have been able to help him, summon a nurse, do something, but instead, she lay inert. Tears streamed from the river of regret. If she had only awakened, she might have helped him. Tortuous thoughts prevailed. How long was Sam there before his heart attack? Did he call out? Did he suffer? Why did he have to die? It was almost too much to bear.

Sam.

Mindlessly, after showering, she stood before her closet. There she saw the black sheath dress, the same dress she had worn to give a poetry reading at the Clearwater Public Library in happier times. Sam had been there, her advocate, her friend. Now she would wear the same dress for a different reason, one filled with the sadness of goodbye. She remembered these things as she began to walk the short distance to Veteran's Memorial Marina Park, but her heart took a detour and she found herself sitting on the bench beneath the Baranoff Oak where she and Sam had sat so often to share their "little talks." At first, she breathed jaggedly, then her breathing slowed, evened out as the tree branches stirred. She lifted her gaze upward past the emerald green leaves and watched the dark, billowing clouds pass overhead. She whispered a prayer for Sam before wending her way to the funeral. As she walked, she looked toward the pier where she saw the solitary silhouette of a young man leaning dejectedly against the balustrade, his gaze trained on the bay. It seemed a lonely pose and Connie felt a kinship with the young man, who seemed forlorn. She sighed and pushed onward.

Sam.

There before her on the freshly mown lawn, Connie saw rows of small white folding chairs were set up for guests. It made her think of Arlington Cemetery. Large wicker baskets of flowers, in the patriot colors of red, white, and blue stood at attention near the lectern. She gasped upon seeing Sam's flag-draped casket. "There he is," she told herself. "There he is." She stood frozen, hand to mouth, stifled a sob. Time stood still.

Glenn approached, offering his arm and escorted her to the first row of seats marked "Family." Connie deferred, questioned sitting in the family section but Glenn assured her it was appropriate, "We are Sam's family. You must know that, Connie." She nodded yes. Drina, Salli and Bill arrived.

Pastor Graham of Safety Harbor Ecumenical Church, pastor to the homeless, delivered an eloquent eulogy. Thoughtfully, he included one of Sam's favorite passages from the poetry of Walt Whitman's "Leaves of Grass": "I know I was even there and slept while God carried me through lethargic mist and took my time . . . Long I was hugged close . . . long and long."

The mourners sat transfixed by the intuitive beauty of the passage of the poem, almost as if Sam had selected it himself for this, his final gathering. Several of Sam's friends from the homeless camp donned their cherished Army uniforms, exemplary of their service in Vietnam. These veterans shared a brotherhood with Sam based upon the horrors of that war which had indelibly marked their hearts and souls. The pastor's message concluded. An eerie silence was punctuated by the crack of the rifle salute, its sharp sound echoing through the filmy air as if confirming the finality of death. Solemnly, the Honor Guard bore Sam's flag-draped coffin to the doleful cadence of Taps, the bugler, a Vietnam vet.

Sam.

There, standing on the small hill overlooking the park, Glenn saw the figure of a young man. Could he be the young man Sam spoke of? Glenn racked his brain trying to remember the young man's name. Will. It was Will. He worked with Sam at the bike shop. Glenn made a mental note to visit the bike shop one day soon. Maybe he could step up, mentor the boy. Sam would want that. Glenn hoped to have a chance to talk with the young man, but he quickly vanished. Regretfully, Glenn wished he had sought out Sam's young friend when he had first learned of Sam's death. Why had he not done that? But he knew the answer. Numb with grief, his mind had failed him. Surely Sam would have wanted this young man in the family section. Glenn sighed. The grieving mind swerves off track under the pressure of loss. It was too late. Now, his duty was to Connie. She was hurting in every way and he was concerned for her safety and well being. Glenn looked with gratitude upon Salli and Bill who now attempted to comfort Drina and Connie. Surely Sam would have been pleased with his service, perhaps he was there in spirit. Yes, surely he was.

The Backpack

IT WAS FRIDAY, THE DAY of Sam's funeral. Distraught, Will wished no communion with anyone attending the service, all strangers to him. It had always been just he and Sam. He liked it that way. Will stood on the little knoll over-looking Memorial Veteran's Park. He saw the neat rows of small white chairs, the flags, the Honor Guard. He held his breath to keep from dissolving into tears and lingered solitarily on the fringes awaiting the formal service to begin. He reflected on how he and Sam had often passed the small park on their way to fish at the pier. The thought had never crossed Will's mind that one day Sam would be laid to rest here.

Will waited for the final goodbye. He watched as the Honor Guard carried Sam's flag-draped casket to the small staging area which was surrounded by large baskets of patriotic floral arrangements. He listened as the cler-gyman spoke of Sam's distinguished career in Vietnam. Sam never told me thought Will, he never said anything about being a hero. Nothing, he said nothing about what he did in Vietnam. Never once. Why? Why didn't he tell me anything? Why didn't he tell me how brave he was? My God, thought Will. Sam was a hero, a real bona-fide American hero. Yet, he said nothing. Will did not understand this and felt a twinge of doubt about the depth of their friendship. But in his heart, he knew that Sam was his true friend. Immediately, Will felt remorse for doubting Sam. He whispered a prayer and focused on the service.

And when the service concluded, he quietly slipped away, feeling lost, confused and alone. Though he wasn't scheduled for work that day, Will found himself heading to the bike shop. Inside, in the back room, Will sat on the familiar bench beside the employee lockers. *Sam.* Slowly, Will pulled the worn, rusting handle of Sam's locker. Inside, he saw Sam's backpack and an old pair of his shoes, muddy spares he kept "in case." Like a movie in his mind, Will replayed the familiar scene where Sam locked up the bike shop, and as he closed the door, how he would heft his backpack onto his shoulder and call out to Will, "Have a good night now; stay out of trouble, yeah." Will gently lifted the faded brown backpack from the locker, needing to find something, some keepsake of Sam's, something to treasure. Maybe it would help fill the emptiness he felt in his heart. Seconds later, there it was, in his hand, Sam's purple heart and a Bronze Star with a V device for Valor, all tucked away in the back compartment. Will gazed upon the medals. How he wished Sam would have shown them to him, talked with him about how it was he earned them. Were all heroes so silent? With a heavy heart, Will clung to the backpack. *Sam.* Friend, mentor, companion. Will sighed, choking back deeply cutting emotion, bereft. Then hesitantly, he unzipped a small compartment in the front of the pack. Something inside, a bottle? Was it medicine? No. Perfume. An old bottle of perfume. That's strange thought Will. Maybe it was Sam's mother's? Whose? Then, it dawned on Will, Sam's wife, the woman he loved, the woman he lost. Again, Will trembled with disbelief, sadness and despite his youth, understood the depth of love it took for Sam to have cherished that perfume all these years. Will lovingly withdrew a well-worn copy of *Walt Whitman, the Complete Poems,* Sam's favorites marked by folded corners, penciled notes. Sam's voice echoed in Will's mind:

> *I celebrate myself, and sing myself,*
> *And what I assume you shall assume,*
> *For every atom belonging to me as good belongs*
> *to you.*

Will repeated the last line to himself. Is it true? Is Sam part of me? Will's tears fell upon the pages. Gently, he dabbed them careful not to tear the aged parchment, parchment so like Sam, precious, yet delicate, more delicate than Will ever realized. Sam's heart, he died of a heart attack. The cruelty of the sentence rang like an unwanted bell in Will's mind, wasn't there a line from literature -- something about, "Ask not for whom the bell tolls, it tolls for thee." Will shook his head as if to clear it. Then, placing the tattered volume back into the bag, something crumpled, something at the very bottom of the backpack, something he had missed. An envelope, an envelope with his name on it. What's this Will wondered and his eyes grew large with curiosity as a warm feeling of connectedness to Sam spread throughout his being. Though gone, Sam had found a way to reach out to him.

Confrontation Overdue

Connie lay on the sofa, achy, miserable, dozing in and out, grieving for Sam when the phone awoke her. She croaked, "Hello?"

"We need to meet," said the voice tersely.

The cold, hard edge of the voice advised her. "What do you want?" she asked, eyes narrowing in distrust.

"To meet. I need that diary."

Connie struggled to sit up, to focus. "Yes, and I want my son," she answered, forcing strength into her voice. The thought of betraying Celeste by exposing her diary to her murderer sickened Connie. Her stomach wrenched. What would she do?

He waited a beat, "I know where he is."

A sharp intake of breath, Connie asked, "Where?"

"Meet me at the Clearwater bus station. Now." He warned, vocal chords tightening.

"You haven't eaten in days, Will, wouldn't you like to sit down have some supper?" asked Mrs. Maloney.

"Not hungry. Thanks, anyway," said Will as he sauntered off to his room.

"You sure you're not hungry, Will?" Tommy called out.

"No, but thanks buddy." Will wanted to be alone. He quietly closed the bedroom door, pulled Sam's letter from the pocket of his jeans, plopped down on the bed. His heart ached for the loss of his friend and mentor. Once again, he unfolded the coarse sheet of paper and studied the scrawl of black ink.

Will, I've written this note because every time I tried to tell you this, I choked at the wheel. I believe I know who your mother is. Now don't get angry. Hear me out. She's living in Safety Harbor, works at the Spa. I know her, she's a good woman. Her name is Connie Mitchell. **(Will paused, no matter how many readings of this note, the mention of her name gripped him, made his chest tighten.)** -- *She's trying to find you. Seems like she made some mistakes when she was young, younger than you are now as a matter of fact. Thing is -- we have to forgive others move on let them redeem themselves. She's going crazy with grief for you. Blames herself. I know this isn't easy on you, but why don't you give her a chance? Get to know her a bit before condemning her.*

> *You know, I made plenty of mistakes, yeah, in my life. I wish someone had forgiven me.*
> **Your friend,**
> **Sam-I-Am**
> **PS Her address is 178 Sabal Street**

Will refolded the letter, tucked it in his jeans, decided to honor Sam's wishes, approach his mother, hear her out. He hopped on his motorcycle. This time he would do more than ride by her house, he would stop, knock on the door, try to make things right. Pulling up to the house, however, Will felt let down, her car was gone. Frustrated, he cut over to Main Street, headed out McMullen Booth. Riding cleared his head, helped him think. But a few minutes into the ride, he spotted Connie's car; he must have just missed her. Burning with curiosity, he pulled next to her and gasped when he saw her face in profile. Vaguely from deep within the memory of his mother surfaced. He gulped hard, trying to swallow the lump in his throat. *She abandoned me.*

The bus station? Where was she going? Will pulled in several spots down from Connie's car, watched as a man approached. He looked mean. Will's heart began to pound as he saw his mother slowly, as if painfully, exit her car. The man clamped his hand on her arm. She tried vainly to pull it free. Wordlessly, they got into the man's car. Pulled out. What's going on? Will wondered.

Connie turned her face away from McHughes, avoiding him, looked out of the passenger window, saw something strange: Sharon Fuller at the ticket window inside the bus station. Connie could recognize her anywhere. Why was she there? Why the dark glasses? Connie dismissed her curiosity. She had more to worry about than that nut case. Reluctantly, she looked at McHughes as he navigated the parking lot and blended into the considerable traffic on Gulf to Bay. His visage: Grim, quite unsettling. Connie realized he had a plan. What was it? If she gave him Celeste's diary, would he really tell her where Will was? Did he even know? Could she outsmart him, find Will? But she did not bring the diary with her. She decided that they would talk, negotiate and though saddened to give up the diary, she realized it was her only power play to get Will back. She hated McHughes but he had big time connections, could pull strings no one else could. He must have done so, located Will, now held his whereabouts in ransom for the diary. Connie thought about the lock of his hair contained within the diary which would lend proof of his DNA. He didn't know that part, she reasoned, she would remove it before giving him the diary. Yes, that was it. Maybe she could glue a dried flower over the spot where the lock of hair was. Cover her tracks. But then she remembered, Celeste had written in the diary about having clipped the lock while he slept. He would know. He would demand it. Things could get really sticky and he looked determined, ugly and mean. She hated him for killing Celeste. She would remove the entire page; he would be none the wiser.

Will discretely followed McHughes out of the parking lot and onto Gulf to Bay. He watched as McHughes' Lexus turned onto a tree-lined street, the entrance to the tony historical district of Clearwater. McHughes doused his headlights, inched up the long narrow driveway which led to the garage located at the back of the property. Quickly, Will shut down his motorcycle and ditched it behind an oleander bush. Will could hear muffled voices, the words indecipherable, yet with a definite combative edge as the man and Will's mother approached the house. Confounded, Will realized his mother was not happy to be here or with this man. What was going on? Will crept to the house, intent on solving the mystery. No stranger to illegal house entry in this or in any posh neighborhood, he easily climbed the trellis to the second story of McHughes' home, deftly pried open a window, stepped over the sash and into the bedroom, heading for the hall. Something stopped him: a whimper. There in the shadows lay a young girl tied to the bed, gagged, her eyes reflecting terror. Will put his finger to his lips, signaling her to be quiet, untied her and whispered, "Stay here. I will help you, give me some time." She nodded fearfully in agreement, trusting Will's earnestness. He left her and tiptoed to the head of the stairs, listening to the adults down below.

"All right. Let's have it. I want the diary," McHughes demanded.

"Not so fast," Connie said, "you need to fulfill your part of the deal first, then you get Celeste's diary and only then. Where's my son! You said you know where he is!"

McHughes bit into his upper lip and gnawed his mustache, "Look, I'm out of patience with you, bitch. He lowered his head as a bull does before charging, rolled evil eyes up to her and in a rasping whisper, "I'll ask again, where is the diary?" A whisper more frightening than a scream.

"Which you will get after you cooperate," said Connie, undaunted.

Will moved further down the staircase, listening.

"Cooperate?" McHughes boomed, thrusting his face close to Connie's. "You're in no position to demand cooperation, *whore*! Oh," he spread his arms dramatically, "I see, by *cooperate*, you mean pay up. Right? How much? How much does it take to keep a whore's mouth shut? He stepped back and with a flourish produced his wallet -- pulled out a wad of cash and threw it about the floor in the manner in which one would disperse chicken feed, steady and repetitive, until it was gone. He stared into the empty wallet, "You've got it all now, *whore*!" he cried and tossed the wallet onto the floor as well.

Connie watched stonily as the money fell. "How much? You think everything's about money, don't you? I don't want your money. I want my son! I came here because you told me--"

Will's eyes grew large. Who is this guy?

McHughes' face reddened. Exasperated, he raked his stubby, nail-bitten fingers across his mouth, desperate to gain control of Connie but bribery and intimidation weren't working. He shook his head, muttered half to him-self, "You are a problem. This is highly unfortunate but extreme measures must be taken. I cannot--"

Will moved to the last stair and began to genuinely fear for his mother's life.

"Cannot what?" Connie spit out, hatred eclipsing her fear.

Lightning fast, McHughes' mood changed from abject frustration to confidence, "Did you know," he harped, "that tonight, according to Greyhound bus records, you purchased a one-way ticket to Miami? You told the clerk you were searching for your son. But something must have happened in Miami because you never returned." A per-verse smile crept over his face.

Connie was stunned. That explained why Sharon was at the bus station. How did she know McHughes? What was the connection? "Sharon?" she said, more a statement than a question.

"That's right, your good buddy, Sharon. She was at the hospital the night the old man died. She missed. You eluded death once, *whore*, but you won't a second time." He took a step forward.

"Missed? What are you talking about!" demanded Connie, her voice rising.

"The old man got in the way, fought to protect you. He got your *medicine*."

"Sam," Connie said, heartbroken. Then, "You filthy bastard."

Will froze, appalled. Sam was killed?

"You know," McHughes said in conciliatory fashion, his eyes roaming Connie's body, "if I weren't running for office, this might not be so sticky, such a problem." He clamped his jaw down, tilted his head sideways staring seemingly into some hidden space. "We might have had a good time, have ourselves a *reunion*."

Connie grimaced. She began to look about the room for an escape route. Could she outrun him? She took a step back, then another. Her breath came in short bursts. A trapped animal.

"Who would even miss you when you're gone?" McHughes hissed, advancing.

A forceful voice: "I would," challenged Will, stepping out from the shadows, granite eyes, locked on McHughes.

McHughes' jaw dropped. The young man standing before him, the resemblance between them was remarkable. Except for the eyes. The eyes were hers. He hated them.

Upstairs, Mandy quietly crept to the doorway of the bedroom, peered about, saw nothing. She ventured further, stepped into the hallway where Miss Snickers lay curled in the corner. Mandy scooped her up and cuddled her, fervently whispered, "I want to go home."

"We're leaving here, old man. We're walking out the door," Will said, unshaken. "Come on, mom," Will reached out for Connie while keeping his eyes on McHughes who defiantly blocked their path, "Get out of the way, old man, or you're going down."

Connie stared in disbelief, her little boy from long ago, now towering over her. The room fell into a slow spin and her knees buckled. Will steadied her, set her gently onto the sofa. From behind, a deep guttural groan emerged from McHughes as he assaulted Will, slamming him against the wall. Father against son. Will restrained him with his left arm and with his right, sank a blow into McHughes' face breaking his nose. Son against father. McHughes tasted his blood and his adrenaline surged. They must die. No going back. For a split second, Will turned to check on Connie. In that instant, McHughes reached for his ankle holstered gun. Connie screamed, "He's got a gun!"

Mandy began to cry and tightly held Miss Snickers but Miss Snickers, conditioned by years with McHughes to recognize intense pressure as a precursor to pain, bolted and scurried down the stairs, across the foyer, into the living room surprising its occupants. McHughes fumbled the gun as Miss Snickers raced across his path. Both Will and McHughes dove for the gun.

Sharon, No Way

SHARON BOUGHT THE TICKET AS instructed but when the bus for Miami pulled in, the exhaust fumes, the tacky guys, frumpy old ladies boarding, the commonality of it all offended her senses. Marilyn would never ride in such a vehicle Sharon thought to herself. Why should she? She tossed the ticket into the trash receptacle and pulled out her car keys. "Ah-oh," she mumbled remembering McHughes' instructions to leave her car at home, take a taxi to the bus station. Well, all the more reason not to board that bus. Relieved that the decision was made, Sharon slid behind the wheel of her car.

"So, what's going on?" asked Mannequin Marilyn, from her perch on the front seat.

"Nothing. I kind of forgot I was supposed to take a cab here. Now Lloyd will be pissed."

"Who cares? I don't, do you? You bought the damn ticket, didn't you? Now let's get out of here, this place gives me the creeps."

"I agree. This isn't working for me either; these people are ugly and I'm not up for this," said Sharon, adjusting the strap of her high heeled sandal. She pulled down the visor, studied her face in the mirror, "Know what I mean?" She started the engine.

"Yes, I do," answered Mannequin Marilyn. "He's got some nerve asking this of you. Who does he think he is, anyway?"

"Humph, yeah. He should take the smelly bus to Miami," said Sharon backing out of the parking spot, knocking down the roped boarding area cones.

"Where is he anyway?" asked Mannequin Marilyn.

Sharon sniffed, pulled her shoulders back, "At his house with Connie the Bitch."

"Doing what? Doing her?"

"No. It's not like that."

"When is it ever *not* like that, huh?" asked Mannequin Marilyn. "When?" she stressed.

Sharon sighed, "You're right. Let's go, I know where he lives, I've been there."

Sharon pulled up to McHughes' house. "This is it, this is his house."

Sharon unbuttoned yet one more button of her blouse and ambled to the front door. She swayed her hips seductively and thought, "I wouldn't mind living in this big house. Maybe that can be arranged." But these high hopes were dashed. No answer to the doorbell she angrily pressed. Was he in bed with Connie the Bitch? Sharon's blood boiled. She stepped out onto the lawn scanning the second story windows. Saw nothing. He must be here she thought. That was the plan, wasn't it? An explosion of sound caught her off guard. What was that? Just as suddenly, the quiet dark street was ablaze with lights. Police! I have to get out of here she thought scurrying to her car but the spiked sling back heels slowed her progress. A young officer stopped her, "We'll need you to stick around a bit, ma'am."

"Don't call me ma'am! I'm not *old*!" she barked.

"Yes, ma'am," the officer replied noting the way she and her friend in the car were scantily dressed, possibly prostitutes. They would be held for questioning.

We Never Really Knew Him

"You seem chipper this morning," said Mary McHughes, "I thought you'd be down with your brother being jailed and all and the family name being dragged through the mud."

"I was until . . ." he said, leaning in for a kiss before pouring a cup of coffee.

"Until?"

Bryce shrugged, "Well, it may sound cold, dear, but it is his problem, isn't it? What can I really say? We've never been close, and this, well, I see this as one extreme example of his freaky ways. As for the family name," he paused, "people have short memories, I'm not worried about it."

"Good! I was worried you would be worried!" she said. Then she asked, "Are you hungry, honey? I can make eggs." She continued spreading peanut butter on bread for the boys' school lunches.

"Just coffee," he said. He sat down at the kitchen table, picked up the *Tampa Bay Times* took in the large picture of Lloyd under arrest. Really, quite shocking. Momentarily,

Bryce felt a pang of pity for his brother, muttered under his breath, "Dumb bastard."

"Hmmm?"

"Oh, nothing, dear." Bryce began to hum as he read the death penalty was in the offing, then smiled smugly and thought: A dead man can't collect an inheritance. The McHughes' fortune would fall one day, undivided, to him. Stirring sweetener into his coffee, he decided that, yes, maybe he would like some breakfast after all. "I'll take those eggs, on second thought, Mary."

"Okay, no problem," she said, getting the frying pan out. "Oh, and hon, what are we going to tell the boys to say when the kids at school ask about Uncle Lloyd?" She, concerned, her children's welfare her focus.

"Tell them to say, we never really knew him. That's what we'll say to anyone that asks. It's true, isn't it?"

"I guess so," Mary agreed and she began to scramble the eggs.

Doomed

BAIL HAD BEEN DENIED: MCHUGHES deemed to be a flight risk by Honorable Judge Bardmoor who delivered his verdict in, of course, rhymed meter.

"Bastard!" McHughes cursed through clenched teeth as he pummeled his fist into his thin gray state-issue polyester mattress. Attempting to control his rising panic, he reviewed events: His father had retained the best legal defense team money could buy. The firm, Sobel, Schwartz and Bancroft recommended he plead temporary insanity in the "Celeste Incident" and the Stand Your Ground defense in the fateful night at his home. How did all this happen? he asked himself. How was he in jail? He concluded he was a pitiable victim of injustice. Was this some sort of a nightmare, a hallucination? He raked his hands through his hair, struggling to find sense in all of this. None of this was his fault: Other people had a habit of getting in the way. What was he supposed to do? Allow himself to be bullied? He had enough of that when he was a kid, his big brother pushing him around but never getting punished for it. Come to think of it, the bullying never occurred when Father was home, only when Mother was there and, of course, she did nothing about it. He winced remembering the beatings Bryce and his buddies inflicted upon him, smeared an old can of shoe polish all over his face. Oxblood. Called him Indian Joe. Mother laughed seeing his face and the stupid feather they stuck in his hair. McHughes brushed away tears. Life had been hard since he was 10 years old when he realized Mother preferred Bryce, AKA, Mr. Perfect.

McHughes sneered, "I bet that smug ass is enjoying seeing me behind bars. But I'll show that bastard. I'll be out of here in no time." He comforted himself with lies and rehearsed more lies: The young whore Celeste? Why, she was doped up when he accidentally pushed her away as she came clawing at him with those nails. The head injury didn't kill her -- she must have suffered a heart attack, druggie that she was. Never mind he had supplied the drugs. No one would know that. How would they?

McHughes considered the accusations of Connie the Whore. She and her illicit son broke into his house. Yes, they did. They committed home invasion. He was within his rights under the Stand Your Ground law to pull the gun. No one got hurt. A bullet pierced the wall. Big deal.

Mandy? Little horny bitch. She *asked* to be tied up, liked it that way, saw it in one of the "X" rated movies they watched together. She didn't count for anything. She was fine, back home with her parents. He reflected on what he foolishly considered the lesser charges, child endangerment, internet stalking, child trafficking, but attempted first-degree murder on two counts, and being charged with the murder of Celeste, that was frightening. He deluded himself believing he might get off with counseling and community service. After all, he reasoned, he had a good defense team and his uncle the gov could surely work something out for him. Bardmoor was a problem, but maybe that lunatic could be recused, bias shown, make a case he always hated Lloyd. Yes, that was it. The wheels turned, yes, a change of venue, that's what he needed. That would make all the difference in the world. He, an upstanding citizen, a man of distinction would surely be recognized by an unbiased court for what he truly was.

Exhausted, he reclined on his bed, thankful to be housed alone for his own protection from the many inmates he had prosecuted. His breathing evened out and was followed by a quickened feeling, a desire for sex. Specifically, sex with Sharon Fuller. Maybe she was crazy but in a good way. He reasoned if more women were like her, living for sexual gratification, that the world would be a better place. More men would be satisfied. There would be fewer rapes. Seduction and Orgasm: The ultimate satisfaction in life. Why could others not see this? Why was everyone so fucking uptight, rigid, spouting rules, more rules, limitations? For God's sake, let there be sex. He turned on his side, faced the wall, touched himself and began to doze off when a delicious dream of Sharon arose. She was at her sexy best. He moaned. But the dream soon turned to a nightmare: Sharon evaporated and a monstrous winged creature materialized -- venomous snakes coiled about the hag's bald head -- Medusa. With the face of Mother. The twisted lips croaked, "It's ruined. You ruined it." The hag pointed an ancient, gnarled finger at him, repeated, "It's ruined."

McHughes felt his body turning to stone. "What's ruined?" he whimpered.

"My life," she answered. "You ruined my life." She vanished in a mist.

A second creature appeared. At first, McHughes could not see clearly but as the dream lens focused, Methuselah materialized. With the face of Father.

"What happened to you?" McHughes cried.

"You! You happened to me. You did this. We're doomed . . . doomed, I say."

McHughes wrenched himself awake, sat bolt upright drenched in sweat, eyes casting about the dank cell like those of a trapped animal. Fear and claustrophobia took hold. Desperate, McHughes assured himself it was only a nightmare. He panted. "I gotta get outta here!"

From the cell next door came a voice, "Me and you both, buddy, me and you both."

Was this to be his social milieu? Talking to prisoners, the scum he put away?

McHughes began to shiver, a cold serpentine chill traveling his spine. He thought of Father and began to understand that Father had always believed in him, supported him. No one else did. Suddenly, without him, the world seemed to be a cold, unwelcoming place, without grace, without inclusion or comfort. What would happen to him now? Futility oozed through his bones the way sludge crawls through storm-torn city streets.

His mind worked full-tilt -- creating deathly scenarios, all of which portrayed him as a victim. Fear tightened its grip and he began to weep, at first in small gasps, then in a low growl, animal-like in its manner. He lay down, drew his knees to his chest and rocked to and fro, whispering all the while, "I did nothing wrong. Nothing!"

At Last

IT WAS MORNING. CONNIE SAT at the kitchen table, pulled the curtains back a bit and watched as peachy pastel clouds shimmered on the horizon. Today was the big day, and though it was early, she knew that soon she and Will would be driving down to Eckerd College where she was to receive a major writing award. She would be sharing her poetry today and her thoughts wound back to the night she read at the poetry slam. She had been so nervous and frightened. Sam had been there, giving her confidence that night. "My dear friend," Connie whispered.

Doodle looked up from her snooze at Connie's feet knowingly, recognizing the sad, tender tone in Connie's voice. She stood on her hind legs, put her paws on the edge of Connie's chair and whimpered. "Come here, baby," Connie said scooping Doodle up onto her lap. She stroked her silky fur as she took stock of the coming events: She was to be presented with a check for $25,000, an award for winning the Hearts of Palm national poetry contest. Her collected poems would be published internationally and translated into 33 languages.

So much had happened recently that Connie shook her head in amazement. To think that Lloyd McHughes had fallen so far, jailed, bail denied. The *Tampa Bay Times* story even mentioned a possibility of the death sentence. Strange, he had seemed so powerful, so well connected only a few short months ago. It was as if their lives were contained in a kaleidoscope, and the hand of an unseen force turned the wheel to new patterns, different formations.

How did all of this come about? Her life seemed miraculous. A steady chain of events -- one by one the links had formed, each building upon the other. From day one when Connie met Salli who impetuously shook down feathers onto her flower bed claiming it was a great fertilizer to the day Salli suggested Connie join the poetry group. Connie took a sip of her coffee thinking how wonderful that advice turned out to be. She thought of the people in the group and how each one of them influenced her life. Momentarily, she flinched thinking of Sharon Fuller. "She's not well, Doodle, so we have to forgive her," said Connie. Doodle responded by licking her hand.

Will sleepily joined her, "Mom, why didn't you wake me?" Connie looked across the tiny kitchen and saw her son standing before her rubbing sleep from his eyes. It was a dream come true. Her eyes filled with tears as she rose to greet him. She held him close and smiled. She thought of the friends and family who would be there today to support her: Mother, Father, Drina, Solana, Salli, Bill and Glenn.

Most of all, Will would be there. Imagine that. Connie's heart sang and a poem formed: *Reunion in Safety Harbor.* At last.

Epilogue For The Brave Reader

ON THE OTHER HAND . . .

YES, ALL WAS WELL WITH Connie Mitchell, reunited with her son and her parents. She had gained many new friends in Safety Harbor and had grown to be an accomplished writer as well as a happy, confident woman.

Not so for Sharon Fuller, now a patient in the very same psychiatric ward where she once worked. Evaluations were still in process but her future looked dim. She seemed not to mind somehow, sitting by the hour watching Marilyn Monroe movies. There were so many of them. So very many. Per doctors' orders, two of the Glass Heads were positioned in her room. She had asked about the other two, and the managing nurse explained that one had not been recovered since her arrest and that another had broken in transit. "Oh, I see," said Sharon, unperturbed. Seemed like nothing really rankled her anymore. No anger. No hateful feelings. Not many feelings at all since the powerful psychotropic drugs were administered. So soothing, so helpful. She talked things over with the Glass Heads. Somehow, they had the right attitude. Somehow, they, too, were calmer than they used to be. No arguing. No jealousy.

But when the night nurse was late dispensing drugs, Sharon's depression would return and the Glass Heads challenged Sharon for they were jealous she spent so much time away from them.

"What are you doing out there all the time? We're stuck in here!" said one.

"Yeah! Who in the day room is your new best friend? You've forgotten us," added another.

Sharon tried to hush them but they would have none of it.

"I want out of here; I want to go home," whined one.

"Me, too," chimed the other. "Isn't there some way out of here? There has to be! Think!"

"I can't think!" screamed Sharon as she raised her hands to cover her ears.

"Yes, you can, and you will," threatened the Glass Heads in unison.

Outside in the corridor, the night custodian mopped the floor and shook his head with pity for the pretty lady in there, making all those voices. Getting all worked up for nothing. Didn't she understand? She would never leave this place. Merriam Pines Hospital was her home now.

Inside the room, things quieted down. Sharon wept. She would like to have felt that she missed her mother, but that would be a lie. She missed and deeply desired nurturance but from whom? How? Strange faces. That's all she saw day-in, day-out now. Even Ray was someone who cared, someone who knew she was alive.

"Try to be patient with me," she begged The Glass Heads, "remember my childhood exactly mirrored Marilyn's. Remember that when you judge me. Watching her movies in the day room, seeing her talk, seeing her walk, I am with my friend. I feel comforted. Do you think we had it easy growing up, getting kicked from foster home to foster home? No one giving a damn?" Sharon's voice level rose with each utterance; the night nurse approached bearing the calming meds. Sharon whimpered, "My life is over."

"I beg your pardon," said the nurse, uncapping the hypodermic.

Sharon sniffed, wiped a tear, "I thought turning 40 that everything would be over for me, you know, my good looks, sex appeal, but I'm finished at 36, just like Marilyn."

"Now you're here. You'll be fine," assured the nurse administering the injection.

"I'm dying!" cried Sharon. "Can't you see? At 36, just like Marilyn." Sharon paled to ghostly white, whispered, "What's today's date?"

"It's August 5th."

"The day Marilyn died," gasped Sharon.

❧ ❧ ❧ ❧ ❧

The rookie police officer who had mistakenly taken Mannequin Marilyn for a prostitute endured endless taunts from the veteran officers who relished reminding him of his mistake. The last straw occurred the day he found Mannequin Marilyn and Glass Head perched on the passenger seat of his patrol car.

"Not funny!" he bitterly exclaimed. Angrily, he drove straight to a donation center and dropped both items off, anxious to be rid of them, whereupon a mother and her young daughter were browsing through the bargains.

"Let's get this for grandma," said the mother.

"What's it for?" asked the daughter.

"It's for when grandma makes dresses, it's kind of a model."

"What's this, mom?" asked the little girl, picking up Glass Head.

"A wig head. Good find. We'll have to clean it up a bit, but grandma's been wanting one for her wig."

Happy with their purchases, mother and daughter strolled to their van carefully pushing the cart which held Mannequin Marilyn and Glass Head. Once at their van, they carefully secured Mannequin Marilyn and Glass Head into the back seat.

"Why are we turning on Regret Lane, mom?"

"Not regret, honey, Egret, like the bird. It's a short cut to grandma's."

"Yes!" shouted the little girl gleefully, thinking about cookies and milk. She turned to the back seat to behold their prize purchases and stared in wonder. Did the Glass Head wink?

"Mama! The wig head blinked. It can move its eyes!"

"No, honey, that's not possible," said the mother.

The little girl turned to look once more.

Blink.

This time the little girl said nothing, nothing at all.

1. Friendship is a key element in this story. What changes and growth have occurred in your life due to the inspiration of friends?

2. Connie became interested in friendship with Drina after Drina shared her butterfly poem. Why was that?

3. Salli was oftentimes confused about her role in life, but what wisdom did she impart to different characters in the book?

4. Was Connie a weak or a strong woman? Give examples to support your belief.

5. When the Department of Children and Families removed Will from Connie, was it wrong of Ruth not to adopt him?

6. Discuss Sam's role in the story.

7. Do you believe Lloyd McHughes would have been a different person had he not harbored anger toward his mother and brother?

8. Discuss the broad meaning of "runaway" -- Celeste and Connie were runaways but were others running away, too?
9. Do you believe Sharon Fuller was a victim or a ruthless sociopath?

Made in the USA
Columbia, SC
20 August 2017